WIZARDS AND WARRIORS . . .
DEMONS AND DEMONESSES . . .
ATLANTIS AND LEMURIA . . .
LOST LANDS AND HIDDEN TREASURES . . .
MARVEL WORKERS AND MIRACLE
MAKERS . . .
CASTLES AND CRYPTS . . .

These are the ingredients of fantasy, the wonderful other world of the imagination. Fantasy is the fey twin of science fiction—it demands only that its reader sit back and let his fancy rove where it will, voyage in and out among the myriad realms of the free imagination, voyage there under the experienced navigation of such star captains as Fritz Leiber and Clark Ashton Smith, of Avram Davidson and L. Sprague de Camp, of Tanith Lee and Lin Carter, and the rest of the unchartered guild of master fantasists.

That's the travel prospectus put forth by this second annual volume of the year's best fantasy stories. Welcome aboard!

Lin Carter in DAW editions:

THE YEAR'S BEST FANTASY STORIES: 1	UY1199—$1.25
UNDER THE GREEN STAR	UY1185—$1.25
WHEN THE GREEN STAR CALLS	UY1267—$1.25
BY THE LIGHT OF THE GREEN STAR	UY1268—$1.25
AS THE GREEN STAR RISES	UY1156—$1.25
IN THE GREEN STAR'S GLOW	UY1216—$1.25
THE IMMORTAL OF WORLD'S END	UY1254—$1.25

The Year's Best Fantasy Stories: 2

Edited by
LIN CARTER

DAW BOOKS, INC.
DONALD A. WOLLHEIM, PUBLISHER

1301 Avenue of the Americas
New York, N. Y.   10019

DEDICATION
To the memory of the late
LEO MARGULIES

FIRST PRINTING, AUGUST 1976

1 2 3 4 5 6 7 8 9

PRINTED IN U.S.A.

ACKNOWLEDGMENTS

"The Demoness" by Tanith Lee appears here in print for the first time. By arrangement with Tanith Lee.

"The Night of the Unicorn" by Thomas Burnett Swann first appeared in the anthology *Nameless Places* (Arkham House, 1975); copyright © 1975 by April R. Derleth and Walden W. Derleth. By permission of Arkham House.

"Cry Wolf" by Pat McIntosh first appeared in *Anduril* for July, 1975; copyright © 1975 by John Martin and *Anduril*. By arrangement with John Martin.

"Under the Thumbs of the Gods" by Fritz Leiber first appeared in *Fantastic* for April, 1975; copyright © 1974 by Ultimate Publishing Co., Inc. By arrangement with Fritz Leiber.

"The Guardian of the Vault" by Paul Spencer appears here in print for the first time. By arrangement with Paul Spencer.

"The Lamp from Atlantis" (orig. "The Lamp") by L. Sprague de Camp first appeared in *The Magazine of Fantasy and Science Fiction* for March, 1975; copyright © 1975 by Mercury Press, Inc. By arrangement with L. Sprague de Camp.

"Xiurhn" by Gary Myers first appeared in *The House of the Worm* (Arkham House, 1975); copyright © 1975 by Gary Myers. By permission of Arkham House.

"The City in the Jewel" by Lin Carter first appeared in *Fantastic* for December, 1975; copyright © 1975 by Ultimate Publishing Co., Inc.

"In 'Ygiroth" by Walter C. DeBill, Jr., first appeared in the anthology *Nameless Places* (Arkham House, 1975); copyright © 1975 by April R. Derleth and Walden W. Derleth. By permission of Arkham House.

"The Scroll of Morloc" by Clark Ashton Smith and Lin Carter first appeared in *Fantastic* for October, 1975; copyright ©

CONTENTS

Introduction

THE YEAR IN FANTASY

1975 was, as you might have expected, a year like any other year, in that there was both good news and bad news. First, the bad news.

The *Silmarillion* still did not get published. This is the long-awaited sequel (or, rather, *prequel*) to *The Lord of the Rings*. Professor Tolkien was still working on revisions to the text up to the time of his death in 1973. The latest information that I have received on this important subject is that the Professor's son, Christopher Tolkien, has resigned his faculty position at Oxford and, in September of last year, moved with his family to France, to live in seclusion there while completing the editing of the *Silmarillion*. Glen Good-Knight of the Mythopoeic Society, who visited the Tolkiens last July, reports that Mr. Tolkien hopes to have the text ready for publication by the end of 1977.

Additional information has also come to light about what will actually be *in* the book, or books. GoodKnight has passed along the news that although the work will bear the overall title of *The Silmarillion*, it will actually be composed of three separate narratives: (1) The *Silmarillion* itself, (2) The *Akallabeth*, which tells the story of the fall of Numenor, and (3) *The Rings of Power*, described as a historical synopsis of events in Middle-earth from the beginning of the First Age to the end of the Third. (The very existence of this last manuscript has been hitherto a secret, known only to Tolkien's family.)

Probably never before in the history of fantastic literature has the appearance of any other single work been so eagerly awaited by so many millions of readers. If Christopher Tolkien completes his editorial work on schedule, 1977 will be a year to remember.

The other item of bad news is that the Conan books remain out of print and unavailable in this country, although eleven of the series of twelve are available in England. At the time of this writing the Conan authors and Howard's estate are trying through the courts to obtain cancellation of the contracts which bind the Conan books to the bankrupt firm of Lancer, so as to offer the series to another publisher. The case is still in litigation; if it is lost, the twelfth volume in the series, *Conan of Aquilonia,* may never be published.

Now for some notes and observations from the brighter side of the news. For the second time in a row, a previously little-known British author named Richard Adams has succeeded in doing something that neither Dunsany, Cabell, Merritt, Lovecraft, Howard, Smith, Lewis or Tolkien ever managed to do—get a fantasy novel on top of the national hardcover bestseller lists!

His first was that astonishing tour de force *Watership Down,* an epic narrative about rabbits. And now he has done it again with *Shardik,* which is much more the sort of straightforward heroic adventure epic we consider the mainstream of fantasy. I have read both, and enjoyed both tremendously, and I am looking forward with intense curiosity to see what Richard Adams will write next.

The critical *and* commercial success of novels such as *Watership Down* and *Shardik* do inestimable good to the cause of modern fantasy because they prove with hard facts and sales figures to publishers and editors reluctant to gamble on such a minority field as fantasy that a large audience does, in fact, exist for such books. The success of *The Lord of the Rings* ought to have demonstrated that to any doubters in the publishing ranks, but until somebody made another huge success in this field, it was always possible to dismiss Tolkien's sales as a fluke, an accident, a freak triumph that could never be repeated.

It is no longer possible to dismiss the success of *LOTR* as accidental.

Even unfortunate events sometimes have happy outcomes. The demise of the Ballantine Adult Fantasy Series was, indeed, unfortunate; but it has led to two or three other eventualities which could not have happened without the cancellation of the reprint of fantasy classics under the Unicorn's Head logo.

One of these was that Ian and Betty Ballantine, severing all connections with the firm they established, which they sold to Random House, have launched a new venture called Rufus Publications. Under that imprint they have begun releasing through Bantam Books a large-format, slick-paper series of handsome art books largely, if not entirely, devoted to fantasy art. Thus far this "Peacock Press" line has printed some remarkably attractive volumes on the work of Dulac, Frank Frazetta, Arthur Rackham and Kay Nielsen. There are more books to come in this series, and they will be heartily welcomed by fantasy buffs.

Another fortunate development of the death of the Adult Fantasy Series is that it has opened the way for another, smaller, less-known publisher to attempt to pick up where Ballantine left off in the reprinting of classic fantasies. The Newcastle Publishing Company of Hollywood, California, has thus far revived some rare and hard-to-find novels by the likes of H. Rider Haggard and William Morris, and has rescued from oblivion a little-known novel called *The Haunted Woman,* by David Lindsay, the author of the celebrated *A Voyage to Arcturus,* and has brought back into print a new edition of Lord Dunsany's *Fifty-One Tales,* under the new title *The Food of Death.* Although they do not enjoy as broad a pattern of distribution as Ballantine, and release only a handful of titles each year, in their way they are carrying on the good work begun under the Sign of the Unicorn's Head.

The third nice thing that came out of the collapse of the Series is, if I may say so, that it has freed me to take up new editorial duties, such as editing DAW Books' *Year's Best Fantasy Stories* anthologies. The idea behind this new series of anthologies is long overdue.

The year saw yet another interesting and significant development, which bodes fair for fantasy in the years ahead. And that is the founding of an annual convention devoted to fantasy alone. There are many conventions yearly devoted to science fiction, of course, but fantasy has never had its own convention.

This past October, over the Halloween weekend, there was held in Providence, Rhode Island, the First World Fantasy Convention. Since Providence is the home town of H. P. Lovecraft, it seemed only logical and fitting to the convention staff to turn the weekend into a celebration of *Weird Tales'* surviving writers. The guest of honor was Robert Bloch, and other celebrities present included such *Weird Tales* writers as Manly Wade Wellman, Frank Belknap Long, Arkham House authors like Joseph Payne Brennan and Ramsey Campbell, and a number of Sword & Sorcery wordsmiths, such as Fritz Leiber, L. Sprague de Camp, Andrew J. Offutt, Karl Edward Wagner, and myself.

It is hoped that the notion of an annual fantasy convention, with its own guest of honor and awards banquet and so on, will catch on and prove popular enough to become a regular part of the fantasy year. The 1976 World Fantasy Convention, incidentally, will be held in New York City.

—LIN CARTER

Hollis, Long Island, New York

THE YEAR'S BEST
FANTASY STORIES: 2

Tanith Lee

THE DEMONESS

Although Tanith Lee has had children's books and collections of her original fairy tales published in this country, her first major novel, The Birthgrave, *appeared only recently. And she is off and running: already her second novel has been published. Not since Ursula K. LeGuin published the first of her Earthsea novels have I been so impressed by the debut performance of a new fantasy writer.* The Birthgrave *is strong, rich, powerful, a work of beauty. For this reason, and one other, I am happy to be able to have Tanith Lee represented in this year's Year's Best.*

The other reason is the story itself, which is a honey. It has never appeared in print until now.

—L. C.

She waited in her high tower.

Day in, day out she waited.

The tower was white and stretched beneath her, far, far, to the sweep of the bleached dunes and the gray glister of the sea.

Her world was all gray, all white, half-tones, glitterings, without shape. A world colorless, and abstract. And she too was white, her foamy dress, her feet, her narrow hands—all white as the chalk hills that ran distantly above the sea. But her long, long hair was red, blood red, red as an eruption of magma out of the white volcanic crystal of her flesh. She did not look at her hair; obscurely she feared it. She bound it on her head in braids.

15

She was waiting, and not certain why she waited, or for whom, or for what.

She did not think of her past or her future, or really of any particular thing. She had no memory, or so it seemed, only an empty page from which words had faded. She watched the gulls dip in on the wind, screaking in their wind voices. She came out of the tower at certain times, and went in again at certain other times. Like a figure on a clock. She had no ambitions or yearnings, nor any hope. She was, in the sense that she existed. She was, but that was all.

Time passed, but time had no meaning. It might have been yesterday or tomorrow when she saw him.

He was riding up the beach in the dawn, a man in gold on a golden horse, its mane like blowing corn, scarlet reins and golden bells on them, its hooves striking up the sand. He dazzled her eyes. He wore a kind of armor that was either too antique or else too recent for her to recognize it. Tassels swung from his shoulders, his hair was ragged and bright like the ripped-out strings of a golden harp.

She felt a quickening as she leaned down from the length of the white tower. *Am I waiting for this man?* He was a burning ant on the beach, but soon he rode under the arch of the tower. An echo came, and then his feet loud on the stairs. She heard him pass through room after room, stopping sometimes. She imagined him examining certain things. But all the while he was drawing nearer. She turned to face the door through which he would come. Her heart beat. Without thinking, she reached up and let down her hair.

He stood still in the doorway looking at her. He was stern; she wanted to make him smile. He stared in her face.

"Where is Golbrant?" he asked her.

She put her hand to her mouth. She shook her head.

"He that passed by here, thirty days gone, riding to Krennok-dol. He that had a harp on his back and a scar like a cross on his brow."

She shook her head once more, and her heart beat fast and she put her hand on her throat and waited.

"Golbrant," he said, his eyes narrow and very bright, "my brother by vow, not blood. He to whom the Sisters said, 'Beware the white woman waiting for death in the tall tower by the sea.' "

He came forward and seized her by the hair, and twisted

it around his hand until the pain filled her skull like a silver cloud.

"Where is Golbrant?" he hissed, and then he met her eyes.

This was how it was to her. His eyes were like a summer garden. She wanted to draw from them those vistas of amber shades and yellow darts of sun, she wanted those hopes, those ambitions and yearnings she saw in them to fill her emptiness, her darkness, with their purpose and their light. She was hungry and thirsty for his reflected life as the fish for water, the wings of the bird for air. And her eyes began to breathe, to drink like beasts at a pool, and she put out her hands to his neck and drew herself against the hard armor, and clung to him tight. He spat a curse at her, and tried to shake himself free of her hands, her eyes, but could not. There was a kind of pleasant deathly heaviness in her embrace, her gaze, like sleep, except where it filled and curdled in his loins. She drew him down. She drowned him in her eyes and her body. He swam in the current of her flesh, and the tide took him away, and he was lost in the tunnel of the pleasure she had to give him. Such pleasure it was no woman before or since had been, would be. It was the whole store of her pleasure, held for him. She was the jar that contained the oceans, the fountainhead; he strove to reach the source and cried aloud to reach it.

But at the last his body checked itself. Out of desire came a great numbness, and then a revulsion of the pale thing wriggling beneath him. He understood then what he would have given her along with the life that ran out of him.

And then he twisted aside. He pulled his body free, and he turned his head, shielding his eyes as if from a dreadful and consuming glare.

"So, what they said of you is true, white woman," he muttered in sick cold anger, more to his own self than to her. "You devour the brain's knowledge and the mind's reason with your look and your womb. Yes, I felt it leaving me, and I would be hollow after as the bone of marrow when the wolf has had it. Is this then how you dealt with Golbrant?"

Her gaze was darkening, dimming, going out. She lay on the ground. She did not understand. And yet there was a faint memory, a memory like a dream, of a man on a dark horse, dark-haired, with a harp on his back with a woman's face, and a jagged criss-cross above his eyes. She had waited for him too, she remembered now, and he had come, across the long rooms, up the stairs of the tower. But he had not flinched aside, the light had passed from him to her. She looked up at the man whom she had almost possessed, for she recollected now, abruptly, what it meant when she lay with men. It was neither a shock nor a surprise, and not abhorrent. It seemed natural, for what did she know of the natural order of things to make this one thing that was hers seem strange and dark and evil?

"He is dead," she said softly, an explanation only.

The golden man drew his sword, swung it to lop her head from her shoulders, but it was not the habit of the warriors of Krennok-dol to kill women, however great their anger. So he halted, and after a moment he sheathed the sword again.

"Live, vampire," he said, his eyes now blind with hate, "but never practice on a man again to take his wits, or I'll see your head on a pole yet."

It could make no sense to her; she was not quite human, human values and laws had no meaning. Yet she stared at him, and she loved him, because he had won free from her and had no need of her any more.

He strode from room to room, searching for his vow-brother, Golbrant, but Golbrant had staggered from room to room when his self and his sanity had gone from him, and had fallen down from the high place into the sea. The waves had carried him off like sour green vinegar dogs, and the vulture gulls had picked at him, and the fish, so that now he was ivory on the ocean floor, with no mark on him any more to say who he was, except the gold harp turning green in the sand at his side.

While the warrior searched, the woman followed him. She could not tell him where Golbrant had gone, could not remember, though no doubt he guessed. She stared at his back, stared at his face when he turned. Her love was all-devouring; she would have eaten him if she could. Her love was like that.

But he thrust her aside, and went down the stairs of the tower, away from her and away. He found the horse and rode it off up the sea road into the chalk stacks that margined the shore.

For three days she wandered in the tower. She did not bind up her long, long hair. She did not go out above the bleached strand. She was no longer waiting. Golbrant and all the other men who had sunk like ships in her deadly embrace, lost their wills and their minds in her eyes and her womb, were quite forgotten again, shadows at the back of her thoughts perhaps, no more. But him she remembered, the warrior on the grain-yellow horse, his narrow bright eyes, his flax hair, his anger and his going away.

On the dawn of the fourth day she went down the stairs of the tower, and out, and up the sea road after him.

She had never left the tower before, not in all her years since she had become what she was. There had been no desire before; now there was a compulsion.

The sun cracked open the gray sky, and the sun and her blowing hair were two bright dabs of scarlet in the colorless land she was leaving.

After some days the land changed color. It changed from white to black. Hills like black crouching crows stood guard on either side of the road. The sky was dark with storms. Now her feet were red as her hair because the sharp black stones bit them like snakes. She was one of those who had no need to eat or sleep, so she simply walked day and night. She followed the hoofprints of the horse, and sometimes there were droppings; here and there a piece of his cloak might have caught on brambles, or she would come to the cold ashes of a fire and run her fingers through them and touch the ash with her tongue because he had lain by them for warmth when they were alive three nights before.

Then there was a black river in the twilight. There was a round blue moon overhead that looked almost transparent, and great clouds beating by like angry birds. And there was an old devil-woman crouched by the rushing water tending a bluish fire and a caldron of death over it. She was wrapped up in something black, only her eyes showed and her skinny hands stuck out, all bone. When she saw the white woman walking along the river bank she screamed out:

"Krennok-dol lies that way! That way! Over the river."

Then the devil-woman left her brew and went up to her, and turned her to look out across the river.

"No way for you to cross. The bridge is down—he did it, knowing you followed after. He was afraid, the horse leaped and struck sparks from its iron feet, knowing the vampire girl came behind them. I gave him a charm to protect him from you, but it will do him no good. Look at you, all hunger. Is this your love then, to follow a man who runs in terror, a man who hates you in his loins and sword arm? Didn't you drive to death his vow-brother, Golbrant the Good?" Here the devil-woman spat. "What is it makes you hurry after the sword stroke which is all he wants to give you?"

But the white woman was already wandering down the bank away from her, searching, searching for a place to cross, though there was none at all, and anyone could see it but her. The devil-woman ran after her, skipping like a ghastly black goat, for she had goat horns on her head, being what she was. She tapped the woman's shoulder.

"Do you know his name even? No. Well, there's too much of him in the world. If you want him, walk into the water and it'll carry you over, unless you're afraid to do it. A long search you will have, but when you find him, he will be yours. Only remember the price he pays for it. Witless he will be then, but what a joy to you—if you keep him from the tall crags and death. Like your child and your man, all in one, for ever and ever."

She heard, and though it was only a shadow on her thoughts, yet she understood. At the brink of the river the devil-woman whispered:

"If you let him go free, you will be dust, for a sword will strike off your head. Let nothing and no one come between. Remember."

Then she thrust with her bony hands, pushing the woman down into the water. The white woman had no fear. Her hair and her dress floated her up, the current bore her downstream, her hands trailed like drowned flowers, and she thought only of him she sought. All night, under the blue-ringed stars, the river pulled her between the hills by silver ropes. Near dawn it cast her up like a white fish-maid on the icy quays that lie below the dol hill.

Six or seven river fishermen found her. They thought she was a suicide and crossed themselves, but before they could run for the priest, she got up and walked away from them up the stone path to the hill, not seeing them.

The hill was green. Things grew on it that were not rank or poisonous in any way, and behind lay a forest. The land of Krennok was a land alive between the dead lands, north, south, east and west. High on the green hill the king's house stood, made of wood, stone and brass. Two hundred pillars upheld the roof in the king's great hall, pillars carved like trees of green marble. Fountains played and pools lay clear as glass, and white birds fluted in the gardens where round fruits grew in clusters under the yellow sky. This was Krennok-dol. At the great gate of bronze hung a bell the size of a warrior, with a tongue the size of a girl-child ten years old.

She had no means to strike the bell; it would take a tall man on a tall horse, striking with his sword, to do it. So she knocked, till her hands bled like her feet, on the bronze door panels.

It was the law in the king's hold that whoever came asking for mercy or justice, or any other kind of boon, should at least get a hearing from him. Consequently the porter came at last and let her in. Her dress and hair were still wet from the river, and she walked over the threshold trailing black river weed from her skirt. She frightened the porter a good deal.

She went up the great stairways into the hall with its forest of pillars. The king and his warriors had come from their dawn prayers, and were sitting eating and drinking at long tables. The king himself sat on his high seat of hammered gold, as he had sat three days before when a warrior came galloping from the sea with red-rimmed eyes and a horse frothing with fear. The king had risen to welcome and embrace him; he loved this warrior perhaps better than the rest, though possibly he had loved Golbrant the Good even more than this his Alondor, that women called the Gold behind their hands.

But Alondor held away from the king.

"There is a curse on me," he said. "God forbid I give it to you like a contagion."

He told them of Golbrant's death in the high tower by the sea. He reminded them of the Sisters, those five dark witches who had come to Krennok-dol five months ago to wail prophecies of death for five warriors. When he spoke of the woman in the tower and what he had done with her, he went white with shame. Later he made confession to the priest. The priest prayed hard, understanding very well what Alondor feared. Having lain with her but given nothing, having failed to kill her when he was able, he had left with her those powers of his pleasure and his hate he had renounced.

And she had come after him, still came, relentless as winter with her cold white desire. If again he stood in her presence he knew he, in turn, would have no power. The succubus would entangle him and destroy him, draining his brain of its life. Such was the shadowy magic of her sexual vampirism, the oldest and most terrible of all the demons in the world. He had not known all this till he was three days on the road and sensed, by a prickling of his skin, a coldness and a frenzy in his loins, what followed and with what ability.

Alondor fled out of Krennok-dol a day before she came there.

As she stood in the king's hall, she looked about for him, and her heart beat. When she saw he was not there, a deadly misery made her falter. Yet only for a moment. Then, forgetting it, remembering only him, she turned to leave the king's house the way she had come.

The king sprang up with an oath and three warriors ran into her path. They raised their swords to strike her down, but again the old stigma caught at their hands. They had never killed or harmed a woman. It came hard to do it now. Then she walked by them with her pale blind eyes.

"Go after!" shouted the king. "Do as he should have done. Remember her foulness and her sorcery! Not a woman but a *thing* under your blades."

They followed her out. On the stairway one looked in her face. He shrank back and could do nothing. Farther down another reached her. He swung her about and the sword swung, but at the last instant she seemed so pitiful, only a poor madwoman.

This is some mistake! he cried to himself, and let her go in an agony of bewilderment.

The third ran for his horse. He followed her across the court, out of the gate, grinning with fury. It seemed to him he was out hunting; he heard the dogs snarling ahead and glimpsed the running white deer leaping down from the green dol hill. When he was near enough, he snatched her on the horse, and rode with her limp in one arm into the forest beyond the hill. There he flung her down and himself over her in an unbearable ecstasy of need. The sword he used on her was flesh, and soon she slid from under him and walked away, barely conscious of what he had done or had become. Days later the king's warriors found him, a wandering madman screaming for his hunting dogs under the thick-leafed boughs.

She walked through a year. For a year Alondor the Gold fled before her. He became a mercenary, hiring out his war skills to many kings whose causes seemed good. Never did he stay long in any one place. He dreamed of fear and lust, and of Golbrant, his vow-brother, whom he had loved better than any man or woman.

The seasons changed. Red leaves fell into her red hair and over her scarred, misused, unnoticed feet, also into the bloody battlefields where he rode. Snows came and went, frost and rain. Beyond the land of Krennok, in the gray dead lands with their twisted trees and tall-spired mountains, he ran, she followed, drawn by instinct and desire, seeing and hearing only him.

In the barren steeples of the north he came at last to the pile of a solitary hold. It was dark and it was gloomy as were the crags around it. A green moon watched as he hammered at the gates. He was sick with the wound a battle two months before had given him, and he was sick of himself and his compulsion to fly the unknown thing which followed. He still had his looks; he was a man to be stared at, but there were white strings in the gold harp hair now, and his eyes ran back deep into his soul, the eyes of a murderer, a victim, or a man possessed by devils. Such was the penalty of an unstruck blow in a tower by the sea.

In a hall where flickering torches burned, he spoke with the lord of the place, but a ringing noise came and went in his head. Finally, from the corner of his eye, he saw a pale shape in the arch of a door. From over the white face to the white shoulders and beyond fell a blood-red curtain. He thought she had found him, she who came after, and terror rose up in his belly and choked him, and struck him, like all enemies, from behind. He fell down in the kind of faint that is an outpost of death.

Yet the woman in the door was not the one he thought. She was the daughter of the hold, her name Siandra, and she wore a scarlet shawl over her head because the hall was cold. She was beautiful as an icon. Her skin was white but her mouth was red, and her hair as black as Golbrant's hair when he rode with the harp on his back toward Krennok-dol. She might have been indeed a sister to Golbrant, for she resembled him very curiously, but she knew nothing of the warriors of the green-growing hill. She had her own kind of waiting, did Sian. When she saw the gold-haired man with nightmares in his eyes, she felt a quickening too. If he had chosen at that time to win her love, he could have done nothing better than fall down like a dead man a few yards from her feet.

She took it on herself to nurse him, and did not find it irksome in the least. Opening his eyes on her face, he felt life turn for him like a page.

Love grew up between them as easily as a child will grow.

As the spring drew on, a night came and took her with it into his chamber. She brought sweetness with her, if not the full draught of the cup. But then, he had known the pleasure of demons, and it was almost good that with this human girl it must be less. Towards dawn he kissed her and said:

"Tomorrow, Sian, I must be gone from you and here."

Tears filled her eyes. She thought the immemorial thought of the discarded.

"No," he said, "not for that. There is a doom on me. I am pursued. If I remain, I die."

"Then let me go with you," Siandra said.

"No. What gift of love is that from me to your sweet self, to make you wander the world homeless at my heels?" His face was pale and he had shut his eyes. "Let me go alone, and have your peace. There's none for me. I have already stayed too long."

If she was sweet, she was strong too, this girl in the north land. She took his hands fast and asked him for the truth, asked him again and again, until he thrust her from him as if he hated her, and told her everything, and then wept on her breast like a child.

"Let her come," Siandra whispered, and her eyes burned.

He was so tired. The year had tired him out. He stayed, for her woman's strength seemed more than any shield or sword in the wide world.

Nights passed. Spring lay on the land, but nothing grew save bright weeds at the door, and birds made nests in the crags of the mountains and the hold. Alondor was the lord's man now. He fought a battle for him and came back with the heads of enemies. The feast ran on into the dark, but for all the wine and meat, he felt a growing cold and uneasiness on him, like a fever coming.

In the close room he paced about while Siandra lay asleep. The moon rose late, the color of yellow bones, and he looked with a turmoil in his belly along the causeway, and saw something standing there, ice-white, holding back its blowing scarlet hair with long white narrow hands on which the nails had grown to talons. She had had no change of garment; her white clothes hung on her like the tatters of a shroud, her feet were carved over with scars. Her face looked up, yearning, her eyes like pools holding only his image. Her love had lasted, was still all-devouring; she would have eaten him if she could. Her love was like that.

Alondor fell on his knees and prayed, but no words came into his mind, only the woman. He felt her draw nearer and nearer across the rocky road, he felt her drift through the gates like white smoke, while the sentries dozed or did not see. He heard her soundless feet on the stairs, and how doors sprang silently wide at her touch.

Siandra woke and sat up in the bed. She looked at him crouching to pray, and heard how his prayers grew weaker and weaker.

She felt terror—*She* is here.

At that instant he got to his feet and the prayers left him altogether. He was a man deprived suddenly of everything—except that one thing which drew him and drew him. Like an automaton, he turned and crossed the room, went out through the door, and his eyes were very bright, his cheeks flushed. He went cheerfully, eagerly, the blood hot as fire in him, lusting, forgetting, caught up in the spell of the white woman who waited, this time, below.

When he was on the stairs, Siandra slid from the bed. If he looked burning and alive, she looked like his death. She snatched up the sword he had left behind and walked trembling, yet soft as a cat, after him.

She was in the house, the woman from the high tower by the sea. She was in a passage, and sensing that now at last he came to her, she had stopped quite still. Her heart beat. She put up her hands to her hair to let it down; finding it loose, she let down her hands instead. She thought she was in the tower, but it had no meaning for her. She thought she heard the sound of the sea sweeping in against the shale beaches; perhaps it was the sound of her own blood, the tide of her body moving in and out. A gull screaked, but it was a stair under his foot. Rounding a corner he came into sight for her. Her heart lifted in her body as if it had no weight or purpose except to lift in her like a bird. A warmth and gladness filled her up like the empty vessel she was, and for the first time since she had become what she was, her lips parted and she smiled. She held out her arms, and he was eager enough to come into them. He had forgotten.

But Siandra was just behind him, holding the sword. She also had the knowledge of old things, old ways—the oldest and most indisputable magic. Even as Alondor reached out to take his own death, Siandra ran between them. She lifted and swung the heavy sword as though it were a grass stem. She knew nothing of Krennok-dol and the warriors, and the chivalry of men who did no harm to a living thing with breasts and a womb, which called itself a woman. She struck for all she held dear and needful, with a selfish, careless, passionate stroke.

What she felt, the woman from the sea, was a long white pain, and then a long scarlet pain. Her head fell from her shoulders in an instant of time, but time had no meaning for her. Her agony lasted many ages. After the passing of these ages, she lay scattered, deaf, dumb, blind and in a million fragments. She knew what it is to be a million separate things, and still to be one.

Siandra shrank back against Alondor, looking away from what she had done, and he held to her, waking from the trance. She had been Golbrant, his vow-brother in that instant, rising out of the sea intact, green-gold harp on back, black hair strings on the strings of the harp, wielding the blow Golbrant had never thought to strike in the tower. This was how Sian finally took his love, more by becoming the past than by ending it.

While they held together, the white woman fell apart like the petals of a blossom. She blew up into their faces like white flour. She was dust as she had been promised she would be by the devil-woman in the blue moonlight. All dust.

The dust circled and pulsed, falling in on itself. Grains disbanded into grains, millions became millions upon millions. Soon there was no more of her to see, neither white nor red.

Yet she was aware. In every minuscule atom her hunger persisted, unassuaged.

Now she is blown here and there, endless varieties of place suck her down and fling her away. She is in everything, her hunger everywhere.

Long after Alondor and his Siandra will be dust of another sort, she will be blown about the world. Into the eyes to cause tears, into the fingernails of murderers, into the crannies of broken hearts to seal up the hurt with more hurting. She has no name. She is in every deed and dream and thought. She is all things and nothing. She is still waiting, and will wait forever, over every inch of the world.

Strangers come and go unharmed up and down the steps of the tall white tower. Gulls build in the ruins. One day every stone will have fallen bit by bit across the sweep of the bleached dunes and into the gray glister of the sea. One day the cliffs too will have fallen. After them, the land. The sea will shrink and drain away, the sky will tumble and the stars go out. And in that last or intermediary dark, she will remain. Still waiting.

Pity her.

Thomas Burnett Swann

THE NIGHT OF THE UNICORN

When I think about Tom Swann I have the weird feeling of looking into a mirror. We were both born about the same time (he in 1928, I in 1930), in the same state (Florida), fought in the same war (Korean), write the same sort of thing (fantasy), began publishing books about the same time (he in 1966, I in 1965), and even from the same publisher (Ace)! After ten years of reading and enjoying a score or so of books and stories by my mirror-image, I could have sworn there was nothing he might write which could surprise me. Boy, can I be wrong! As the next story easily proves: it is, in every way, completely unlike anything of his that I have ever seen before. It's like an initial work by a brand-new, unfamiliar writer. Yet, in its way, it has the old Swann magic . . .

—L.C.

It was the night of the unicorn, and the villagers of Cozumel, the capital and only town of a small island off the Yucatán peninsula, had begun to gather in the square. The maidens wore their brightest prints, lemon and turquoise and hyacinth, so that the animal could see their dresses even if not their virginal countenances and give them the approval of his notice. Somewhat more sedate in dress, their mothers maintained that haughty vigilance which had thus far safeguarded the daughters for marriage, while the young men of the town, casual in figured American sport shirts, looked impishly at the girls who would one day become their wives.

Maria stood in the doorway of her basket shop, debating if she should join the rest. The night of the unicorn! The words sang themselves in her brain, like an old Mayan chant to the god of swallows. It was said that a hundred years ago, a unicorn had emerged from the Mayan-haunted jungles of the interior and walked through the town, acknowledging the purest women with a nod of his golden horn or the press of his warm muzzle. He had never returned. But the villagers still celebrated in the hope that they could once again lure him from the jungle. Besides, Maria guessed, they loved a holiday and the chance to wear finery.

"Shall we go?" asked Mico, appearing quietly beside Maria in the door. At seventeen, his face looked adolescent but his eyes, gray and deep and a little sad, looked forty. He was small and copper-skinned like most of the islanders, with short-cut prickly hair. Also like them, he worked for tourists in the season, gigging lobsters or guiding photographers into the interior of the island where Mayan temples still thrust their stone jaguars through matted lianas. But a seriousness of purpose, almost a solemnity, distinguished him from the other youths, who laughed when he drew out his English grammar and announced that one day he would go to school in America. Maria loved him as a brother. Only Mico had befriended her since she had come to the island a year ago to open her shop.

"Shall we go?" he repeated. "The unicorn may truly come this year. My father saw strange tracks beside the Temple to the Jaguar."

"It is my dream to see the unicorn," Maria sighed. "But he will probably ignore me." It was not a secret that Maria, in Mérida, had sold her body and thus amassed the money with which, at forty-one, she had come to Cozumel to open a basket shop. She had come to forget her tawdry past. But the men of Cozumel remembered her from Mérida. Since she was still beautiful, with the slenderest figure on the island and with curious slanted eyes as purple as a murex shell, they paid her unpleasant attentions. What was worse, their jealous wives refused to buy her baskets, and her shop was threatened with failure. With a few hundred dollars, she could purchase curios for the tourist trade; but she lacked such a sum and the poor baskets she imported from Mérida were fit only for the islanders who refused to buy them. Her money would soon be gone. What then? The prospect of returning to Mérida alarmed her.

"He will not pass you by," said Mico firmly. "If he comes at all, he will come to you."

She touched his cheek and smiled. "Let us go."

He took her arm and they walked toward the square. A breeze from the sea brought the stench of lobster shells rotting in the harbor. Was there something else, Maria asked herself, a fragrance of jungle flowers and the sweet moistness of buried temples? For an instant, figures tumbled to clarity within her mind, a silken unicorn surrounded by jaguars, boars, and coatis. When the unicorn raised his head, the scythe of his golden horn flashed in the green light.

"Mico, is there something in the air tonight?"

Mico sniffed. "Yes," he said matter-of-factly. "There are pigs and chickens and asses—" Indeed, they were passing a wire-fenced yard where children huddled with pigs under sapodilla trees and roosters drowsed in the branches. Ahead of them in the street, an ass and a mongrel sniffed at a tuft of garbage.

"You're right, of course. I thought for a moment—"

"You thought it was the unicorn," said Mico, apologetic because he had not guessed her meaning. "Tonight he will surely come."

"What will he look like, Mico?" Sometimes she tried to draw him into moods of fantasy, though she loved him no less because he was more a realist than a dreamer.

"A lordly beast, my father says. His horn will catch the lamplight and gleam like a crescent moon above the white clouds of his mane. He will move up the street like a Mayan priest in a sacred procession. And he will pause beside the innocent—"

"If I could only glimpse him," she sighed. "Just a glimpse, no more."

"When he comes," Mico continued, "he will pause beside *you*." Maria claimed Mayan blood, and Mico had often compared her to the ancient corn goddesses who came from the jungle to teach the natives agriculture. "He will pause and dip his horn—"

"Maria, go home," screeched a female voice, its owner concealed in a blur of faces. "You will frighten the unicorn!"

Suddenly Maria saw that the people in the street, both men

and women, were staring at her. The men spoke loudly, careful that she should catch their gross compliments:

"Maria's kiss is worth a dozen unicorns. . . ."

"In Mérida they called her the Crimson One. . . ."

Maria lowered her head but she did not turn aside or slow her pace. "We will stand apart," she whispered to Mico. "There is no need that the unicorn see us. Only that we see him." They sought the shelter of a bougainvillea bush, its moon-silvered blossoms, purple by daylight, exploding earthward. Beyond the bush a row of streetlights kindled the village to a garish orange. But the sacred circle of the bougainvillea seemed inviolate to the work of man, aloof from his artificial lamps, his overpainted houses, and his strident outcries. Within this circle, companioned only by the moon, Maria and Mico awaited the unicorn.

In the streets, in the doorways of the shops, the crowd continued to chatter, first about the unicorn, then about lobsters and tobacco and silks from Mérida, the tourists who would soon be coming from the United States and the new guest houses built to accommodate them. In a little while they seemed to forget the unicorn. Had anyone really expected to see him after a hundred years, Maria wondered, except herself and Mico? Perhaps even Mico was humoring her out of politeness. A good boy, yes, but practical, his dreams extending no farther than a school in America.

And then she saw the animal in the street. He was walking toward her. He came slowly, deliberately, looking to neither side of him. At first she could not understand why the crowd had failed to take notice, for an unmistakable horn rose above his head.

"The unicorn!" she cried. "It is the unicorn, Mico!" Why did no one see him? Why did even Mico stare, like a stupid owl, into the distance? For an instant modesty restrained her. Then she forgot herself. She began to run, weaving among the crowd, brushing against the virgins, who drew back as if she had dirtied their dresses. She scarcely felt the jagged pebbles under her thin shoes. A bicycle came toward her and swerved to avoid a collision. The driver was too astonished to swear.

At last she knelt before the animal and stretched out her hand to touch his horn. How lordly he looked, even in the garish lamplight! How imperial was his bearing, how like a king's! She hesitated, suddenly aware of her daring, frozen

with her fingers inches from his horn. She, the fallen, impor-
tuning a unicorn! But slowly, with infinite majesty, he pressed
his muzzle against her cheek, and she felt the warm salt
wetness of her own tears.

A babble of voices stabbed at her ears. The people are
startled, she thought, because the unicorn has honored me,
the least pure, and overlooked the virgins. The voices rose
into a howling unison, and then she realized that the crowd
was laughing at her. Laughing and calling her unicorn an
ass!

"You profane him," she shouted. "You profane the holy
unicorn!"

Mico hurried to her side. "Are you sure he is a unicorn?"
he whispered. "Look at him again."

She looked at the animal closely for the first time, no
longer blinded by tears and wonder. Imperial? On the contrary, he was small, gray, mottled with age and mud. There
was little to distinguish his body from that of an ass. But his
horn. That was the irrefutable mark of his kingship! Only a
unicorn boasted such a horn. But she looked again, and she
saw that, though he truly held a horn, it was dirty and
crooked, and it might have grown there as a freak of nature
or it might have been placed there as a hoax.

Boys, emboldened by their sisters, began to scoop garbage
from the street and hurl it at Maria and her unicorn. A
banana peel struck her face and another struck the animal
where the horn sprouted from his head. He began to look
baffled and frightened, not kingly at all. A simple-minded ass
in the midst of a hostile crowd, Maria thought. Well, no
matter. She would not let the crowd make fun of him. Facing
his attackers, she returned the banana peels and shouted,
"You leave this animal alone! Whatever he is, you have no
right to hurt him!"

She felt Mico's hand on her shoulder. "The animal has
gone, Maria. His horn fell off and he ran away." He presented the horn to her, the dirty crescent which somehow had
been fastened to the head. She clutched the horn and began
to run, tears in her eyes, tears of shame for her own embarrassment and, even more, for the helpless animal harassed by
the crowd. She did not stop until she had come to her house
and run through the clean, spare kitchen into a garden where
a pool, no wider than a well, reflected a mahogany tree, a
moon, and a riot of stars. Beside the pool, she fell to her feet

and the horn slipped from her fingers. Breathless, Mico overtook her and waited for her to speak. For a long time she was silent. Mico retrieved the horn and began to wash it in the water.

"Why are you doing that?" she asked finally. "You know it is false. Someone has played a trick on me."

"It is very heavy," he said. "I want to see what it is made of."

The hard surface of the horn glittered beneath a coating of mud and filth. In the pool, among a hundred stars and beside the golden scimitar of the moon, a second scimitar materialized, richer than the first.

He handed the horn to Maria. "I believe it is made of gold."

She looked at him, unbelieving. She took the horn in her hand and marveled at its weight and its hard, smooth texture. A small treasure in gold! Her mind leaped: precious curios from the mainland to sell the tourists, an education for Mico.

"But shouldn't we return it to the unicorn?" she asked doubtfully.

"He will grow another. This one he meant for you."

"Then we must thank him! He is probably heading for the interior. If we hurry, we can overtake him."

But they were too late. Beyond the village, they found his tracks vanishing into the jungle and knew that he had eluded them. Swallows and frogs muffled whatever hoofbeats they might have heard.

"We'll never find him now," sighed Maria. "And we never told him how grateful we were."

As if to reassure her, a lordly cry thundered among the orchids and cacti, and briefly, goldenly, a pair of eyes poised in the black and silver night. The swallows and frogs fell silent.

"Good-bye, king unicorn," Maria whispered. "A king has no need of a crown. He carries kingliness in his heart."

"So does a queen," said Mico.

Pat McIntosh

CRY WOLF

I don't know why so many of the new major writers in fantasy are women, but they all seem to be. In the last few years we've seen the emergence of such important talents as Katherine Kurtz, Patricia A. McKillip, Sanders Anne Laubenthal, Tanith Lee—and Pat McIntosh. It all seems mighty suspicious to me, but maybe that's just my natural chauvinism rearing its ugly head. Anyway, like Tanith Lee, Pat McIntosh is also a young lady, also British, and also a whale of a writer. In last year's Year's Best it was my pleasure to bring you the first of her stories about Thula, a girl warrior of the Order of the Moon. And here's the second.

—L.C.

I heard his voice before I turned in at the archway by the inn, indistinct through the thick walls, with a clipped accent I did not recognize. The one that answered had the local accent, as thick as the local cider; as I rode through the archway the first voice spoke again.

"But the slate is up at the door. Are you certain there are no rooms?"

"Her be forgetful to tak un down." The Amyner struck a light and set it to a lantern, which sputtered into life as the third of the three men in the yard turned to look at me.

"Hello," he said. "You after a room too? I think we're out of luck."

This one was clearly from my own part of the world, and

34

he took me for a boy. In the lantern light, hair and mustache glinted red.

"Be no rooms," said the ostler, as if he was prepared to go on repeating it.

The redhead stepped to his horse's head and gathered up the reins, saying, "Wolf, let's go and see if the gate-ward'll let us out. There was a good spot a mile or so back."

The inn door flew open and a volley of sound poured out. Then a girl shot down the wooden steps to land sprawling in the yard, and the inn-wife appeared in the doorway flourishing a broom and still screeching curses.

"Let me see thy sour-apple face again!" she shouted. "Just once more in my clean inn, thee gall-weevil leaf-blighted barren strumpet! And if that city trash come nosing round here again the constables I'll set on him. Out!"

The girl, already at the archway, turned and shrieked something indistinct but venomous, then left hastily as the inn-wife made to come down the steps. She watched the empty archway for a moment, then turned back into the inn with a satisfied air.

"Applesweet," called the redhead. She paused, and turned ponderously, peering into the lamplight. The redhead returned his reins to the man called Wolf and went forward. "Mind me, applesweet? Changed thee have not, saving better. Knew thy voice on the first word, that I did."

The dialect of Amyn sat oddly on his Westlands tongue but the inn-wife appeared to think otherwise. With a shriek of delight she cast herself down the steps at him; he caught her, staggering, and patted her ample bottom.

"Barlach!" she exclaimed. "Truly it be thee?"

"Is that you forget me so quick? Truly me—no, not here, shock himself you will. Has thee room for himself, applesweet?"

She cast a quick glance beyond him at the man called Wolf, straightened, and bobbed a curtsy.

"Got a lovely room, now she'm left. Two beds, and both clean sheets, it has. Come thee and see," she said to the redhead, and started up the steps onto the inn. He came back to where the man called Wolf was still holding the reins of both their horses.

"Well?" he said. "I'm provided for—" He grinned in the lampilght. "D'you want to share?" he said to me.

I stared at him. I knew my answer, of course. Any mem-

ber of the Order, said the rules, who shall wittingly and
willingly share a room, a bed, or a blanket with a man shall
be held excommunicate until suitable expiation. . . . I looked
at the mounted man, and he pushed back his hood and
smiled at me. In the lamplight his face was pale and dia-
mond-shaped, and his eyes, smiling, drew the heart out of
me. Blinded, I smiled back, and nodded.

"Fine," said the redhead. "You see to the horses, then."

I dismounted, and led Dester and my packhorse into the
stable, wondering whether I had run mad. I had been sane
enough when I rode in at the archway, and now here I was,
Thula, warrior of the Order of the Moon as Alkris, sworn
to remain virgin and eschew the company of men, about to
share a room with one. I put my horses in the stalls the
ostler pointed to, and unlashed my saddlebags from Dester's
saddle. There was enough money in them to buy a half share
in the inn.

"Well, friend?" said the man called Wolf. I turned, and he
was looking at me with those disturbing eyes. I moved toward the door, and slipped on rotted straw. He put out a
quick hand to steady me, and at his touch the world swirled
and went dark about me.

*I lay flat—in a bed, perhaps—and about me were hooded
figures, faceless in the light of a spider-lamp that glimmered
faintly on the wooden bowl before my face. I must drink or
choke on the bitter liquid it held; I raised my hand to push
it away, without success, and panic rose in my throat as I
saw my hand. Not square-fingered and short-nailed, but long
and thin, taper-nailed, a scar across the knuckles . . .*

"Easy," said the man called Wolf. "How long since you
ate?"

I pulled away from him. The vision had passed, but not
the feeling of panic, and I was trembling.

"I'm all right," I said. "Dizzy for a moment. I need a
drink."

We crossed the yard in silence, I with my thoughts in
turmoil. We are taught to regard such visions as having
meaning, but what should this one tell me . . . ?

The room was a good one, although not so good as the
inn-wife claimed; she was insisting that the High King of the
Westlands himself slept in it frequently when we arrived.

"Gonseir the Usurper?" said Barlach. "It looks it, applesweet. Wolf, that's three crescents. If we pay two and the youngster pays one—"

"I should pay one and a half," I objected.

"The Wolf gets the bigger bed," Barlach said. "He'd never get into this one. Got a crescent?"

"Please," I said, embarrassed. "I can't—"

"Fair's fair," Barlach argued. "If you like to share the other bed, you can—"

"Barlach," said the Wolf quietly. The redhead turned to look at him, said, "Oh, all right," and accepted my one-and-a-half crescents. The inn-wife, paid, leered lovingly at Barlach and puffed off down the stairs. I put my saddlebags down on the small bed and looked around. Fresh water and a basin stood on the table between the beds.

"Ale before supper, Barlach?" asked the Wolf. He had removed cloak and hood and stood clad in black; a single heavy black plait swung as he turned his head, and his eyes gleamed pale under dark brows.

"I've a thirst like a lime kiln," said the redhead. The Wolf turned to me, one eyebrow raised. I shook my head.

"I'll wash first," I said. "I'll follow you down."

As they left, I realized for the first time their relative heights. Barlach was smaller than me, six inches or so, which made him five feet three at the most, but broader and heavier, solidly made; the Wolf was a foot taller than his friend and the leanest man I had ever seen. They made a strange pair.

The door closed behind them and I turned to the ewer and basin. What was I doing, I wondered. Had I indeed run mad? I was now excommunicate; moonlight falling on me would kill me; I must not pray to the Lady—I ought to be on my knees shaking and weeping and begging to First Star to intercede for me. . . . Instead I was calmly washing the dust off my face and wondering what the tall man with the light eyes would say if he knew I was a girl. And what he would do.

I looked at the door. Firmly shut. And I was covered in dust. I decided to risk a proper wash, and pulled off my padded tunic and, with another glance at the door, my shirt and the linen band that goes under it. The cool water was blissful on my throat and shoulders; I reached for the soap and began to remove the rest of the dust.

I was finished and rinsed and reaching for my linen towel

when hasty feet sounded along the corridor. I grabbed at the towel as the door burst open.

"Wolf, have you got—" began the redhead, and halted. He stared at me, took in what he had seen, and stepped inside. I felt the slow tide of color rise in my face and spread down my neck. Helplessly I stared back at him, almost mesmerized.

"Devern's golden ball," he said, closing the door behind him. "Well, now, gorgeous. You're on the wrong track. The Wolf's under an oath, he'll have no use for you. Why not make do with me?"

I had never seen anything like his expression. I clutched the folds of linen against me and said with difficulty,

"Please—it wasn't like that! I don't—I mustn't—"

"Or were you planning to knife him in the night?" He stared at me, frowning. Then the frown cleared and the other, more alarming expression returned. "No, you weren't. Come on, then," he said, trying to coax me, taking a step forward. I retreated, though my knees threatened to give way. Unarmed and half-naked I was awash with panic.

Again feet came along the corridor, light and hasty. The door flung open and the Wolf appeared. He glanced swiftly at me, at Barlach and back; frowning, he stepped in and closed the door. Panic died before despair; I had been mistaken in him, and here was my end, force and ignominy and falling on my sword.

Then his glance sharpened. Comprehension dawned. He took Barlach by the shoulder and swung him around, turning himself to face the door.

"Let you dress, madam," he said quietly. Heart pounding, knees trembling, I rubbed myself half-dry and obeyed, wrestling with clinging linen and dust-caked wool. At last I said,

"You can turn around now."

My voice sounded small in my own ears. He released Barlach and turned to face me, and I found myself going scarlet again.

"I will sleep in the stables," he said harshly, and moved to lift his saddlebag. "Best you leave before us in the morning. I will not ask your name, lest this come to the ears of your superiors."

His tone had shaken me, but he could not maintain it, and his eyes did not match it. I had fallen from grace already, what was a little more?

"I want to ride with you," I said. He stared at me, his face going rigidly expressionless. Barlach produced an appalling snigger.

"I've told you, sweetheart," he said. "The Wolf has no use for you. Why not make do with me—?"

The Wolf dropped the saddlebags and struck him backhanded. He sat down on the kist behind the door, rubbing his mouth and looking startled; the Wolf turned to me and said, still without expression, "We are not for such as you. I am—I am under judgment on a matter of league with Darkness, and Barlach—" He halted, and glanced over his shoulder at the redhead, who smiled deprecatingly.

"You should see the village where we lived for six months," I said.

"Your shield-sister is dead?" he said, more gently. I nodded, and there was another pause. The Barlach came to his feet.

"Oh, hell's teeth, let's go and eat," he said. "I'm hungry."

The Wolf looked at him, and back at me.

"Aye," he said. "Let us eat."

I came forward to obey. I could argue in the morning. Barlach looked me up and down and snorted, disapproving.

"I like 'em well covered, anyway," he said.

We ate at one end of the long table in the public room. It was stuffy, full of Amyner peasants, and noisy, but a row of empty bowls showed that the other guests had already eaten well. Barlach disappeared shortly, to help the innwife at the tap of the great cider barrel in the corner; to judge by the sounds that reached us now and then, he was little help. We two left at the table ate stew with thick barley bread. The Wolf, finishing first, sat in silence, looking at his hands clasped on the table. They were as pale as his face, with no line at the cuffs of his shirt such as I had on each wrist; they were long and thin, taper-nailed, and as he reached for his cider-mug I saw the long scar across the knuckles.

Something lurched inside me. I stared, transfixed; then, finding him looking at me with faint concern, I said the first thing that came into my head.

"The scar on your hand—troll?"

He looked down at it and shook his head, half smiling.

"Na, not that one. This was a troll." He touched his upper

arm as if it were still tender, and I recalled that he had not used that arm all evening. There was a tear in shirtsleeve, clumsily mended, and a bloodstain partly washed out. "A week since," he added, feeling the silence. "Perhaps three days' hard ride." There was another pause; I finished my stew. "You know trolls?"

"Trolls killed Fenala," I said. "I got the trolls."

"Where was that?"

"A long way. North of Rhawn Dys—other side of the Mountains."

"You have crossed the Mountains alone?" he said.

"Well, I wasn't alone when I set out," I said. He quirked one eyebrow and looked interested, so I told him the story of how I crossed the Mountains. Bits of it made him laugh; once or twice he made a dry comment that made me laugh. Behind me the taproom filled with villagers, cider fumes and noise, but isolated in its center we continued to talk of the Mountains, of merchants, of the trading road through the Isthmus to the Southlands . . .

Then the Wolf, who could see the tap and the crowd around it, broke across something I was saying.

"Madam," he said softly, "in a moment there will be fighting. When I say the word, go quickly and stay in our room. Open only to Barlach or to me. Is that clear?"

"I can use a knife," I said. He looked at me like a man not used to being disobeyed.

"Battle, even with trolls, is one thing," he said. "A drunken brawl is another." His glance went beyond me again. "Go now. Quickly." He got to his feet and without staying to see that I obeyed made his way quietly through the crowd about the tap. A silence fell, in which I heard Barlach's voice.

"Let go of me, pig-feet," he said clearly.

"Tak they filthy hands off of she," said an Amyner voice, "or mak thee I will."

"Let go of me first," said Barlach.

"What business is it of thine, brother?" said the inn-wife shrilly. "Is that I gave thee leave to meddle wi' my doings?"

"Be quiet, woman," said the Amyner voice. "Now tak thy hands off of she, thee city trash, afore I mak thee."

The Wolf had reached them now, and seemed about to join in the discussion when a man by the door shouted:

"Werewolf!"

The Wolf stiffened. My heart began to thump unpleasant-ly—I had once before seen a shapeshifter taken, but that was in an Eastlands city, and the Peacekeepers had arrived before blood was shed. Here, anything might—

"Where be werewolf?" demanded somebody. "Where?"

"There! Him i' the black tunic!"

Over the heads of the crowd the Wolf's narrow black-clad shoulders were rigid. I stared, and the men nearest him laid hands on him. Those farther away backed away a little, and I saw Barlach come up in a rush to help his friend. Someone clipped him on the side of the head with a cider mug, and he went down, and the man by the door shouted,

"Kill the filthy shapeshifter!"

"He be no werewolf!" the inn-wife protested. "Know him I do, all on us do!"

"He bear the marks," said the man. He was marked him-self, a livid birthmark like a horse-track on one cheek, and his eyes were wild and burning. Cloth ripped, and some-body swore, and as the crowd fell back again the Wolf stood passive in the hands of his captors, tunic and shirt torn to the waist. Everyone knows the marks of the werewolf: hair on the back and none on the chest, different teeth, the extra nipples down the belly like a wolf. They made no attempt to count his teeth. I saw the meaning of his nickname, and a chill wave of horror washed through me.

"Kill the filthy shapeshifter!" someone shouted. They all took up the cry. I should have left, but I stayed where I was, shaking. I had left my young charge with a werefalcon in the Mountains, but a bird was a bird. A wolf killed people. They told tales—especially in the north, nearer to the Wolf-land—things I had heard jumped to my mind. And I had nearly shared a room with that. . . .

"Hang the brute!" someone yelled. The man near the door seemed to have vanished. I got to my feet and slid to the door, and through it, and ran along the passage and up the stairs and into the room. Mother of mares, what an escape! I might have been torn to pieces while I slept!

Common sense took over. In the first place, being torn to pieces was likely to wake one; in the second, he had or-dered me out of a possible brawl. Not trying to reason out why this made a difference, I went back to the door and opened it. Voices rose in ciderous discord, arguing about what to do with him. They could not hang him, Grum's cow had eaten the rope. They could not burn him, for fear of firing the thatch this dry weather. Knifing only worked with a silver blade, everyone knew that.

Someone suggested drowning, and they all took that up. Hope leapt in me. They must open the gates to take him down to the river, and in the mood they were in they would not close them. With much shouting they settled on that, and I left the door and hastily stuffed soap-box and linen towel into my saddlebag. The Wolf's heavy fur cloak and hood, their bag, was that everything—?

In the dark stable, Dester snorted at me, and nudged an en-quiring muzzle into my hand. At any other time I would have cursed into Outer Darkness any ostler who left him to eat his supper around his bit; now I only prayed that all four horses were yet bridled, and almost wept with relief to find it so. It can be hard to bit and bridle a strange horse in haste. Their two were easily identified, the ugly black the Wolf had ridden and a nappy half-broken chestnut who threatened to bite as I clapped his saddle on his back. I tightened the girths with trembling fingers; the packhorse, my gift from Fenist the Falcon, grumbled sleepily and tried to blow himself out, but I thumped him in the ribs and he subsided. Gathering up the four sets of reins, I led the horses out across the yard.

As I came to the archway the rabble of villagers poured past in the street; it had taken them until now to find cords enough to bind him, and as he passed I saw by moonlight the knots and tangles about his arms. I could not tell if he had seen me but it mattered little. As they battled loudly with the gates, I led the horses out and tied them up before the inn.

Inside, all was deserted. The inn-wife sobbed in the dis-tance, and in the taproom Barlach lay in a gaudy heap on the floor, cider dark in his hair. I shook him, but he showed no sign of rousing, so I grabbed the back of his orange tunic and tugged. He slithered across the floor, limp and amazing-ly heavy, rushes piling up before him. Mother of mares, I prayed, let his tunic hold, for I like him, no matter what he said to me, and he is the Wolf's friend.

The tunic held, while I towed him across to the door, and somehow down the steps to where the horses shied away, snorting. My packhorse seemed the best steed; something gave me strength to lift him across the pack-saddle before the horse could avoid me. I lashed him on with the unused stirrup-leathers from my saddlebag and mounted Dester, four sets of reins wound around my hand. The gates at the end of the silent street stood wide open. I turned the beasts, and nudged Dester forward with my knees.

We came forth at the canter, into the open beyond the fence. Down yonder, away to the right, was a group of men shouting and splashing in the moonlit river. I drew my sword with my free hand and shouted a war-cry, and we bore down on the gaggle of villagers like an army—four horses, one unconscious man, and a frightened war-maid. Many of the Amyners scattered, leaving something dark in the river. I let go the other horses' reins, and two of them shied off, frightened by the shouting, but the ugly black one the Wolf had ridden chased the few Amyners who tried to stand ground. I halted Dester in the water and leaned down.

He was beyond struggles, lying limply in a foot of water. I reached for him, trying to get some purchase on arm or shoulder, and his black horse left off chasing peasants and to my surprise splashed into the river, bent his head and got the slack of the Wolf's tunic in his teeth and heaved. I grabbed at the limp body as it came up dripping moonlight, and getting some purchase in the ropes about his arms dragged him across my saddle-bow. No time to see to him now: the peasants, seeing the avenging army to be but one rider and three uncontrolled horses, were returning. I shouted, and flourished my sword, and turning Dester's head for the road kicked him in the ribs. The other horses, seeing him running, came after, and we went off down the road like the Wild Hunt.

A mile from the village I first noticed the ravens. The urgency was wearing off, and we were doing a hand-canter, so that I had time to look around; and there were three birds flapping along near us, wheeling across the moon, quite plainly ravens. I wondered vaguely what ravens should be doing out at this hour, but my attention was for the Wolf, who was beginning to stir across my knees. I touched his arm, meaning to say something reassuring, and through torn wet linen my fingers found cold and clammy skin. Once again the world swirled and went dark about me.

I faced a man, one who though seated I could discern to be tall, who regarded me with piercing eyes from under a

broad-brimmed hat. Gems hung bright from the hat, catch-
ing the light of the candle-crown I knew was over my head,
and a slow voice spoke, and I felt myself answer.

Then I snatched my hand away, and I was on Dester's
back, a half-drowned man across my knees, with the
strange feeling that the man in gem-hung hat knew all the
paths of my mind and how I trod them. . . .

There was a good place to stop. I turned Dester and
walked him down onto the grassy slope between the stream
and the road. The Wolf's black horse spoke to the other
beasts, or so it seemed, for in response to its half-threatening
snicker they wheeled off the road and stood obediently waiting to be tethered for the night. I unloaded my two prizes,
and tethered the beasts hastily, not letting them drink yet.
Barlach, when I checked him, was twitching slightly; I covered him with his own blanket against the dew, and turned
to the Wolf.

He was wholly unconscious again, soaked to the skin, cold
and clammy to the touch as I cut the ropes away. Fresh
blood spotted his sleeve over the troll-wound, but it seemed
to me the first thing was to warm him. I got the dry wood
out of my pack-saddle and began to build a fire.

By the time the water boiled he was rousing. I put various
herbs to infuse in the pan, this and that against fevers and
chills, and when he groaned I lifted it from the fire and
poured some into my pewter mug. Setting it near him I
knelt beside him and, without thinking, put my hand on his
cheek to turn his head. He groaned again, and his eyes
opened, and his gaze met mine.

*This time, more than ever, I was not myself. I was sitting
in a high wooden chair, carved and uncomfortable, facing
the tall man with the piercing eyes, who sat in another such
chair. Between us, to left and right, were long tables, and
men seated behind them, watching us. The man before me
was speaking, eyeing me closely from under his gem-hung
hat, but I could not understand the words. Then he said,
"You who are accused, the first test, for tainting of thought,
intent and memory, gave no result. The second test, for
tainting of purpose, gave no result. This test will show if
you are tainted by Darkness in blood, bone and sinew, and
by the writing in the nail. Do you submit to this final test?"*

*I nodded, because I had obeyed when this truly hap-
pened.*

"The test is carried out within a Ring of Feeling," he said, and the words echoed in my head, ring-of-feeling, ring-of-feeling—the swirling happened again, and there were chalked lines about me and a gleaming and glowing in the air. I saw this and knew it illusion, there was only chalk on the marble floor; but I felt raw, mind and body, not hurting but as if anything that did hurt would be too much to bear, like a crab without a shell. The man in the hat said, *"Hold out your left hand."*

I did so, and hands took it; it was pale and long-fingered, and they twitched it expertly into position on a slab of marble, and before I fully realized what came next the hinged chopper cracked down on my little finger. It went through bone and muscle cleanly, someone caught the severed joint in a little silver bowl, and my hand was allowed to swing free, down inside the glowing ring. A demon of pain, fearsome even in memory, devoured hand and arm, and darkness covered me.

A series of images. A dwarf, strangely dressed, mixing this and that in little bowls on a table before the man in the hat. Two rats, a white and a black, in a cage before my feet, one eating boiled flesh, the other refusing his share. A sickening smell, and the stomach-churning, sudden knowledge that this was my flesh, the scraps of muscle from the severed joint. The same with the bone. . . . The dwarf working over another little bowl, stirring with a glass rod, heating it over a tiny brazier, adding wine vinegar and water-of-sulphur. The phrase rose in my mind again: *the Writing in the Nail.*

The dwarf facing me.

"You had a brush with Darkness," he said. *"Six weeks since."* The words echoed in my mind; my hand hurt, and the world looked strange.

"We were here," said Barlach's voice. *"Talking to Gonseir the Bastard."*

I saw indistinctly the man with the birthmark whom I had seen in the inn, his eyes furious, the birthmark pulsing redly.

Then my sight cleared, and I was kneeling over the Wolf, staring down at him in the moonlight. My left hand resting on his cheek had four whole fingers attached to it.

"You went away," he said. I drew a shaking breath, and let it go. Whatever it meant, that was a dream. This was reality —two hurt men to see to, and this one soaking wet.

"I was afraid you'd think that," I said. I raised his head, and lifted the cup which was still scalding hot. "Try and drink this, it's hot."

He drank a little, then rolled over on all fours, stomach heaving. I set down the cup and held his head, and he retched till his belly was empty and then subsided against me, shivering. I found I was holding his left hand in mine; it was long-fingered, pale in the moonlight, and the last joint of the little finger was missing. *The wound was still tarred over.*

It came to me with a lurch. These visions had no meaning for me—they were his, memories rather than dreams, of some sort of trial. What had he said? "I am under judgment on a matter of league with Darkness." Mother of mares, no wonder his judges had wanted the Oracular Joint!

I pushed him down on the turf and reached for the cup again. He drank obediently and said, "I mind I was in the water."

"You were," I said. "I thought you were drowned. I frightened the men with the flat of my sword, but that horse of yours chased them off—like a dog after rabbits. They were more scared of it than of me."

He laughed, almost light-headedly.

"Squirrel is wise," he said. "Wise as the Wizard's ravens."

"We've got three of those," I said. "Ravens I mean."

"Ravens?" he said quickly.

"Yes," I said. "Flapping round us all the way here. They've gone now, but—"

"Ravens!" he muttered. "The message. It must be—!" He stared about him at the silent sky. "You are certain? They were not owls?"

"I saw them against the moon," I said.

Mother of mares, the Moon! I had broken the Rules, I should have run mad by now, riding about in the moonlight like this—and yet I had prayed to her, and she had answered. Or at least Barlach's tunic had held. Were my teachers all wrong, was I specially favored—?

I realized the Wolf was shivering.

"You should change," I said. "I'll be down by the river. Shout if you need me."

Barlach groaned beyond the fire. The Wolf jumped, and I turned and peered at the redhead, still lying inert under his blanket.

"It's Barlach," I explained. "He's not hurt, except for a bang on the head."

"Can you do everything?" he asked. His tone of rueful amusement made my face burn.

"I'm scared of thunder," I said. He laughed at that, and began getting to his feet. The torn tunic fell open, and I remembered why it had been torn.

"I'll be down by the stream," I repeated, and went off across the short turf.

Down by the water I found a flat stone to sit on, and for some time stared at the black-and-silver water without seeing it. All the things that had happened this evening went round and round in my head, images of Barlach, the peasants crowding about the pool, the Wolf's bare chest in the moonlight, and over all his compelling eyes by lamplight in the yard. I liked him, I was drawn to him, when he smiled I would be his bond-servant for life, but he was a werewolf, half animal, a shapeshifter—my nurse's tales danced in my mind.

Then suddenly all the spinning images fell into a pattern. The moon had showed me all these; she had lit my way out of the inn-yard, she had given me light by the river, and now she had reminded me what this man was. I was being given a choice: to go with him, follow my liking, forsake the training of my youth; or ride away and leave him and go with the moonlight. For the first time in my life, I found the moonlight cheerless.

But supposing, against all better judgment, I did as I wanted and rode with him. If the rules are broken, how shall the Order survive? I would be in the displeasure of the Moon, that I had served since I was seven years old. . . . And anyway, he had refused my earlier request: maybe he would refuse this one. Suddenly I decided. I would not speak. I would go up the bank, and collect my horses, and ride on before they left, never seeing him again. I would go down to Maer-Cuith and tell them at the Temple that Fenala was dead; they would find me another girl to ride with, and we would go out and combat evil under the moon. . . .

Twigs snapped. I turned, and he stood against the stars; I rose to my feet, and the moon came out. I had been so engrossed in my thoughts I had not noticed the clouds coming up.

"You'll be all right here," I said. "I'll go on now, my horses should be rested."

"I assure you," he said, and his voice was smiling, "I stopped eating little girls for breakfast when I left my mother's country."

"That's not—" I began, and stopped guiltily.

"For one thing," he pursued drily, "I dislike meat first thing in the morning."

I couldn't help it, I giggled.

"I prefer a light breakfast myself," I agreed. He sat down, as if his legs had given way, and my voice said of its own accord, "I never met a werewolf before. I didn't think—" I regained control and changed that to, "When the man with the birthmark shouted Werewolf—"

"Birthmark?" he said quickly.

"Yes, the man by the door." I thought quickly. "No, he kept out of your sight. Six feet, dark hair, wild eyes, a mark like a horseshoe on his cheek." I drew it on my own cheek to make it clear, and he took a long unsteady breath.

"Gonseir," he said. "Gonseir the Bastard. My loving cousin."

"Gonseir?" I said. There was a short silence. Then I said, "He was in your dream. The third one."

He glanced at me, unsurprised.

"I felt your fear, when Barlach surprised you," he said. "Clear across the yard, I felt it. My dream, lady—if you saw that, you saw that I have been on trial," he said, as if the words tasted bad. "My cousin, who is High King of the Westlands, can think of no better way to be rid of me than to impeach me before the Order of White Sorcery on a charge of league with Darkness." He shivered, his hands working together. I saw that he was rubbing at the damaged finger as if there were a ring missing from it. "By the laws of the Order, if I am innocent, he must submit to the same trial, but he thought it worth the attempt."

"And you are innocent?" I said. Try as I might I could not keep the question out of my voice. He nodded.

"I know myself to be innocent. But my cousin is less than sane, and he has many resources, and speech with him can mark one like a brush with Darkness. They were to decide today."

"But surely," I said, "if he tried to get you the other way just now, the judgment must be for you?"

"The ravens will tell me," he said, and his voice was weary. I suddenly remembered my decision. I moved to go past him, saying,

"I wish you luck. The moon shine on you."

He put up his hand and caught my wrist. His fingers went right around it. I stared down at him, and he said, "I have an oath on me as binding as yours. I would not harm you."

The Moon came out—when had it gone in?—and in the same moment Barlach called from the fire. I slipped from his slackened grasp and went up the bank. By the time he followed me, Barlach was sitting up cursing and feeling his head, which was not broken despite all he said.

"I think he'll live," I said over his shoulder to the Wolf. "His tongue isn't damaged, anyway."

"No bones broken, small brother?" said the Wolf.

"Only my head," said the redhead. "Devern's brass ball, if I ever drink Amyn cider again—" He was silent, staring before him. The Wolf turned, and I likewise, as a second and a third raven flopped down to join the one on the turf.

"Greetings to the emissary of the Wizard," said the Wolf, and went down on one knee. The first bird waddled forward and ducked its head in a travesty of a bow.

"My son," it said. "Gonseir's charges against you stand not proven."

The second bird joined it, and in the same outlandish accents recited, "Wherever this finds you, make all haste to join me."

The third raven came clumsily across the grass and halted at the Wolf's knee. "Gonseir is suspended," it said. "Take your ring and walk in light."

Gold glittered on its leg. The Wolf lifted it gently, his hands trembling, and worked the ring over its claw. It croaked, and bit him, but at length he set it free and held up the ring. Getting to his feet he slid the ring onto his damaged finger and turned to us.

"Walk in light," he said. Barlach scrambled up and sprang at him, hugging him and then punching him in the ribs so that he swayed.

"Careful," I said. "He was nearly drowned."

"Drowned?" said Barlach blankly. "Hey—how'd we get here, anyway?"

"We were brought," said the Wolf, one arm still across

Barlach's shoulders, "by the lady whose name we still do not know."

"Thula," I said.

"Thula," he repeated. "What way do you ride, Thula? We must make all speed westwards, since the Wizard summons me."

Barlach groaned, and muttered something about the Wizard, but I stared at the Wolf. Here was my decision, made and unmade in my head a dozen times, being taken for me. All the sanctuaries and holy places of the Westlands lay south from here, not west. They rode on an errand with no place for me. South down the moon's path was my road.

"South," I said, and my voice cracked. He looked at me a long moment, while Barlach stared from one to the other of us. Then he bent his head.

"So be it," he said. "Let us break the fire."

But when the fire was broken, the horses watered, all made ready to leave, he came to me where I tested Dester's girth.

"Thula," he said, and his hand was held out. "It is in my heart that we shall meet again, and before too long. I do not know our plans, and only the Moon knows what comes to you, but the Bunch of Grapes in Maer-Cuith is a good place."

"A good place for what?" I said. The clasp of his hand made my heart thump, but when that wore off he was saying,

"Have you a coin? Any coin will do."

"What for?" I asked, searching my pockets. "If you're planning to go back and pay the reckoning—"

"Na!" He was laughing. "Only, there is this I wish to give you, and I do not wish to cut the friendship."

I found a half-copper crescent, and gave him it, and he put in my hand a dagger, a good one, blue Southron steel with a shagreen hilt. He closed my hands over it, and bent and kissed my closed fingers, and swinging about went and mounted his horse.

"Come, Barlach," he said, and they moved off, crossed the road, set off westward in the moonlit countryside. I watched them until the Moon changed shape and wavered and spilled over, and he did not look back.

Fritz Leiber

UNDER THE THUMBS OF
THE GODS

Fritz Leiber is neither a young lady, nor a Britisher, and he's certainly no newcomer to fantasy. He is, in fact, the finest living fantasy writer, and he can prove it, too. Not only with delightful tales like the next, which he seems to turn off with unearthly ease and grace, but also with a solid testimonial in the form of a bronze statuette called "the Gandalf," awarded him in Australia by the membership of the 1975 World Science Fiction Convention. The little statue is more formally known as The J. R. R. Tolkien Memorial Award for Achievement in Fantasy, and Fritz won the Grand Master award for his entire career. His achievement is a massive and enduring sequence of novels and stories about Fafhrd and the Gray Mouser, which he has been steadily adding to for thirty-seven years. And here is the latest chapter in that enormous—and enormously entertaining—epic.

—L.C.

Drinking strong drink one night at the Silver Eel, the Gray Mouser and Fafhrd became complacently, even luxuriously, nostalgic about their past loves and amorous exploits. They even boasted a little to each other about their most recent erotic solacings (although it is always very unwise to boast of such matters, especially out loud; one never knows who may be listening).

51

"Despite her vast talent for evil," the Mouser said, "Hisvet remains always a child. Why should that surprise me?—evil comes naturally to children, it is a game to them, they feel no shame. Her breasts are no bigger than walnuts, or limes, or at most small tangerines topped by hazelnuts—all eight of them."

Fafhrd said, "Frix is the very soul of the dramatic. You should have seen her poised on the battlement later that night, her eyes raptly agleam, seeking the stars. Naked save for some ornaments of copper fresh as rosy dawn. She looked as if she were about to fly—which she can do, as you know."

In the Land of the Gods, in short in Godsland and near Nehwon's Life Pole there, which lies in the southron hemisphere at the antipodes from the Shadowland (abode of Death), three gods sitting together cross-legged in a circle picked out Fafhrd's and the Mouser's voices from the general mutter of their worshippers, both loyal and lapsed, which resounds eternally in any god's ear, as if he held a seashell to it.

One of the three gods was Issek, whom Fafhrd had once faithfully served as acolyte for three months. Issek had the appearance of a delicate youth with wrists and ankles broken, or rather permanently bent at right angles. During his Passion he had been severely racked. Another was Kos, whom Fafhrd had revered during his childhood in the Cold Waste, rather a squat, brawny god bundled up in furs, with a grim, not to say surly, heavily bearded visage.

The third god was Mog, who resembled a four-limbed spider with a quite handsome, though not entirely human face. Once the girl Ivrian, the Mouser's first love, had taken a fancy to a jet statuette of Mog he had stolen for her and decided, perhaps roguishly, that Mog and the Mouser looked alike.

Now the Gray Mouser is generally believed to be and have always been complete atheist, but this is not true. Partly to humor Ivrian, whom he spoiled fantastically, but partly because it tickled his vanity that a god should choose to look like him, he made a game for several weeks of firmly believing in Mog.

So the Mouser and Fafhrd were clearly worshippers, though lapsed, and the three gods singled out their voices because of that and because they were the most noteworthy worshippers these three gods had ever had and because they were boasting. For the gods have very sharp ears for boasts, or for declarations of happiness and self-satisfaction, or for assertions of a firm intention to do this or that, or for statements that this or that must surely happen, or any other words hinting that a man is in the slightest control of his own destiny. And the gods are jealous, easily angered, perverse, and swift to thwart.

"It's them, all right—the haughty bastards!" Kos grunted, sweating under his furs—for Godsland is paradisial.

"They haven't called on me for years—the ingrates!" Issek said with a toss of his delicate chin. "We'd be dead for all they care, except we've our other worshippers. But they don't know that—they're heartless."

"They have not even taken our names in vain," said Mog. "I believe, gentlemen, it is time they suffered the divine displeasure. Agreed?"

In the meanwhile, by speaking privily of Frix and Hisvet, the Mouser and Fafhrd had aroused certain immediate desires in themselves without seriously disturbing their mood of complacent nostalgia.

"What say you, Mouser," Fafhrd mused lazily, "should we now seek excitement? The night is young.

His comrade replied grandly, "We have but to stir a little, to signify our interest, and excitement will seek us. We've loved and been forever adored by so many girls that we're bound to run into a pair of 'em. Or even two pair. They'll catch our present thoughts on the wing and come running. We will hunt girls—ourselves the bait!"

"So let's be on our way," said Fafhrd, drinking up and rising with a lurch.

"Ach, the lewd dogs!" Kos growled, shaking sweat from his brow, for Godsland is balmy (and quite crowded). "But how to punish 'em?"

Mog said, smiling lopsidedly because of his partially arachnid jaw structure, "They seem to have chosen their punishment."

"The torture of hope!" Issek chimed eagerly, catching on. "We grant them their wishes—"

"—and then leave the rest to the girls," Mog finished.

"You can't trust women," Kos asserted darkly.

"On the contrary, my dear fellow," Mog said, "when a god's in good form, he can safely trust his worshippers, female and male alike, to do all the work. And now, gentlemen, on with our thinking caps!"

Kos scratched his thickly matted head vigorously, dislodging a louse or two.

Whimsically, and perhaps to put a few obstacles between themselves and the girls presumably now rushing toward them, Fafhrd and the Gray Mouser chose to leave the Silver Eel by its kitchen door, something they'd never done once before in all their years of patronage.

The door was low and heavily bolted, and when those were shot still wouldn't budge. And the new cook, who was deaf and dumb, left off his stuffing of a calf's stomach and came over to make gobbling noises and flap his arms in gestures of protest or warning. But the Mouser pressed two bronze agols into his greasy palm while Fafhrd kicked the door open. They prepared to stride out into the dismal lot covered by the eroded ashes of the tenement where the Mouser had dwelt with Ivrian (and she and Fafhrd's equally dear Vlana had burned) and also the ashes of the wooden garden house of mad Duke Danius, which they'd once stolen and occupied for a space—the dismal and ill-omened lot which they'd never heard of anyone building on since.

But when they'd ducked their heads and gone through the doorway, they discovered that construction of a sort *had* been going on (or else that they'd always seriously underestimated the depth of the Silver Eel) for instead of on empty ground open to sky, they found themselves in a corridor lit by torches held in brazen hands along each wall.

Undaunted, they strode forward past two closed doors.

"That's Lankhmar City for you," the Mouser observed. "You turn your back and they've put up a new secret temple."

"Good ventilation, though," Fafhrd commented on the absence of smoke.

They followed the corridor around a sharp turn . . . and stopped dead. The split-level chamber facing them had surprising features. The sunken half was close-ceilinged and otherwise gave the impression of being far underground, as if its floor were not eight finger-joints deeper than the raised section but eighty yards. Its furniture was a bed with a coverlet of violet silk. A thick yellow silk cord hung through a hole in the low ceiling.

The chamber's raised half seemed the balcony or battlement of a tower thrust high above Lankhmar's smog, for stars were visible in the black upper background and ceiling.

On the bed, silver-blonde head to its foot, slim Hisvet lay prone but upthrust on her straightened arms. Her robe of fine silk, yellow as desert sunlight, was outdented by her pair of small high breasts, but depended freely from the nipples of those, leaving unanswered the question of whether there were three more pairs arranged symmetrically below.

While against starry night (or its counterfeit), her dark hair braided with scrubbed copper wire, Frix stood magnificently tall and light-footed (though motionless) in her silken robe violet as a desert's twilight before dawn.

Fafhrd was about to say, "You know, we were just talking about you," and the Mouser was about to tread on his instep for being so guileless, when Hisvet cried to the latter, "You again!—intemperate dirksman. I told you never even to *think* of another rendezvous with me for two years' space."

Frix said to Fafhrd, "Beast! I told you I played with a member of the lower orders only on *rare* occasions."

Hisvet tugged sharply on the silken cord. A heavy door dropped down in the men's faces from above and struck its sill with a great and conclusive jar.

Fafhrd lifted a finger to his nose, explaining ruefully, "I thought it had taken off the tip. Not exactly a loving reception."

The Mouser said bravely, "I'm glad they turned us off. Truly, it would have been too soon, and so a bore. On with our girl hunt!"

They returned past the mute flames held in bronze hands to the second of the two closed doors. It opened at a touch to reveal another dual chamber and in it their loves Reetha and Kreeshkra, whom only short months ago they'd been seeking near the Sea of Monsters, until they were trapped in the Shadowland and barely escaped back to Lankhmar. To the left, in muted sunlight on a couch of exquisitely smoothed dark wood, Reetha reclined quite naked. Indeed, extremely naked, for as the Mouser noted, she'd kept up her habit, inculcated when she'd been slave of a finicky overlord, of regularly shaving all of herself, even her eyebrows. Her totally bare head, held at a pert angle, was perfectly shaped and the Mouser felt a surge of sweet desire. She was cuddling to her tender bosom a very emaciated-seeming but tranquil animal, which the Mouser suddenly realized was a cat, hairless save for its score of whiskers bristling from its mask.

To the right, in dark night a-dance with the light of camp-fire and on a smooth shale shore of what Fafhrd recognized to be, by the large white-bearded serpents sporting in it, the Sea of Monsters, sat his beloved Kreeshkra, more naked even than Reetha. She might have been a disquieting sight to some (naught but an aristocratically handsome skeleton), except that the flames near which she sat struck dark blue gleams from the sweetly curved surfaces of her transparent flesh casing her distinguished bones.

"Mouser, why have you come?" Reetha cried out some-what reproachfully. "I'm happy here in Eevamarensee, where all men are as hairless by nature (our household animals too) as I am by my daily industry. I love you dearly still, but we can't live together and must not meet again. This is my proper place."

Likewise, bold Kreeshkra challenged Fafhrd with "Mud Man, avaunt! I loved you once. Now I'm a Ghoul again. Per-haps in future time . . . But now, begone!"

It was well neither Fafhrd nor Mouser had stepped across the threshold, for at those words this door slammed in their faces too, and this time stuck fast. Fafhrd forbore to kick it.

"You know, Mouser," he said thoughtfully, "We've been enamored of some strange ones in our time. But always most intensely interesting," he hastened to add.

"Come on, come on," the Mouser enjoined gruffly. "There are other fish in the sea."

The remaining door opened easily too, though Fafhrd pushed it somewhat gingerly. Nothing startling, however, came into view this time, only a long dark room, empty of persons and furniture, with a second door at the other end. Its only novel feature was that the right-hand wall glowed green. They walked in with returning confidence. After a few steps they became aware that the glowing wall was thick crystal enclosing pale green, faintly clouded water. As they watched, continuing to stroll, there swam into view with lazy undulations two beautiful mermaids, the one with long golden hair trailing behind her and a sheathlike garb of wide-meshed golden fishnet, the other with short dark hair parted by a ridgy and serrated silver crest. They came close enough for one to see the slowly pulsing gills scoring their necks where they merged into their sloping, faintly scaled shoulders, and farther down their bodies those discrete organs which contradict the contention, subject of many a crude jest, that a man is unable fully to enjoy an unbifurcated woman (though any pair of snakes in love tell us otherwise). They swam closer still, their dreamy eyes now wide and peering, and the Mouser and Fafhrd recognized the two queens of the sea they had embraced some years past while deep diving from their sloop *Black Treasurer*.

What the wide-peering fishy eyes saw evidently did not please the mermaids, for they made faces and with powerful flirts of their long finny tails retreated away from the crystal wall through the greenish water, whose cloudiness was increased by their rapid movements, until they could no longer be seen.

Turning to the Mouser, Fafhrd inquired, eyebrows alift, "You mentioned other fish in the sea?"

With a quick frown the Mouser strode on. Trailing him, Fafhrd mused puzzledly, "You said this might be a secret temple, friend. But if so, where are its porters, priests, and patrons other than ourselves?"

"More like a museum—scenes of distant life. And a piscesium, or piscatorium," his comrade answered curtly over shoulder.

"I've also been thinking," Fafhrd continued, quickening his steps, "there's too much space here we've been walking through for the lot behind the Silver Eel to hold. What *has* been builded here?—or there?"

The Mouser went through the far door. Fafhrd was close behind.

In Godsland Kos snarled, "The rogues are taking it too easily. Oh, for a thunderbolt!"

Mog told him rapidly, "Never you fear, my friend, we have them on the run. They're only putting up appearances. We'll wear them down by slow degrees until they pray to us for mercy, groveling on their knees. That way our pleasure's greater."

"Quieter, you two," Issek shrilled, waving his bent wrists, "I'm getting another girl pair!"

It was clear from these and other quick gesticulations and injunctions—and from their rapt yet tense expressions—that the three gods in close inward-facing circle were busy with something interesting. From all around other divinities large and small, baroque and classical, noisome and beautiful, came drifting up to comment and observe. Godsland *is* over-crowded, a veritable slum, all because of man's perverse thirst for variety. There are rumors among the packed gods there of other and (perish the thought!) superior gods, perhaps invisible, who enjoy roomier quarters on another and (oh woe!) higher level and who (abysmal deviltry!) even hear thoughts, but nothing certain.

Issek cried out in ecstasy, "There, there, the stage is set! Now to search out the next teasing pair. Kos and Mog, help me. Do your rightful share."

The Gray Mouser and Fafhrd felt they'd been transported to the mysterious realm of Quarmall, where they'd had one of their most fantastic adventures. For the next chamber seemed a cave in solid rock, given room-shape by laborious chipping. And behind a table piled with parchments and scrolls, inkwells and quills, sat the two saucy, seductive slave-girls they'd rescued from the cavern-world's monotonies and tortures: slender Ivivis, supple as a snake, and pleasantly plump Friska, light of foot. The two men felt relief and joy that they'd come home to the familiar and beloved.

Then they saw the room had windows, with sunlight suddenly striking in (as if a cloud had lifted), and was not solid rock but morticed stone, and that the girls wore not the scanty garb of slaves but rich and sober robes, while their faces were grave and self-reliant.

Ivivis looked up at the Mouser with inquiry but instant disapproval. "What dost here, figment of my servile past? Tis true, you rescued me from Quarmall foul. For which I paid you with my body's love. Which ended at Tovilysis when we split. We're quits, dear Mouser, yes by Mog, we are!" (She wondered why she used that particular oath.)

Likewise Friska looked at Fafhrd and said, "That goes for you too, bold barbarian. You also killed my lover Hovis, you'll recall—as Mouser did Ivivis' Klevis. We are no longer simple-minded slaves, playthings of men, but subtle secretary and present treasurer of the Guild of Free Women at Tovilysis. We'll never love again unless I choose—which I do not today! And so, by Kos and Issek, now begone!" (She wondered likewise why she invoked those particular deities, for whom she had no respect whatever.)

These rebuffs hurt the two heroes sorely, so that they had

not the spirit to respond with denials, jests, or patient gal-
lantries. Their tongues clove to their hard palates, their
hearts and privates grew chilly, they almost cringed—and
they rather swiftly stole from that chamber by the open door
ahead . . . into a large room shaped of bluish ice, or rock of
the same hue and translucence and as cold, so that the flames
dancing in the large fireplace were welcome. Before this was
spread a rug looking wondrously thick and soft, about which
were set scatteredly jars of unguents, small bottles of perfume
(which made themselves known by their ranging scents), and
other cosmetic containers and tools. Furthermore, the in-
vitingly textured rug showed indentations as if made by two
recumbent human forms, while about a cubit above it floated
two living masks as thin as silk or paper or more thin, holding
the form of wickedly pretty, pert girl faces, the one rosy
mauvette, the other turquoise green.

Others would have deemed it a prodigy, but the Mouser
and Fafhrd at once recognized Keyaira and Hirriwi, the invisible frost princesses with whom they'd once been separately
paired for one long, long night in Stardock, tallest of Nehwon's northron peaks, and knew that the two gaysome girls
were reclining unclad in front of the fire and had been playfully anointing each other's faces with pigmented salves.

Then the turquoise mask leapt up betwixt Fafhrd and the
fire, so that dancing orange flames only shone through its staring eye holes and between its now cruel and amused lips as it
spoke to him, saying "In what frowsty bed are you now dead
asleep, gross one-time lover, that your squeaking soul can be
blown halfway across the world to gape at me? Some day
again climb Stardock and in your solid form importune me. I
might hark. But now, phantom, depart!"

The mallow mask likewise spoke scornfully to the Mouser,
saying in tones as stinging and impelling as the flames seen
through its facial orifices, "And you remove too, wraith most
pitiful. By Khahkht of the Black Ice and Gara of the Blue—
and e'en Kos of the Green— I enjoin it! Blow winds! and out
lights all!"

Fafhrd and the Mouser were hurt even more sorely by
these new rebuffs. Their very souls were shriveled by the
feeling that they were indeed the phantoms, and the speaking
masks the solid reality. Nevertheless, they might have summoned the courage to attempt to answer the challenge
(though 'tis doubtful), except that at Keyaira's last com-

mands they were plunged into darkness absolute and man-handled by great winds and then dumped in a lighted area. A wind-slammed door crashed shut behind them.

They saw with considerable relief that they were not con-fronting yet another pair of girls (*that* would have been unen-durable) but were in another stretch of corridor lit by clear-flaming torches held in brazen wall brackets in the form of gripping bird-talons, coiling squid-tentacles, and pinching crab-claws. Grateful for the respite, they took deep breaths.

Then Fafhrd frowned deeply and said, "Mark me, Mouser, there's magic somewhere in all this. Or else the hand of a god."

The Mouser commented bitterly, "If it's a god, he's a thumb-fingered one, the way he sets us up to be turned down."

Fafhrd's thoughts took a new tack, as shown by the chang-ing furrows in his forehead. "Mouser, I never squeaked," he protested. "Hirriwi said I squeaked."

"Manner of speaking only, I suppose," his comrade con-soled. "But gods! what misery I felt myself, as if I were no longer man at all, and *this* no more than broomstick." He in-dicated his sword Scalpel at his side and gazed with a shake of his head at Fafhrd's scabbarded Graywand.

"Perchance we dream—" Fafhrd began doubtfully.

"Well, if we're dreaming, let's get on with it," the Mouser said and, clapping his friend around the shoulders, started them down the corridor. Yet despite these cheerful words and actions, both men felt they were getting more and more into the toils of nightmare, drawing them on will-lessly.

They rounded a turn. For some yards the right-hand wall became a row of slender dark pillars, irregularly spaced, and between them they could see more random dusky slim shafts and at middle distance a long altar on which light showered softly down, revealing a tall, naked woman stretched on it, and by her a priestess in purple robes with dagger bared in one hand and large silver chalice in the other, who was in-toning a litany.

Fafhrd whispered, "Mouser! the sacrifice is the courtesan Lessnya, with whom I had some dealings when I was acolyte of Issek, years ago."

"While the other is Ilala, priestess of the like-named god-dess, with whom I had some commerce when I was lieutenant to Pulg the extortioner," the Mouser whispered back.

Fafhrd protested, "But we *can't* have already come all the way to the temple of Ilala, though this looks like it. It's half-way across Lankhmar from the Eel," while the Mouser recalled tales he'd heard of secret passages in Lankhmar that connected points by distances shorter than the shortest distance between.

Ilala turned toward them in her purple robes and said with eyebrows raised, "Quiet back there! You are committing sacrilege, trespassing on most holy ritual of the great goddess of all shes. Impious intruders, depart!" While Lessnya lifted on an elbow and looked at them haughtily. Then she lay back again and regarded the ceiling while Ilala plunged her dagger deep into her chalice and then with it flicked sprinkles of wine (or whatever other fluid the chalice held) on Lessnya's naked shape, wielding the blade as if it were as aspergillum. She aspersed her thrice—on bosom, loins, and knees—and then resumed her muttered litany, while Lessnya echoed her (or else snored) and the Mouser and Fafhrd stole on along the torchlit corridor.

But they had little time to ponder on the strange geometries and stranger religiosities of their nightmare progress, for now the left-hand wall gave way for a space to a fabulously decorated, large, dim chamber, which they recognized as the official residence room of the Grandmaster of the Thieves' Guild in Thieves' House, half Lankhmar City back again from Ilala's fane. The foreground was filled with figures kneeling away from them in devout supplication toward a thick-topped ebony table, behind which there stood queenly tall a handsome red-haired woman dressed in jewels and behind her a trim second female in maid's black tunic collared and cuffed with white.

" 'Tis Ivlis in her beauty from the past, for whom I stole Ohmphal's erubescent fingertips," the Mouser whispered in stupefaction. "And now she's got herself a peck more gems."

"And that is Freg, her maid, looking no older," Fafhrd whispered back hoarsely in dream-drugged wonderment.

"But what's she doing here in Thieves' House?" the Mouser pressed, his whisper feverish, "where women are forbidden and contemned. As if *she* were grandmaster of the Guild . . . grand-mistress . . . goddess . . . worshipped . . . Is Thieves' Guild upside down? . . . all Nehwon turvy-topsy . . . ?"

Ivlis looked up at them across the heads of her kneeling

followers. Her green eyes narrowed. She casually lifted her fingers to her lips, then flicked them sideways twice, indicating to the Mouser that he should silently keep going in that direction and not return.

With a slow unloving smile, Freg made exactly the same gesture to Fafhrd, but even more idly seeming, as if humming a chorus. The two men obeyed, but with their gazes trailing behind them, so that it was with complete surprise, almost with starts of fear, that they found they had walked blindly into a room of rare woods embellished with intricate carvings, with a door before them and doors to either side, and in the one of the latter nearest the Mouser a freshly nubile girl with wicked eyes, in a green robe of shaggy toweling cloth, her black hair moist, and in the one nearest Fafhrd two slim blondes a-smile with dubious merriment and wearing loosely the black hoods and robes of nuns of Lankhmar. In nightmare's fullest grip they realized that this was the very same garden house of Duke Danius, haunted by their earliest deepest loves, impiously reconstituted from the ashes to which the sorcerer Sheelba had burned it and profanely refurbished with all the trinkets wizard Ningauble had magicked from it and scattered to the four winds; and that these three night-fillies were Ivmiss Ovartamortes, niece of Karstak like-named, Lankhmar's then overlord, and Fralek and Fro, mirror-twin daughters of the death-crazed duke, the three she-colts of the dark to whom they'd madly turned after losing even the ghosts of their true loves in Shadowland. Fafhrd was wildly thinking in unvoiced sound, "Fralek and Fro, and Freg, Friska and Frix—what is this Fr'-charm on me?" while through the Mouser's mind was skipping likewise, "Ivlis, Ivmiss, Ivivis (two Iv's—and there's e'en an Iv in Hisvet)— who are these girl-lets of the Iv . . .?"

(Near the Life Pole, the gods Mog, Issek, and Kos were working at the top of their bent, crying out to each other new girl-discoveries with which to torment their lapsed worshippers. The crowd of spectator gods around them was now large.)

And then the Mouser bethought him with a shiver that he had not listed amongst his girl-lings of the Iv the archgirl of them all, fair Ivrian, forever lost in Death's demesne. And Fafhrd likewise shook. And the nightfillies flanking them pouted and made moues at them, and they were fairly catapulted into the midst of a pavilion of wine-dark silk, beyond whose unstirring folds showed the flat black horizons of the Shadowland.

Beauteous, slate-visaged Vlana spat full in Fafhrd's face, saying, "I told you I'd do that if you came back," but fair Ivrian only eyed the Mouser with never a sign or word.

And then they were back in the betorched corridor, more hurried along it than hurrying, and the Mouser envied Fafhrd death's spittle inching down his cheek. And girls were flashing by like ghosts, unheedingly—Mara of Fafhrd's youth, Atya who worshipped Tyaa, bovine-eyed Hrenlet, Ahura of Seleucia, and many many more—until they were feeling the utter despair that comes with being rejected not by one or a few loves, but by all. The unfairness of it alone was enough to make a man die.

Then in the rush one scene lingered awhile: Alyx the Picklock garbed in the scarlet robes and golden tiara a-swarm with rubies of the archpriest of an eastern faith, and kneeling before her costumed as clerk Lilyblack, the Mouser's girlish leman from his criminous days, intoning, "Papa, the heathen rage, the civilized decay," and the tranvestite archpriestess pronouncing, "All men are enemies . . ."

Almost Fafhrd and the Mouser dropped to their knees and prayed to whatever gods may be for surcease from their torment. But somehow they didn't, and of a sudden they found themselves on Cheap Street near where it crosses Crafts and turning in at a drab doorway after two females, whose backs were teasingly familiar, and following them up a narrow flight of stairs that stretched up so far in one flight that its crazy warpage was magnified.

In Godsland Mog threw himself back, blowing out his breath and saying, "There! that gets them all," while Issek likewise stretched himself out (so far as his permanently bent ankles and wrists would permit), observing, "Lord, people don't appreciate how we gods work, what toil in sparrow-watching!" and the spectator gods began to disperse.

But Kos, still frowingly immersed in his task to such a degree that he wasn't aware of the pain in his short burly thighs from sitting cross-legged so long, cried out, "Hold on! here's another pair: to wit, one Nemia of the Dusk, one Eyes of Ogo, women of lax morals and, to boot, receivers of stolen property—oh, that's vile!"

Issek laughed wearily and said, "Quit now, dear Kos. I crossed those two off at the very start. They're our men's dearest enemies, swindled them out of a precious loot of jewels, as almost any god around could tell you. Sooner than seek them out (to be rebuffed in any case, of course) our boys would rot in hell," while Mog yawned and added, "Don't you ever know, dear Kos, when the game's done?"

So the befurred short god shrugged and gave over, cursing as he tried to straighten his legs.

Meanwhile, the Eyes of Ogo and Nemia of the Dusk reached the summit of the endless stairs and tiredly entered their pad, eyeing it with disfavor. (It *was* an impoverished, dingy, even noisome place—the two best thieves in Lankhmar had fallen on hard times, as even the best of thieves and receivers will in the course of long careers.)

Nemia turned round and said, "Look what the cat dragged in." Hardship had drastically straightened her lush curves. Her comrade Ogo-Eyes still looked somewhat like a child, but a very old and ill-used one. "Wow," she said wearily, "you two look miserable, as if you'd just 'scaped death and sorry you had. Do yourselves a favor—fall down the stairs, breaking your necks."

When Fafhrd and the Mouser didn't move, or change their woebegone expressions, she laughed shortly, dropped into a broken-seated chair, poked out a leg at the Mouser, and said, "Well, if you're not leaving, make yourself useful. Remove my sandals, wash my feet," while Nemia sat down before a rickety dressing table and, while surveying herself in the broken mirror, held out a broken-toothed instrument in Fafhrd's direction, saying, "Comb my hair, barbarian. Watch out for snarls and knots."

Fafhrd and the Mouser (the later preparing and fetching warm water) began solemn-faced to do those very things most carefully.

After quite a long time (and several other menial services rendered, or servile penances done) the two women could no longer keep from smiling. Misery, *after* it's comforted, loves company. "That's enough for now," Eyes told the Mouser. "Come, make yourself comfortable." Nemia spoke likewise to Fafhrd, adding, "Later you men can make the dinner and go out for wine."

After awhile the Mouser said, "By Mog, this is more like

it." Fafhrd agreed. "By Issek, yes, Kos damn all spooked adventures."

The three gods, hearing their names taken in vain as they rested in paradise from their toils, were content.

Paul Spencer

THE GUARDIAN OF
THE VAULT

Paul Spencer is an old-time fantasy buff and Oz en-thusiast who lives in New Jersey and works for a book publisher there. As a collector and connoisseur of fantastic literature, I know and admire his taste and expertise. (It is entirely due to Paul that Evangeline Walton and Hope Mirlees enriched the late, lamented Ballantine Adult Fantasy Series with their fine books, which he recommended to my attention.) And now, after reading the enclosed story which follows, I have other things about Paul Spencer to admire, such as his innate storytelling skill and gift for sur-prise endings.

Incidentally, this is a new story and appears here in print for the first time.

—L.C.

Narac was still trembling as he climbed out onto the roof. With shaking hands he steadied himself against one of the crenellations; the stone, warm in the sun, was soothing under his fingers. The open sky, the vast, sparsely wooded plain stretching toward the city of Poseidonis quieted his nerves, as he had hoped when he pelted up the stairs from the somber confines of the tower. Gradually his pulses slowed. With a sigh he relaxed and turned, leaning against the wall. Beyond the far side of the tower the plain continued toward the sea, lost in silvery haze.

66

Then he chilled again. Scarcely five paces from him, in the center of the roof, yawned the open trapdoor, quickening thoughts of what lay below: that sudden bellowing from beneath—the crash against the symbol-encrusted disk of stone that sealed the shaft—the terror that It was about to smash through once more into the world of men.

Before Keroth's death, the two Guardians had bolstered one another's courage, if only through reluctance to display their fear. Now, thought Narac wryly, no sense of shame restrained his impulse to flee. Not that the roof would provide any real sanctuary if It were actually to rise from Its prison . . .

Narac turned back toward Poseidonis and scanned the horizon. Probably it was too soon to expect Keroth's replacement. Only a few hours had passed since Keroth's pyre had blackened the roof yonder as it sent into the night the flaming signal that a Guardian had died and another of the Chosen must be sent. Indeed, the horizon remained empty. Narac's heart constricted as he faced the possibility of another night alone below.

Yet courage, he reminded himself, was one of the qualities that had placed him among the Chosen. And there was no sane choice. Already he had been away from his post too long, inviting what he most feared. He turned back toward the trapdoor.

But the seaward expanse was no longer empty. Far off he saw a cluster of tiny figures, moving in a curious swarming motion. As Narac paused and studied the distant shapes he sensed they were moving out of the haze and in the direction of the tower. They were still too far away for him to be sure. It was no concern of his, in any case; the only visitors to the tower would come from the city.

He was still dangerously wasting time, avoiding the descent. With a grimace that was part self-contempt and part apprehension, he clambered through the trapdoor and hastened down the stairs.

The stone disk was still in place. There was no danger, now that Narac had returned. He knew it well, but his nerves were not yet convinced.

They must learn. Deliberately Narac turned his back on the great disk and contemplated the mess he had caused when he rose in panic, knocking over the table and spilling his meal.

The stew made a great blotch on the flagstone floor. Narac concentrated on spooning it back into the bowl.

A crashing thud—and Narac was on his feet, whirling to face the sigil-stone. It remained in place. The sounds continued, louder, faster, not from the shaft but from behind him. It was a pounding at the door.

Narac turned from the seal and approached the metal-reinforced portal. Now he could hear another sound mingled with the beating on the wood: a high-pitched voice, calling unintelligibly. A woman.

Those running figures in the distance . . .

Narac drew his sword, and with one hand heaved back the bolt from across the door. As he lifted the latch and pulled inward, a woman, red-haired and white-robed, collapsed over the threshold. Beyond, Narac glimpsed several figures in chain armor and bright-feathered helmets.

Bending, he pulled the woman by one arm until both her feet were over the threshold; then with a grunt he shoved the door closed. As he slid home the bolt, the door shook to new and multiplied poundings and there was a muffled outcry of frustrated curses. Narac, his back against the door, paid no attention, but watched the woman push herself to her knees and then to her feet. She turned, tossing her long hair back with both hands, and faced him.

She was tall, her greenish eyes on a level with Narac's, and lithely shaped, her features pleasing. But it was her hair that absorbed Narac's attention. It rippled almost to her waist, a cascade tinted far closer to scarlet than he had ever seen on a human head, and it formed twin arches meeting in a peak above her forehead.

The hint of the foreign was echoed by her robe: cut high across her chest from shoulder to shoulder, it was loose at the top, and gathered at the waist with a golden cord, then spread in pleated folds almost to her insteps. Its elegant simplicity suggested high station, even without the colorful embroidery favored by the aristocrats of Atlantis. As she stood there panting, one slim-fingered hand rested on her chest as though to control the pounding of her heart. She seemed too breathless to speak.

Outside, the pounding and shouting had ceased.

Narac slid his sword back into the scabbard and crossed his arms. "Who are you, and those men? And why are they pursuing you?"

Her eyes had been studying him as closely as his had studied her. Now they dropped; her hand fell to her side, and her shoulders slumped. She sighed; then straightened and met his gaze again. "My name is Aelitha. My father is King of the Flaming Islands, far over the sea." She spoke slowly, sounding the words with an alien tinge. "Those men are from the ship that attacked my father's galley. I was being taken to Borealis, to wed with King Haemestes. Instead, the chief of these pirates claimed me. When they landed for water and provisions, I escaped. And they pursued."

She turned, glancing around the single room—the table, the cupboards, the beds, the rack of scrolls, the fireplace with its hanging pots, the weapons hung on the wall. Then she noticed the great embossed disk in the center of the floor, and looked again at Narac with a puzzled frown. "What place is this?"

It was a moment before he could answer. "You must indeed be from far away!" He hesitated, tempted by the opportunity to converse. But what of the danger?

He bounded up the few steps to the window-slit at the left of the door. A cautious glance revealed the armored pirates sitting cross-legged a few yards from the door, their leader standing over them with folded arms, staring at the tower. They seemed resigned to a long wait. Perhaps reinforcements were expected from the ship.

Narac descended thoughtfully. "There is no immediate threat, but later they may storm the tower. Help from Poseidonis may already be on its way—perhaps in time, perhaps not. Meanwhile, the door is bolted and arms are at hand. There seems to be time to talk." He invited her with a gesture to sit at the table. As she did so, he remembered with a pang the trapdoor to the roof, and ran up the stairs to shoot its bolts. He was conscious of a tingling excitement, almost exhilaration. Danger from a human source came as a relief to his nerves.

"A replacement for my companion who died yesterday will soon be here," he explained as he descended again. "And the Chosen are always attended by an armed guard. The lives of the Chosen are precious, and there are lawless men in the countryside. We have only to wait. The walls are as thick as a man is high, and the doors are heavy and strongly bolted. Will you have wine?"

She smiled and tossed her crimson hair in refusal.

Narac sat across from her, carefully maintaining an air of confidence. Much depended on what reinforcements might join the pirates before the Atlantean guard arrived, but this was no thought to share with the woman. He groped for neutral conversation, while he automatically kept his right hand close to his sword hilt.

"This tower is unknown to you? Shall I explain its meaning, and the importance of my mission?"

This time she inclined her head. "Please." Her hands were relaxed in her lap, but her beautiful green eyes studied him keenly as he took up the tale, quoting much of the priestly narrative he had been taught.

"In the time of my father's father's father, two great wizards dwelt in the city of Poseidonis, capital of the island Poseidonis and of the realm of Atlantis. Each quested after hidden knowledge, superhuman power. One, Agastor, was a blasphemer who sought to converse with demons—with those he believed dwelt beyond the worlds ruled by the gods. The other, Numidon, was a lover of wisdom who sought the gods' aid in achieving great power for good.

"From the godly researchers of Numidon came rich rewards. Power to use birds and beasts to send messages in Numidon's voice. Power over the spirits of pain and death, to lift ailment from the sick. Power to banish the demons that work mischief among mankind. But the fruits of Agastor's impious toil—"

A bellow from beneath shattered the sentence—the petrifying combination of profoundest roar and shrillest scream with which It protested Its imprisonment. Narac grasped the edge of the table and gritted his teeth while ripples of terror wriggled down his spine. Aelitha's eyes widened and her hands clenched. For a moment she and Narac stared at one another.

Narac let out his breath. "That, too, the tale will explain." He rubbed together his sweaty palms and continued:

"After years of forbidden researches, passing from the summoning of sprites and minor devils to contact with mighty powers, Agastor spoke at last with a being from realms beyond the sway of the gods themselves. An apprentice who fled in dismay and remorse babbled of a great black smoke that was also a doorway, of an inhuman voice that was both unthinkably distant and unbearably loud, of Agastor bargaining in some unearthly tongue, of shapeless movement within the blackness—and then he died, in midspeech.

"What bargain Agastor struck, none knows, nor whether the mage yet lives in this world or some other. None has seen him since that apprentice fled. But in his place another strode from Agastor's house on that blackest of days. Strode, but not on legs, and as It strode It grew, and with each stride swelled to greater height and girth, while all Its lengthening arms clutched and crushed, feeding its widening mouths on men and women and babes and on the very stone of the buildings over which It stepped, while between chewings It roared and screamed at once a cry of cosmic triumph.

"It grew until It overtopped the mighty statue of Poseidon, grew until Its bright crest brushed the clouds. Then It stamped on Poseidonis, flattening homes and temples, storehouses and palaces, crushing the city walls, and smearing the city's pavements with our people's bodies. And the air quivered with Its bellowing shriek—a shriek like that sound we heard just now, but full of glee."

Aelitha's eyebrows arched; she stared at the disk in the center of the floor.

"Fortunate indeed," Narac went on, "that Numidon's house lay in a quarter It had yet to reach. Numidon alone in Poseidonis knew the demon's name and nature, knew in what powers to put his trust. Strengthened in spirit and deed by his friendship with the gods, he matched his magic against the demon's might.

"He sent forth lightnings that shook the monster's strength and held It still. Yet even as It stood in frozen weakness, others like It swelled out of the air around It with bellowings and mighty stampings, twins that multiplied before the eyes of those in the city that still lived. The moment's hope gave place to despair, in all hearts but Numidon's. With stronger lightnings he smote the first of the monsters. All of Its eyes withdrew, all of Its limbs relaxed. Stunned by Numidon's godly power It stood like some vast misshapen statue. And all Its twins were gone, mere phantoms conjured by the might of Its will."

"And this thing lies beneath us?" Aelitha whispered.

Narac nodded. "Numidon's magic hollowed the shaft and melted the rock of Its sides to an impassable substance that exists nowhere in nature. From that same magicked rock he shaped the disk that seals the shaft. And when his power from the gods had dwindled the demon and thrust It within the shaft, his magic closed the monster's prison with the stone and embossed upon the disk the sigil of eternal confinement."

The woman pushed back her chair and crossed to the disk. "Strange symbols indeed. They seem within the stone as much as upon it. And so, however It bellows and strives, this demon cannot emerge?"

Narac arose and moved to her side. "The seal alone cannot hold It, nor can the shaft, not for long. Numidon's wisdom was beyond the understanding of other men, but he spoke of a cosmic law that oversways all magic and the gods themselves. For every power that binds, he said, there is another that loosens, and as the years pass the demon may find a counterspell. But he taught that the spell holding the disk in place will endure if the disk is constantly guarded. Someone must stand vigil for every hour of every day and every night, or the demon may loosen the spell."

"And you—?" She touched his chest.

"I am Narac, a Guardian, one of the Chosen." Pride rang in his voice. "Each year eight Guardians are selected from the young men of all Atlantis. They are judged for intelligence, piety, courage, and integrity. Four serve in alternate months, two at a time. The other four stand ready in case illness, accident, or even incompetence should make replacements necessary. If not, they serve in the following year.

"It is a wearing task, to watch the sigil-stone. The demon cannot emerge while our vigilance lasts, yet Its howls and enraged smashings against the stone shake a man's faith in Numidon's magic, as if nothing could restrain the force of the demon's fury.

"Much of the while, all is quiet. There is exercise and conversation, games and reading and prayers—many prayers. Yet the time passes with tiring slowness, and at every moment a portion of one's being trembles in anticipation of the next howling, the next battering against the barrier.

"At least one Guardian must be awake at all times, and therefore one must wake while the other sleeps, and then vigilance is most needful.

"Last night, when Keroth and I were near the end of our second period of monthly service, Keroth slipped on the stairs that lead to the roof, fell, and smashed his skull." He paused, remembering the sound and the sight. "With the smoke of Keroth's pyre scarcely passed into the heavens, I wait alone for one of the Chosen, with an escort of soldiers, to come as his replacement."

He smiled, enjoying her beauty and relishing her rapt attention. "You can understand, then, that your presence is even more welcome than it would be otherwise."

An answering smile began to curve her lips, when a crash made both go tense—a crash, not from the disk but from the door. Narac found his sword leaping to his hand, as he whirled to face the assault.

Another crash, more thunderous than before. "Some kind of battering ram!" Narac muttered.

He glanced up at the trapdoor and weighed contingencies. To open the trap might admit men from the roof, if they had scaled the tower. Yet the reflexes of the Chosen had to be of the quickest, and Narac was inclined to trust his ability to slam and bar the trap. He turned to Aelitha. "Watch the sigil, while I see what is happening outside."

Sword at the ready, he climbed the stairs and slowly, soundlessly slid back one bolt, then the other. Poised for quick withdrawal, he held his breath and pushed the trap upward, almost vertical. Another crash resounded from the door.

Above was blue of sky. Narac put one foot on the next step and ventured a glance through the opening. The roof was empty. Below sounded another assault on the door.

Narac glanced down. Aelitha was standing beside the sigil, staring at it rather than at him or the door. Pleased, Narac stepped out onto the roof and crossed to the shelter of a crenellation.

A quick look down showed him two men holding horizontally the log they had been using to batter at the door. While he talked with Aelitha, they must have obtained it from the woods not far inland from the tower. At a fresh crash, he peered down again; the two were reeling back with their ram from the still-solid door. Narac was reassured by the relative smallness of the two-man ram. The thick, sturdily bolted door could long stand against it.

Then it occurred to him to wonder why there were only two men. Surely he had seen at least three when he had pulled Aelitha through the door and when he had looked through the window-slit. His heart sank, for the third man had surely been sent for reinforcements from the ship. With enough of the pirates, the tower could be forced—through the main entrance in time, through the trapdoor much more quickly, once the pirates gained the roof.

Crouching, he ran to the landward side and looked toward the city. Why was the replacement taking so long?

His heart quickened. Far along the road to Poseidonis was a trailing cloud of dust. Straining his eyes, Narac persuaded himself he could make out moving dots that must be men. His fingers drummed on the parapet. Yes—yes, there were tiny dark shapes against the brown ribbon of the highway. Keroth's replacement and the guard, most probably; friends beyond question, since they came from the Atlantean capital.

Narac crawled swiftly to the trapdoor, slid through the opening, and shoved home the bolts. While he descended the stairs as quickly as memory of Keroth's fall permitted, Aelitha turned from the sigil with questioning brows.

"Help is in sight!" he announced, and put a reassuring hand to her shoulder. Recollection of her noble birth made the hand leap away, but her smile brought an answering smile to his lips.

A crash more thunderous than before echoed through the tower.

Narac whirled toward the door. The metal fastenings were commencing to bend, the ponderous bolt was straining inward. Then the door relaxed, and Narac could visualize the warriors outside retreating in preparation for another shattering blow.

"With only two men?" he whispered.

He turned back to the woman and, heedless of etiquette, grasped her arms. "We have no time to wait for help. I must go outside and delay them long enough for rescue to arrive."

"Alone?" Her eyes were wide.

Again the door resounded and the bolt bulged.

Aelitha pulled from his grasp and ran to the wall where weapons hung. "I, too, can wield a sword!"

But he was upon her before she could touch the hilt. "No! You must take my place as Guardian!"

He pointed to the disk. "There would be time for It to become aware It was unguarded, and to break through! You must stay and watch to maintain the spell!"

Another smashing blow upon the door; a crack opened within the great bolt. Hard upon the blow, a thud slammed against the sigil. Aelitha's eyes flashed to the disk. She clasped

Narac's right hand in both of hers and pressed her mouth to his cheek. "If you dare to go, I dare to stay!"

Exhilaration tingled along his limbs. "Help me open the door. Then swiftly close it behind me and shoot the bolt, if you can. While I keep these men occupied, you guard the sigil."

She nodded, with a glance at the desk. From it came another crash, louder than before.

Narac unsheathed his sword. The weeks of tense boredom were over with a vengeance, he reflected. Now was a time that demanded heroism—an opportunity to justify the faith placed in him as a Guardian. Aelitha's scarlet-haired beauty, and the excited light in her eyes, gave the moment an added zest. He strode to the door, the princess at his heels.

Ignoring repeated thunder from the sigil, Narac heaved the bolt from the latch, and Aelitha grasped the door's handle. Her eyes met his; on her lips was a suggestion of a smile. Narac shifted his grip on the swordhilt, while with his left hand he too grasped the door.

At his nod, both of them heaved backward, and the door, with a shriek, moved inward.

Narac took a deep breath and slid through the opening. The two pirates, apparently resting, stood with the ram vertical between them. Seeing Narac, they let it fall. Its tip crashed to the ground scarcely an inch from him. By dropping it, he realized with a surge of hope, the pirates had abandoned their most potent weapon. With a shout, he leaped at them.

Knocking aside the sword of the man on the right, he dodged the other man's savage slash and sent him sprawling with a kick. Then he lost track of what was happening, in automatic response to a storm of blows, first from the man still standing, then also from the other as he came again to his feet. Narac's blade leaped with a will of its own, now warding off attack, now diving to bite at exposed flesh or hack at resisting armor. He felt nothing from the wounds he knew he must be taking.

Now and again he danced back, retreating to catch his breath, then doggedly met the others' onslaught again. Armored as the pirates were, outnumbering him as they did, his chances of defeating them were slim, but he clung to the memory of the approaching rescuers. If he could but hold the two at bay—if the third did not return with reinforcements—

Thought vanished in his leaping, whirling defense, his plunging attack. But a moment later, with his back to the tower, he could see beyond the men the cluster of Atlanteans, clearly visible on the road. Sunlight glittered from their armor, their spearpoints. Soon the pirates must notice them, and flee. Unless their companions arrived. . . .

With new energy he slashed and stabbed, and astonishment and dismay showed in his opponents' faces.

The view along the road to the city was open. There were no pirates, and there were no approaching rescuers.

Then they vanished.

For a moment Narac stood dumbfounded. Then he whirled, seeking his foes behind him. Between him and the tower was empty air. Even the battering ram was gone.

Narac became aware of the sweat running down his body. His legs began to shiver. In the back of his mind an unthinkable association of ideas began—the demon's power to conjure phantoms—

The ground heaved, sending him asprawl on his back.

As he lifted himself dazedly on one elbow, the tower split. A jagged line opened in its side and cracks spiderwebbed all around the walls. The crenellated parapet opened like a flower, the great stone building blocks leaped apart, and something dark and shrieking expanded up from the toppling ruins.

Now cracks opened in the heaving ground, with a great roaring, and ran branching across the plain, while the thing rising from the ruins swelled skyward with writhing limbs and howling mouths. And as the largest and most formidably fanged of the mouths shouted shrill feminine laughter from Its scarlet-crested head, the deluded Narac, last of the Guardians, realized with utter and final clarity how cataclysmically he had failed his trust.

L. Sprague de Camp

THE LAMP FROM
ATLANTIS

It's hard to introduce stories by Sprague, because just when you've summed up his accomplishments in handy capsule form and think you have him pat, he busts out in a new direction and adds fresh laurels to his already overburdened brow. The latest sheaf of laurels he earned by writing a serious, formal, full-scale biography of H. P. Lovecraft, which he wanted to call Eldritch Yankee Gentleman *but the Messrs. Doubleday insisted on calling, simply,* Lovecraft, *figuring nobody would be able to pronounce "Eldritch." Well, maybe they were right. Anyway, while rummaging through the detritus of Lovecraft's career, Sprague discovered the germ of this story in a plot-idea which Lovecraft always meant to work up, about a lamp from Lost Atlantis, found in modern times, and the havoc it might wreak. He's turned this notion into a smooth, understated, very un-Lovecraftian story which follows next.*

—L.C.

I stopped at Bill Bugby's Garage in Gahato and got young Bugby to drive me to the landing above the dam. There I found Mike Devlin waiting for me, in an aluminum rowcanoe with an outboard motor. I said:

"Hello, Mike! I'm Wilson Newbury. Remember me?"

I dropped my gear into the boat, lowering the suitcase carefully lest I damage the box I was carrying in it.

"Hello, Mr. Newbury!" said Mike. "To be sure, I remember you." He looked much the same as before, save that the wrinkles on his brown face were a little deeper and his curly hair a little grayer. In old-fashioned lumberjack style, he wore a heavy flannel shirt, a sweater, an old jacket, and a hat, although the day was warm. "Have you got that thing with you?"

I sent the car back to Bugby's to keep until I needed it again and got into the boat. "The thing Mr. Ten Eyck wanted me to bring?" I said.

"I do mean that, sir." Mike started the motor, so that we had to shout.

"It's in the big bag," I said, "so don't run us on a stump. After fetching that thing all the way from Europe, and having nightmares the whole time, I don't want it to end up at the bottom of Lower Lake."

"I'll be careful, Mr. Newbury," said Mike, steering the boat up the winding course of the channel. "What is that thing, anyhow?"

"It's an antique lamp. He got me to pick it up in Paris from some character he'd been writing to."

"Ah, well, Mr. Ten Eyck is always buying funny things. After his troubles, that's about all he's interested in."

"What's this about Al's having been married?" I asked.

"Sure, and didn't you know?" Although born and reared in Canada, Mike still sounded more Irish than most native-born Irishmen. I suppose his little home town in Nova Scotia had been solidly Irish-Canadian. "He married the Camaret girl—the daughter of that big lumberjack." Mike chuckled, his faded blue eyes searching the channel ahead for snags. "You remember, when she was a little girl and the teacher in Gahato asked all the childer what they wanted to be when they grew up, she said: 'I want to be a whore!' It broke up the class for fair, it did."

"Well, what happened? Whatever possessed Al—"

"I guess he wanted a husky, hard-working cook and housekeeper, and he figured she'd be so pleased to marry a gentleman that she'd do what he wanted. Trouble was Melusine Camaret is a pretty hot piece—always has been. When she found Mr. Ten Eyck couldn't put it to her night and morning regular, she up and ran off with young Larochelle. You know, Pringle's foreman's son."

A big blue heron, disturbed by the racket of the outboard,

flapped away up the channel. Mike asked, "How was the Army, Mr. Newbury?"

I shrugged. "Just manning a desk. Nobody bothered to shoot at me. I sometimes feel I was lucky the war ended when it did, before they found what a nincompoop they'd put into an officer's uniform."

"Ah, sure, you was always the modest one."

The channel opened out into Lower Lake. The lake was surrounded by the granite ridges of the Adirondacks, thickly clad in hardwoods and evergreens—mostly maple and pine. Here and there, a gray hogback or scar showed through the forest. Most of the marketable timber had been cut out early in the century and its place taken by second growth. The postwar shortages, however, had made it profitable to cut stands that theretofore had stood too far back from transportation to be profitable. While much of the land thereabouts had gone into the Adirondack State Park and so was no longer cuttable, enough remained in private hands to keep the lumber trucks rolling and the saws of Dan Pringle's mill in Gahato screaming.

We cut across Lower Lake to Ten Eyck Island, which separated Lower Lake from Upper Lake. On the map, the two lakes made an hourglass shape, with the island partly plugging the neck between them.

Alfred Ten Eyck, in khaki shirt and pants, came to the dock with a yell of "Willy!" He had a quick, nervous handshake, with a stronger grip than I expected.

We swapped the usual remarks about our not having changed a bit, although I could not say it sincerely of Alfred. While he had kept his slim, straight shape, he had pouches under his eyes. His sandy hair was graying; although, like me, he was still in his thirties.

"Have you got it?" he asked.

"Yes, yes. It's in that—"

He had already grabbed my big suitcase and started for the old camp. He went up the slope at a pace that I almost had to run to keep up with. When he saw me lagging, he stopped to wait. Being out of condition, I came up panting.

"Same old place," I said.

"It's run down a bit," he said, "since the days when my folks entertained relays of friends and relatives all summer. In those days, you could hire help to keep it up—not that Mike doesn't do two men's work."

The trail was somewhat overgrown, and I stumbled on a clump of weeds. Alfred gave me a wry grin.

"I have an understanding with Nature," he said. "I leave her alone, and she leaves me alone. Seriously, anytime you want to help us clear out the trails, I'll give you a corn hook and tell you to go to it. It's all you can do here to keep ahead of the natural forces of growth and decay."

Camp Ten Eyck was a big two-story house, made of huge handhewn logs, with fifteen or sixteen rooms. There was a tool kit beside the front door, with tools lying about. Mike and Alfred had evidently been replacing a couple of porch boards that had begun to rot.

Most Adirondack camps are of wood, because lumber is relatively cheap there. The Adirondack climate, however, sees to it that a wooden house starts to fall apart almost as soon as it is completed. Some of the big logs that made up the sides of Camp Ten Eyck had spots so soft that you could stick your thumb into them.

While I caught my breath, Alfred said, "Look, I'll show you your room, but first would you please get *it* out? I want to see it."

"Oh, all right," I said. I set the suitcase on one of those old-fashioned window seats, which filled the corners of the living room, and opened it. I handed Alfred the box.

"You'll notice it's properly packed," I said. "My sister once sent us a handsome antique luster vase from England, in just a flimsy carton, and it got smashed to pieces."

Alfred cut the cords with shaking hands. He had to go out to get a chisel from his tool chest to pry up the wooden lid. Then he burrowed into the excelsior.

While he worked, I looked around. There were the same old deerskins on the couches and window seats, the same deer heads staring glassily from the walls, the same stuffed fox and owl, the same silver-birch banisters with the bark on, and the same lichens on whose white nether surfaces amateur artists had scratched sylvan scenes.

I was surprised to see that the big, glass-fronted gun case was empty. As I remembered it from the thirties, the case had held an impressive array of rifles, shotguns, and pistols, mostly inherited by Alfred from his father and grandfather.

"What happened to all your guns?" I said. "Did you sell them?"

"The hell I did!" he said, working away. "You know that

no-good cousin of mine, George Vreeland? I rented the place to him one year, and when I got back I found that he had simply sold most of the guns to the *natives*." (Alfred always snarled a little when he said "natives," meaning the year-round residents of the country.)

"What did you do about it?"

"Nothing I could do. George was gone before I got back, and the last I heard he was in California. Then, when I was away last winter, one of our local night workers made off with the rest, including my sailing trophy. I know who did it, too."

"Well?"

"Well, what? No matter how good my proof was, do you suppose I could get the goddamn *natives* to convict him? After what happened to me with Camaret?"

"What about Camaret? I don't know this story."

"Well, you knew I'd been married?"

"Yes. Mike mentioned it."

Alfred Ten Eyck gave me a brief account of his short-lived union with Melusine Camaret. He said nothing about his own sexual inadequacy, for which I cannot blame him.

"The day after she flew the coop," he said, "I was walking along the street in Gahato, bothering absolutely nobody, when Big Jean comes up and says: 'Hey! What you do wit my leetla girl, *hein?*' And the first thing I know, he knocks me cold, right there in the street."

(That was not how the folk in Gahato remembered the event. They say that Alfred answered: "Now look, you dumb Canuck, I don't know what that floozie has been telling you, but—" and then Camaret hit him.)

"Well," Alfred went on, "when I came to, I swore out a warrant and had the trooper run Jean in. But the jury acquitted him, although half the village had seen him slug me. I heard they figured that if Big Jean wanted to belt his son-in-law, that was a family fight and none of their business."

(The villagers' version was that since Jean Camaret was built like a truck and had a notoriously violent temper, anyone fool enough to pick a fight with him deserved what he got.)

Waving an arm to indicate the surrounding mountains, Alfred glowered at me. "They can't forget that fifty years ago, everything you could see from here was Ten Eyck property, and they had to get a Ten Eyck's permission to so much

as spit on it. Now the great Ten Eyck holdings are down to
this one lousy little island, plus a few lots in Gahato; but
they still hate my guts."

(In fact, several members of the Ten Eyck family still
held parcels of land in Herkimer County, but that is a minor
point. Alfred did not get on well with most of his kin.)

"I think you exaggerate," I said. "Anyway, why stay here if
you don't feel comfortable?"

"Where should I go, and how should I earn a living?
Jeepers! Here I at least have a roof over my head. By collect-
ing a few rents on those shacks on Hemlock Street in Gahato
—when the tenants don't talk me out of them with hard-luck
stories—and now and then selling one of the remaining lots,
I get by. Since I can't sell them fast enough to get ahead of
my expenses and build up some investments, I'm whittling
away at my capital; but I don't seem to have any choice. Ah,
here we are!"

Alfred had unwrapped the page from *Le Figaro,* which en-
folded the lamp. He held up his treasure.

It was one of those hollow, heart-shaped things, about the
size of the palm of your hand, which they used for lamps in
Greek and Roman times. It had a knob-shaped handle at the
round end, a big hole in the center top for refilling, and a
little hole for the wick at the pointed or spout end. You can
buy any number of them in Europe and the Near East, since
they are always digging up more.

Most such lamps are made of cheap pottery. This one
looked at first like pottery, too. Actually, it was composed
of some sort of metal but had a layer of dried mud all over
it. This stuff had flaked off in places, allowing a dull gleam of
metal to show through.

"What's it made of?" I asked. "Ionides didn't seem to
know, when he gave me the thing in Paris."

"I don't know. Some sort of silver bronze or bell metal, I
guess. We'll have to clean it to find out. But we've got to be
careful with it. You can't just scrub an antique like this with
steel wool, you know."

"I know. If it has a coating of oxide, you leave it in place.
Then they can put it in an electrolytic tank and turn the
oxide back into the original metal, I understand."

"Something like that," said Alfred.

"But what's so remarkable about this little widget? You're
not an archaeologist—"

"No, no, that's not it. I got it for a reason. Did you have any funny dreams while you were bringing this over?"

"You bet I did! But how in hell would you know?"

"Ionides told me that might happen."

"Well, then, what's the gag? What's this all about?"

Alfred gave me another glare from his pale-gray eyes. "Just say I'm fed up with being a loser, that's all."

I knew what he meant. If the word "loser" applied to anybody, it was Alfred Ten Eyck. You know the term "Midas touch"? Alfred had the opposite, whatever that is. He could turn gold into dross by touching it.

Alfred's father died while Alfred was at Princeton, leaving him several thousand acres of Adirondack land but hardly any real money to live on. So Alfred had dropped out of college and come to Herkimer County to try to make a go of the country-squire business. Either he lacked the right touch, however, or he had the most extraordinary run of bad luck. He sold most of the land, but usually on unfavorable terms to some smarter speculator, who thereupon doubled or tripled his money.

Alfred also dabbled in business of various kinds in Gahato. For example, he went partners with a fellow who brought in a stable of riding horses for the summer-visitor trade. It turned out that the fellow really knew very little about horses and imported a troop of untrained crowbaits. One of his first customers got bucked off and broke her leg.

Then Alfred put up a bowling alley, the Iroquois Lanes, with all that machinery for setting up the pins after each strike. He did all right and sold out at a handsome profit to Morrie Kaplan. But Morrie was to pay in installments. He had not had it a month when it burned up; and Morrie, who was no better a businessman than Alfred, had let the insurance lapse. So Morrie was bankrupt, and Alfred was left holding the bag.

Then came the war. Full of patriotic fire, Alfred enlisted as a private. He promptly came down with tuberculosis in training camp. Since antibiotics had come in, they cured him; but that ended his military career. Maybe it was just as well, because Alfred was the kind of fellow who would shoot his own foot off at practice.

"Okay," said Alfred, "let me show you to your room. Mike and I just rattle around in this big old place."

When he had settled me in, he said, "Now what would

you really like to do, Willy? Drink? Swim? Hike? Fish? Or just sit in the sun and talk?"

"What I'd really like would be to go for a row in one of those wonderful old guide boats. Remember when we used to frog around the swamps in them, scooping up muck so we could look at the little wigglers under the microscope?"

Alfred heaved a sigh. "I don't have any more of those boats."

"What happened to them? Sell them?"

"No. Remember when I was in the Army? I rented the island to a family named Strong, and they succeeded in smashing every last boat. Either the women got into them in high heels and punched through the hulls, or their kids ran them on rocks."

"You can't get boats like that any more, can you?" I said.

"Oh, there are still one or two old geezers who make them through the winter months. But each boat costs more than I could afford. Besides the outboard, I have only an old flat-bottom. We can go out in that."

We spent a couple of very nice hours that afternoon, out in the flatbottom. It was one of those rare days, with the sky crystal-clear except for a few puffy little white cumulus clouds. The old rowboat tended to spin in circles instead of going where you wanted it to. When, not having rowed for years, I began to get blisters, I gave my place to Alfred, whose hands were horny from hard work.

We caught up on each other's history. I said, "Say, remember the time I pushed you off the dock?" and he said, "Whatever happened to your uncle—the one who had a camp on Raquette Lake?" and I said, "How come you never married my cousin Agnes? You and she were pretty thick. . . ."

I told Alfred about my inglorious military career, my French fiancée, and my new job with the trust company. He looked sharply at me, saying:

"Willy, explain something to me."

"What?"

"When we took those tests in school, my IQ was every bit as high as yours."

"Yes, you always had more original ideas than I ever did. What about it?"

"Yet here you are, landing on your feet as usual. Me, I

can't seem to do anything right. I just don't get the hang of it."

"Hang of what?"

"Of life."

"Maybe you should have gone into some line that didn't demand such practicality—so much realism and adaptability. Something more intellectual, like teaching or writing."

He shook his graying head. "I couldn't join the professorate, on account of I never finished college. I've tried writing stories, but nobody wants them. I've even written poems, but they tell me they're just bad imitations of Tennyson and Kipling, and nobody cares for that sort of thing nowadays."

"Have you tried a headshrinker?" (The term had not yet been whittled down to "shrink.")

He shook his head. "I saw one in Utica, but I didn't like the guy. Besides, chasing down the line to Utica once or twice a week would have meant more time and expense than I could afford."

A little breeze sprang up, ruffling the glassy lake. "Oh, well," he said, "time we were getting back."

The island was quiet except for the chugging, from the boathouse, of the little Diesel that pumped our water and charged the batteries that gave us light and power. Over drinks before dinner, I asked:

"Now look, Al, you've kept me dangling long enough about that damned lamp. What *is* it? Why should I have nightmares while bringing the thing back from Europe?"

Alfred stared at his Scotch. He mostly drank a cheap rye, I learned, but had laid in Scotch for his old friend. At last he said:

"Can you remember those nightmares?"

"You bet I can! They scared the living Jesus out of me. Each time, I was standing in front of a kind of chair, or maybe a throne. Something was sitting on the throne, only I couldn't make out details. But when it reached out toward me, its arms were—well, kind of boneless, like tentacles. And I couldn't yell or run or anything. Each time, I woke up just as the thing got its snaky fingers on me. Over and over."

"Ayup, it figures," he said. "That would be old Yuskejek."

"That would be *what?*"

"Yuskejek. Willy, are you up on the mythology of the lost continent of Atlantis?"

"Good lord, no! I've been too busy. As I remember, the occultists try to make out that there really was a sunken continent out in the Atlantic, while the scientists say that's tosh, that Plato really got his ideas from Crete or Egypt or some such place."

"Some favor Tartessos, near modern Cadiz," said Alfred. (This happened before those Greek professors came up with their theory about the eruption of the volcanic island of Thera, north of Crete.) "I don't suppose a hard-headed guy like you believes in anything supernatural, do you?"

"Me? Well, that depends. I believe what I see—at least most of the time, unless I have reason to suspect sleight-of-hand. I know that, just when you think you know it all and can see through any trick, that's when they'll bamboozle you. After all, I was in Gahato when that part-time medium, Miss—what was her name?—Scott—Barbara Scott—had that trouble with a band of little bitty Indian spooks, who threw stones at people."

Alfred laughed. "Jeepers Cripus, I'd forgotten that! They never did explain it."

"So what about your goofy lamp?"

"Well, Ionides has good connections in esoteric circles, and he assures me that the lamp is a genuine relic of Atlantis."

"Excuse me if I reserve my opinion. So what's this Yuskejek? The demon-god of Atlantis?"

"Sort of."

"What kind of name is 'Yuskejek,' anyway? Eskimo?"

"Basque, I believe."

"Oh, well, I once read that the Devil had studied Basque for seven years and only learned two words. I can see it all —the sinister Atlantean high priest preparing to sacrifice the beautiful virgin princess of Ongabonga, so the devil-god can feast on her soul-substance—"

"Maybe so, maybe not. You've been reading too many pulps. Anyway, let's go eat before I get too drunk to cook."

"Doesn't Mike cook for you?"

"He's glad to, when I ask him; but then I have to eat the result. So most of the time I'd rather do it myself. Come along. *Mike!*" He roared. "Dinner in twenty minutes!"

By mutual unspoken consent, we stayed off Atlantis and its lamp during dinner. Instead, we incited Mike to tell us of the old lumbering days and of some of the odder lumberjacks he had known. There was one who swore he was being trailed, day and night, by a ghostly cougar, or puma, although there hadn't been one of those animals in the Adirondacks since the last century. . . .

We let Mike wash the dishes while Alfred and I settled down in the living room with the lamp. Alfred said:

"I think our first step is to get this crud off. For that, suppose we try an ordinary washcloth and a little water?"

"It's your gimmick," I said, "but that sounds reasonable."

"We have to be oh-so-careful," he said, wetting his cloth and rubbing gently. "I wish we had a real archaeologist here."

"He'd probably denounce you for buying looted antiquities. Someday, they tell me, governments will clamp down on that sort of thing."

"Maybe so, but that time hasn't come yet. I hear our brave boys looted half the museums in Germany during the occupation. Ah, look here!"

Much of the mud had come off, exposing a white, toothlike projection. Alfred handed me the lamp. "What do you make of it?"

"I need a stronger light. Thanks. You know, Al, what this looks like? A barnacle."

"Let me see! Jeepers Cripus, you're right! That means the lamp must have been under water—"

"That doesn't prove anything about its—its provenance, I think they call it. It could have been a lamp of Greek or Roman times, dropped overboard anywhere in the Mediterranean."

"Oh," said Alfred, dampened. "Well, I wouldn't dare work on it longer this evening. We need full daylight." He put the thing away.

That night I had the same nightmare again. There was this throne, and this dim character—Yuskejek or whatever his name was—sitting on it. And then he stretched out those rubbery arms. . . .

A knocking awoke me. It was Alfred. "Say, Willy, did you hear something?"

"No," I said. "I've been asleep. What is it?"

"I don't know. Sounds like someone—or something—tramping around on the porch."

"Mike?"

"He's been asleep, too. Better put on your bathrobe; it's cold out."

I knew how cold Adirondack nights could get, even in July. Muffled up, I followed Alfred downstairs. There we found Mike, in a long nightshirt of Victorian style, with a lantern, a flashlight the size of a small baseball bat, and an ax. Alfred disappeared and, after fumbling in one of the chests beneath the window seats, reappeared with a .22 rifle.

"Only gun on the place," he said. "I keep it hidden in case the goddamn *natives* burgle me again."

We waited, breathing lightly and listening. Then came the sound: a bump—bump—bump—pause, and then bump—bump—bump—bump. It sounded as if someone were tramping on the old porch in heavy boots, the kind everyone used to wear in the woods before the summer people started running around in shorts and sneakers. (I still like such boots; at least the deer flies can't bite through them.)

Perhaps the sound could have been made by a horse or a moose, although we haven't had a moose in the region for nearly a century. Anyhow, I could not imagine what either beast would be doing, swimming to Ten Eyck Island.

The sound was not especially menacing in itself; but in that black night, on that lonely spot, it made my short hair rise. The eyes of Alfred and Mike looked twice their normal size in the lantern light. Alfred handed me the flashlight.

"You fling open the door with your free hand, Willy," he said, "and try to catch whatever it is in the beam. Then Mike and I will go after it."

We waited and waited, but the sound did not come again. At last we went out and toured the island with our lights. There was no moon, but the stars shone with that rare brilliance that you get only in clear weather in high country. We found nothing except a raccoon, scuttling up a tree and turning to peer at us through his black bandit's mask, with eyes blazing in the flashlight beam.

"That's Robin Hood," said Alfred. "He's our personal garbage-disposal service. It sure wasn't him that made that racket. Well, we've been over every foot of the island without seeing anything, so I guess . . ."

There were no more phenomena that night. The next day, we cleaned the lamp some more. It turned out quite a handsome little article, hardly corroded at all. The metal was pale, with a faint ruddy or yellowish tinge, like some grades of white gold.

I also took a swim, more to show that I was not yet middle-aged than for pleasure. I never cared much for swimming in icewater. That is what you get in the Adirondack lakes, even in the hottest weather, when you go down more than a foot or so.

That night, I had another dream. The thing on the throne was in it. This time, however, instead of standing in front of it, I seemed to be off to one side, while Alfred stood in front of it. The two were conversing, but their speech was too muffled for me to make out the words.

At breakfast, while demolishing the huge stack of pancakes that Mike set before me, I asked Alfred about it.

"You're right," he said. "I did dream that I stood before His Tentacular Majesty."

"What happened?"

"Oh, it's Yuskejek, all right—unless we're both crazy. Maybe we are, but I'm assuming the contrary. Yuskejek says he'll make me a winner instead of a loser, only I have to offer him a sacrifice."

"Don't look at me that way!" I said. "I've got to get back to my job Monday—"

"Don't be silly, Willy! I'm not about to cut your throat, or Mike's either. I have few enough friends as it is. I explained to this spook that we have very serious laws against human sacrifice in this country."

"How did he take that?"

"He grumbled but allowed as how we had a right to our own laws and customs. So he'll be satisfied with an animal. It's got to be an animal of real size, though—no mouse or squirrel."

"What have you got? I haven't seen anything bigger than chipmunks, except that coon."

"Jeepers, I wouldn't kill Robin Hood! He's a friend. No, I'll take the outboard down to Gahato and buy a pig or something. You'd better come along to help me wrassle the critter."

"Now I know we're nuts," I said. "Did you find out where the real Atlantis was?"

"Nope, didn't think to ask. Maybe we'll come to that later. Let's shove off right after lunch."

"Why not now?"

"I promised to help Mike on some work this morning."

The work was cutting up a dead poplar trunk into firewood lengths. With a powered chain saw, they could have done the job in minutes; but Mike distrusted all newfangled machinery. So they heaved and grunted on an old two-man crosscut saw, one on each end. I spelled Alfred until my blisters from rowing began to hurt.

The weather had other ideas about our afternoon's trip to Gahato. It is a safe rule that if it rains anywhere in New York State in summer, it also rains in the Adirondacks. I have known it to rain some every day for eight weeks running.

We had had two fine days, and this one started out clear and balmy. By ten, it had clouded over. By eleven, thunder was rumbling. By twelve, it was raining pitchforks with the handles up, interrupting our woodcutting job on the poplar.

Looking out the windows, we could hardly see to the water's edge, save when a particularly lurid flash lit up the scene. The wind roared through the old pines and bent them until you thought that any minute they would be carried away. The thunder drowned half of what we said to one another. The rain sprayed against the windows, almost horizontally, like the blast from a fire hose.

"Yuskejek will have to wait, I guess," I said.

Alfred looked troubled. "He was kind of insistent. I told him there might be a hitch, and he mumbled something about 'Remember what happened last time!' "

The rain continued through the afternoon. The thunder and lightning and wind let up, so that it became just a steady Adirondack downpour. Alfred said:

"You know, Willy, I think we really ought to take the boat to Gahato—"

"You *are* nuts," I said. "With this typhoon, your boat would fill before you got there."

"No, it's an unsinkable, with buoyancy tanks, and you can bail while I steer."

"Oh, for God's sake! If you're so determined on this silly business, why don't you take Mike?"

"He can't swim. Not that we're likely to have to, but I don't want to take the chance."

We argued a little more, in desultory fashion. Needless to say, neither of us really wanted to go out in that cataract. Alfred, though, had become obsessed with his Atlantean lamp and its attendant spirit. Perhaps the god had been evoked by our rubbing the lamp, like the jinn in the *Arabian Nights*.

Then Alfred grabbed my arm and pointed. "Look at that!"

I jumped as if stuck; the spooky atmosphere had begun to get to me. It was a relief to see that Alfred was pointing, not at the materialized form of Yuskejek, but at an enormous snapping turtle, plodding across the clearing in front of the house.

"There's our sacrifice!" cried Alfred. "Let's get him! *Mike!*"

We tore out the front door and went, slipping and sliding in the wet, down the bank to Lower Lake in pursuit of this turtle. We ringed the beast before it reached the lake. Looking almost like a small dinosaur, it dodged this way and that, showing quite a turn of speed. When we got close, it shot out its head and snapped its jaws. The *glop* of the snap sounded over the noise of the rain.

The turtle was snapping at Mike when Alfred caught it by the tail and hoisted it into the air. This took considerable strength, as it must have weighted at least twenty pounds. Alfred had to hold it almost at arm's length to keep from being bitten. The turtle kept darting that hooked beak in all directions, *glop, glop!* and flailing the air with its legs.

"Watch out!" I yelled. "That thing can castrate you if you're not careful!"

"Mike!" shouted Alfred. "Get the ax and the frog spear!"

We were all soaked. Alfred cried, "Hurry up! I can't hold this brute much longer!"

When the tools had been brought, Alfred said, "Now, Mike, you get him to snap at the end of the spear and catch the barbs in his beak. Willy, stand by with the ax. When Mike hauls the head as far out of the shell as it'll go, chop it off!"

I had no desire to behead this turtle, which had never done anything to me. But I was a guest, and it was just possible that the lamp and its nightmares were kosher after all.

"Don't you have to do some ritual?" I asked.

"No, that comes later. Yuskejek explained it to me. Ah, got him!"

The turtle had snapped on the frog spear. By twisting the

little trident, Mike hauled the head out out of the shell. Then—

"Mother of God!" shouted Mike. "He's after biting off the shpear!"

It was true. The turtle had bitten through one of the tines of the trident—which may have been weakened by rust—and freed itself.

Instantly came a wild yell from Alfred. The turtle had fastened its beak on the flesh of his leg, just above the knee. In the excitement, Alfred had forgotten to hold the reptile out away from his body.

As the turtle bit into his leg through his trousers, Alfred danced about, tugging at the spiny tail. Then he and the turtle let go together. Alfred folded up on the ground, clutching his wounded leg, while the turtle scuttled down the slope and disappeared into the rain-beaten waters of Lower Lake.

Mike and I got Alfred back to Camp Ten Eyck, with a big red stain spreading down the front if his soaking pants leg. When we got the pants off, however, it did not look as if a trip to the doctor in Gahato would be needed. The turtle's jaws had broken the skin in four places, but the cuts were of the sort that a little disinfectant and some Band-Aids would take care of.

With all the excitement, we more or less forgot about Yuskejek and his sacrifice. Since Alfred was limping, he let Mike get dinner. Afterwards we listened to the radio a bit, read a bit, talked a bit, and went to bed.

The rain was still drumming on the roof when, some hours later, Alfred woke me. "It's that stamping noise again," he said.

As we listened, the bump—bump—bump came again, louder than before. Again we jerked open the door and sprayed the light of the flash and the lantern about. All we saw was the curtain of rain.

When we closed the door, the sound came again, louder. Again we looked out in vain. When we closed the door again, the noise came louder yet: boom—boom—boom. The whole island seemed to shake.

"Hey!" said Alfred. "What the hell's happening? It feels like an earthquake."

"Never heard of an earthquake in this country," I said. "But—"

There came a terrific *boom*, like a near-miss of a lightning bolt. The house shook, and I could hear things falling off shelves.

Mike risked a quick look out and wailed, "Mr. Ten Eyck! The lake's coming up!"

The shaking had become so violent that we could hardly stand. We clutched at the house and at each other to keep our balance. It was like standing in a train going fast on a bad old roadbed. Alfred looked out.

"It *is!*" he shrieked. "Let's get the hell out of here!"

Out we rushed into the merciless rain, just as the water of Lower Lake came foaming up to the porch of Camp Ten Eyck. Actually, it was not the lake that was rising but the island that was sinking. I stumbled off the porch to find myself knee-deep in water. A wave knocked me over, but I somehow shed my bathrobe.

I am, luckily, a fairly good swimmer. Once I was afloat, I had no trouble in keeping on the surface. There were no small waves of the kind that slap you in the face, but big, long, slow surges, which bobbed me up and down.

There was, however, a vast amount of debris, which had floated off the island when it submerged. I kept bumping into crates, shingles, sticks of firewood, tree branches, and other truck. I heard Mike Devlin calling.

"Where are you, Mike?" I yelled.

By shouting back and forth, we found each other, and I swam to him. Remembering that Mike could not swim, I wished that I had had more lifesaving practice. Fortunately, I found Mike clutching a log—part of that poplar they had been sawing up—for a life preserver. With some pushing on my part, we got to shore half an hour later. Mike was sobbing.

"Poor Mr. Ten Eyck!" he said. "Such a nice, kind gentleman, too. There must have been a curse on him."

Whether or not there was a curse on Alfred Ten Eyck, his corpse was recovered the next day. He was, as he had admitted, a loser.

The surges had done many thousands of dollars' damage to other people's docks, boats, and boathouses on Upper and Lower Lakes and the Channel. Because of the downpour, however, all the other camp owners had stayed in and so had not been hurt.

The state geologist said the earthquake was a geological

impossibility. "I should have said, an anomaly," he corrected himself. "It was obviously possible, since it happened. We shall have to modify our theories to account for it."

I did not think it would do any good to tell him about Yuskejek. Besides, if the story got around, some camp owner might be screwy enough to sue me for damages to his boat-house. He would have a hell of a time proving anything, but who wants even the silliest lawsuit?

The Atlantean lamp is, I suppose, at the bottom of the lake, and I hope that nobody dredges it up. When Yuskejek threatens to sink an island if disappointed of his sacrifice, he is not fooling. Perhaps he can no longer sink a place so large as the supposed Atlantis. A little islet like Ten Eyck is more his present-day speed.

I do not, however, care to needle that testy and sinister old deity to find out just what he can do. One such demonstration is enough. After all, Atlantis is supposed to have been a *continent*. If he got mad enough . . .

Gary Myers

XIURHN

*Speaking of Lovecraft, you know his early Dreamlands
yarns were heavily inspired by Lord Dunsany's little fables
of kingdoms at the Edge of the World, under Pegāna's
shadow. No one ever seems to have thought of writing
stories inspired by both Lovecraft and Dunsany simultane-
ously, working in a style that is a meld of each writer's
early period. Only Gary Myers, a young Californian whose
talents were discovered and encouraged by August Derleth,
who thought it was a grand idea. I heartily agree, and
here's a new tale of those dubious, small lands which lie
halfway between Pegāna and Kadath.*

—L.C.

Opposite the grim onyx temple of Unattainable Desires,
in the Street of the Pantheon in Hazuth-Kleg, sacred to the
Moon, there stood long the low, terrible house of Skaa that
figures oddly in myth. Skaa dwelt all alone in her terrible
house and worshipped her carven idols, and chanted and
lighted unwholesome candles and made the Voorish sign. But
there are those who do not scruple to consult witches, and
Thish was used to dealing with persons of doubtful character
in his business, which was nothing less than robbery.

He had heard it whispered by certain jewel merchants, before his knotted cords silenced them completely, that the gem
of immeasurable worth is kept by the Night in fabled Mhor.
He heard it first in Celephais, from a fat jeweller seeking to
buy his own life with that peculiar knowledge, and Thish had

95

not trusted his whimperings. But in Vornai he was less sure, and in Ulthar's scorpion-guarded shops he wondered whether it might be true, and in the yak caravan on Kaar's sunny plain he could doubt no longer; the ruby-merchants who come to Dylath-Leen he robbed not. The truth and other pertinent matters, he knew, might be read in the mouldering *Pnakotic Manuscripts* wherein is recorded all things it is better that men should not know, but he did not wish to pay the Guardian's price to peruse that hateful tome. Less perilous would be to consult one who had already paid the Guardian's price.

In that low house shadows dwelt, despite the flickerings of a little oddly-painted clay lamp. Thish did not like the way those shadows behaved, and Skaa's eyes that shone like the nethermost stars of some nameless gulf were less than reassuring. He entered by that disturbing door which stands open at all seasons between dusk and dawn, and did what was expected of clients, and in turn was told what he wished to know. For beyond the unknown East, mumbled Skaa, there must certainly lie that great, silent vale which is the Night, whence he sends forth his shades at evening to slay the bleeding sun, and whither flee all dreams when the sun returns at dawning. And in that shadow-guarded vale (if one may believe the queer sayings of them that mouth strange secrets to any who may hear) is the high, haunted tower of stone wherein the myth Xiurhn sits and mutters dreams to himself and watches over the gem of immeasurable worth. As no other in the World is this gem, for it was made by the craft of the Other Gods as supplication to the mindless daemon sultan Azathoth, and cut in a semblance of some droll blending of sloth and vampire bat whose pulpy, sinister head is slyly concealed behind its folded wings. It is better that mortals do not think of it, for the Other Gods are not as men (whose tiny souls are bound to them by silver threads), but find earthly focus in certain horrible links, and the noxious soul of Xiurhn haunts the Dark Jewel. It would not be pleasant to meet Xiurhn or his soul, and the Other Gods have shocking methods of punishment. Yet it is known that the yellow-skulled priests of Yuth possess a talisman they anoint in adoration of N'tse-Kaambl, that is useful in protecting those who would profane what belongs to the Other Gods. And Skaa told how one might come to Yuth and the talisman; and casting at the witch's webbed feet his payment in opals, Thish hurried out into the winding cobbled streets beneath the stars.

When Skaa opened the little bag and found only pebbles, for Thish was a robber of note, she drew a pattern known to the skull-faced priests of Yuth and nailed it to the brow of her messenger, who made an obeisance and vanished in a rustle of leathery wings. She described then a sign in the dark with her forefinger above the worthless rocks to change them into opals, and gave no more thought to the thief.

In seven nights a stealthy shadow passed on stockinged feet through the third and most secret vault of that abhorred monastery where the priests of Yuth celebrate the mass of Yuth with curious torments and prayer. When the yellow-skulled priests found the strangled witch with the knotted cord still about her throat and the talisman gone from its proper place on the altar, they only laughed softly and returned to their curious tortures.

That even the East must end if one only travels far enough, all sane men know, despite what philosophers may say; but Thish on his journey watched the four seasons of Earth come in file down through the fields of man and the fields that know him not, come each and pass and come again. And queerer and queerer grew the lands as one rode further East. Beyond the last of Six Kingdoms Thish beheld the dark, mordant forests of trees whose knotted roots fasten like leeches to the mold and moan and bleach the earth, and in whose loathly shadows the inquisitive brown Zoogs caper and leer; and evil bogs whose pale, luminous blooms are fetid with swollen worms having astonishing faces. The deserts on the thither side of Gak are all strewn with the gnawed, untidy bones of absurd chimeras. Thish spent a week in crossing those deserts, and day by day prayed to his gods that the gnawers might remain comfortably hidden. Beyond the deserts is the city it is not well to enter, for the portcullis mimes teeth entirely too well to be canny. And upon a time Thish led his famished zebra across the barren, stony ridge which is the East's farthest border, and peered down to see the Night lapping evilly below, a sluggish, viscid pool in fabled Mhor.

There he turned free his zebra. Already the bleeding sun failed at his back, and then sinister Night would rush terribly up from that vale with strange intent, and Thish did not need to be told what hellish spawn might lurk in the dusk athirst for that which he could ill afford. He lighted a little oddly painted clay lamp that did not belong to him, and sitting

down on a broad, flat rock, with his back to the stone and his
jeweled sword at his side, he drew his cloak up to his eyes and
waited. But Thish did not have to wait long. . . . For then
with many a subtle flap and whisper the shadows sprang,
amid a bitter cold of the star-spaces. An object with clammy
feelers and wings splattered against his brow. Queer half-
glimpsed shapes of nightmare clamored just beyond his feeble
light, he heard the brief, frenzied screams of his zebra out in
the dark with the titter he hoped but did not really believe
was the wind. Then that shadowy horde had wriggled obscenely over the high ridge and into the World beyond, and
Thish was left all alone to creep down the treacherous slope,
bearing his lamp before him. The very stones oozed a horrible dew of fluid shadows, and were pitted everywhere with
fiendish burrows, and the burrows were not always unoc-
cupied. Thish stumbled more often than he must have liked,
for the little lamp could not dispel the blackness, only its vile
children, and once his hand slipped down into one of the burrows. . . . Later he found those worn steps at the base of the
tower, where something began to slither nastily behind him,
snuffling in the dark and disturbing ancient bones. Thish was
glad he could not see what he suspected. He could only gibber
a meaningless prayer to the talisman in his pocket, and froth
and scramble madly up the dizzy stair on his hands and knees
in the dark, while the little suspicious noises behind him got
bigger and bigger, and something wet twisted the lamp from
his nerveless fingers and swallowed it with bestial slobberings
and panted on his neck until his bleeding hands found the
brazen tower door and pulled it shut behind him. Something
knocked on the door and chuckled ominously.

Crouching there in the dark with his sword and mumbling
to himself of a Dark Jewel of immeasurable worth kept by
the Night in fabled Mhor, of amorphous Xiurhn, whose noxious soul it is, who sits in a high tower in the dark and talks
with those Other Gods whose methods of punishment the
theif had most reason to fear, but who cannot abide the talisman sacred to that goddess N'tse Kaambl whose splendor
hath shattered worlds, Thish in the dark of his own shattered
mind never knew when that talisman left his fingers at the
silent beck of the yellow-skulled priests. . . .

And then Xiurhn came downstairs with his soul to answer
that peristent knocking.

Lin Carter

THE CITY IN THE JEWEL

Writers get ideas for stories in the strangest situations, in the weirdest ways. At the World SF Convention in St. Louis, or somewhere, a few years back, I was playing Title Chains with a circle of fans. Title Chains is a game where you say "The Moon Pool" and the next guy in the circle has to think of another fantasy/weird/or sf story whose title uses one of the words from the last title, as, for example, the next guy might say "The Moon is a Harsh Mistress" or "The Pool of the Stone God," and so on around the circle. My mind numb after hours of this, when some fan fed me "The City and the Stars" I responded, automatically, "The City in the Jewel." The fan, Dan Hatch, looked blearily at me and grumbled, "There's no such story." "Well, there ought to be," I grumbled back, "'cause it's a good title."

So I wrote it. And dedicate this story to Dan Hatch and everybody else who ever played Title Chains in a hotel lobby at a worldcon at four in the morning, and in so doing joined The League of the Burnt-Out Minds.

—L.C.

1. As The Sun Died

The fierce tropic sun of old Lemuria had long since passed the zenith of day.

Now it descended the dome of heaven to perish in its pyre of crimson vapors that lit the dim west with flame.

In all this desolate land of jagged, jumbled rock, nothing lived, nothing moved, but—shadows!

99

The level shafts of flaming light struck across the vast tableland of the plateau and drew long ink-black shadows from the circle of standing stones amidst the waste.

Seven they were, and twice taller than a man: tapering columns of dark volcanic stone, rough-hewn, coarsely porous. They stood in a circle on the plain of broken rock, and the red rays of the sinking sun drew long tapering shadows from them. Seven long black narrow shadows . . . like the fingers of a monstrous, groping hand.

Glyphs were deep-cut in the ringed monoliths. Ages of slow time had all but worn them smooth. Yet still were they faintly legible, were there any eye to read them in this shadowy land of stone and silence.

That which stood amidst the circle of standing stones caught the red rays of sunset and flashed with gemmy brilliance.

It was a vast rugged mass of crystal, cloudy, misted: a huge gem of green and sparkling silver, so large that the arms of a full-grown man could scarce encompass it.

Into nine hundred uneven geometric facets was the glimmering crystal cut. Each facet was engraven with a curious sigil; each sigil was subtly alike each other, yet no two were precisely the same.

As the sun died in thunderous glory on the western horizon, the faceted stone caught the last beams and burst ablaze with sparkling splendor.

Amidst the shimmering radiance, the strange sigils glowed weirdly, as if sentient. Like watchful eyes, cold, alert, intent, they peered through the purpling shadows.

No man alive on earth in all that distant age could read those carven signs on the monstrous jewel, nor spell the sense of those deep-carved and age-worn glyphs upon the seven monoliths.

But something pulsed amidst the blazing radiance of the stone and as it lay bathed fully in the sunset flames.

Power!

Vast, awesome, magical.

And . . . *deadly*.

2. *When Dragons Hunt*

For five hours now the boy had fled for his life, and now he had reached the very end of his strength.

His numb legs would move no farther and he fell, gasping for breath, in the coarse rubble that bestrew the plateau.

His lungs were afire and his throat ached rawly and thirst was like a raging torment within him. But he could flee no more.

Against the blaze of sunset, the dragons circled. Black horrid shapes with snaky necks and ragged, batlike wings. They had caught the hot scent of manflesh shortly past midday and they had hunted him lazily down the high mountain pass that cleft all this mighty range, the Mountains of Mommur, and across this bleak and desolate tableland, until they had worn him to the point of exhaustion.

Now they swung lazily, wings booming like sails on the quickening breeze, cold ferocity flaring in the mindless reptilian eyes that shone through the gathering dusk like yellow coals.

Sprawled panting amidst the broken stones the boy glared up at them, his strange gold eyes blazing lionlike through tangled black locks. He did not fear them and would fight them to the last with every drop of strength in his bronzed and brawny form. But he was doomed, and he knew it.

His savage people, a tribe of the cold north, had a saying. *When dragons hunt, the boldest warriors hide.*

He was young, perhaps seventeen or a trifle less, and nearly naked, his brown hide bare save for high-laced sandals and a rag of cloth twisted about his loins. His breast and strong arms, back, belly and shoulders were scored with old scars and white with road dust, for he had come far—halfway across the world, it seemed, from that gore-drenched battlefield whereon all his people had died save he alone. Down from the wintry tundras of the frozen Northlands had he come, alone and on foot, battling savage beasts and even more savage men, and the scars of many battles marked him.

Strapped in a worn old scabbard across his broad young shoulders, a great Valkarthan broadsword lay. It was his only weapon: and it was useless against the winged death that hovered, lazily flapping, against the sky of darkening crimson. Had he but a bow he could perchance have struck down the flying horrors that had playfully, catlike, lazily hunted him all afternoon down the bleak mountains to this desolate plateau.

Here, in a brief red scarlet flare of agony, he would die. And here his bare white bones would lie bleaching to powder under the Lemurian skies for ever.

But he knew no fear, this bronzed boy who lay helpless, panting, exhausted.

This boy—Thongor.

3.   Where Horror Dares Not Pass

Suddenly a cold hand went gliding across his hot thigh. He jerked about, nape prickling with primal night-fears, one capable fist seizing the hilt of the two-handed broadsword. Then he relaxed, panting.

It was a cold black shadow had crept across his flesh, dark and stealthy. A long tapering shadow, like a pointing finger.

Curious, the boy raised himself on one arm and peered about to see the source of that shadow.

He threw his tangled black mane back from his face and stared with amazement.

Stared at the ring of dark columns that encircled a low cube of black stone like a rude altar. And stared at that which glittered and flashed thereupon.

He was staring directly into the sunset, but that roiling mass of crimson flame was less brilliant than the immense and sparkling jewel that stood amidst the monoliths.

Cold wind swept over him in a gush!

Fetid, hot breath blew stinkingly in his face. He flinched— ducked—as one of the scaly horrors of the upper sky swung low, snapping yellowed fangs at his flesh.

The dragons were bolder, now. Or, perhaps, hungrier.

He staggered to his feet, levering himself erect with one hand braced against a broken boulder.

He would meet death face to face, standing on his two feet like a man, he thought grimly.

They swung about far above, the twin bat-winged horrors, circling for the kill.

He glared about for a place to stand, a tall stone to set his shoulders against, and suddenly he bethought him of that circle of smooth lava pillars. The monoliths were set close together: the bat-winged horrors would not be able to come at him from above or behind it if he set his shoulders against one of those pillars; they could only come at him from in front, and then they would face the glittering, razory scythe of that mighty broadsword wherewith he and his forefathers had fought against many a foe. Perhaps he had a chance after all.

Staggering a little, his aching legs still numb with bone-weary exhaustion, he headed for the ring of standing stones and the sparkling enigma they guarded and enclosed.

He drew the great sword. He set his back against the rough cold stone and took his stand. He threw back his head and hooted a challenge to the winged predators of the sky.

They swerved and came hurtling down at him, the flapping black shapes. He could see the flaring coals of their burning eyes and the immense grinning jaws lined with yellowed fangs, the long snaky neck stretched hungrily for him, clawed bird-feet spread to cling and rip—

Ignoring the ache of weariness in chest and arms and shoulders, the boy swung up the great sword as the flying dragons flashed for him—

—And swerved aside!

Puzzled, the boy's strange gold eyes narrowed thoughtfully. He watched through tousled black locks as the flying reptiles curved in their flight, veered away, and flapped off hesitantly, to rush down at him again.

Again they came swooping down.

And again they veered to one side at the last moment.

It was strange. It was more than strange, it was a little frightening. It was as if those horrid dragons of the sky—*feared* the circle of standing stones!

Propped against the rough pillar, leaning weary arms on the cross-hilt of the great sword, the boy, Thongor, watched as the sunset died to smoldering coals. The skies darkened as Night rose on black wings up over the edges of the earth to shroud the great continent in shadow.

The dragons hovered and circled, and, at length, flapped away and were lost in the gathering darkness.

Then the boy turned to explore this peculiar ring of monoliths . . . where even the fanged predators of the sky dared not come near. This circle of stones which mailed dragons of might dared not pass!

4.   *The City In The Jewel*

Thongor examined the seven stone pillars. They were of cold dead rock, dark, volcanic, rough and porous to the touch. With curious fingers the young Barbarian traced the strange hieroglyphs wherewith they were inscribed. He could make nothing of the curious symbols, but, then, as for that, he could neither read nor write. He had no way of guessing that those inscriptions were in a long-dead tongue whose last living speaker had perished from the earth untold aeons before. . . .

He next approached the low altar.

It was a six-sided cube of black rock and it bore no carvings.

Atop it, the great gem flashed and twinkled.

Never had the boy seen a mass of crystal so immense. He bent over it curiously, and the cold shifting lights that moved within bathed his features in a restless glow.

It was a strong young face, square of jaw and broad of brow and cheekbone. Scowling black brows curved over lion-like eyes. Sun and wind had burnt it to the hue of old leather; there was strength in that face, and intelligence, and breeding. Though how a half-naked wild boy from the savage wildernesses of the wintry Northlands had come by that breeding, none could say.

He was curious of the carven sigils which adorned the glassy surface of each of the odd-angled facets, and he stretched out his hand to trace them—

And jerked back numb, tingling fingers with a little cry! A cold electric shock stabbed at him as his outstretched fingers touched the slick glassy surface—a weird thrilling force.

Frowning, puzzled, he bent over the glittering, flashing gem and peered deep into it.

Deep and deep . . . through the angled mirrors of the faceting . . . down through twinkling mists of dim green and sparkling silver dust . . . to the strange pulsing core of the monstrous gem, where cold phosphorescent fires coiled and glared.

But something happened. The crystal—changed!

The mists thinned—faded—evaporated.

Had the touch of his fingers closed a contact between the boy and the forces that slumbered, locked deep within the mystery jewel?

Had his nearness triggered some dormant, age-old spell— some mystic sorcery whose secret was traced in the weird sigils wherewith the facets of the gem were hewn?

Sparkling mists coiled—cleared—whipped away!

Suddenly the clouded green crystal was clouded no more. Now it was clear and pellucid as glass . . . and the boy's eyes widened in amazement as he stared down upon that which was now clearly visible in the very core of the gigantic gem. He stared down upon . . .

A city! A city there in the heart of the jewel!

It was exquisite; elfin. Tiny delicate minarets and needle-pointing spires of dainty glistening ivory. Swelling bells of domes twinkling with goblin lights. Delicious little houses, peak-roofed and gabled, with stained-glass windows no bigger than his thumbnail.

A faërie princedom in the frozen heart of a gem!

Breathless with awe and wonder, the savage boy stared down at little crooked streets cobbled as if with cowrie shells; at curved flights of alabaster stairs a fingerjoint in width; at elfin gardens of miniature trees where tiny brooks meandered like shimmering strips of blue satin ribbon.

All of exquisite ivory it was, walls fretted like lace, thread-thin, lit with tiny silver lamps like acorn shells. He stared down at courts tiled with malachite; at walls of rosy coral, towers of glistening jade, slender arcades of delicate marble pilasters, beams of ebony, scrolled carvings over windows, balconies, balustrades—so tiny it hurt the eye to search their detailwork.

It was an elfin mirage—a goblin vision—a glimpse into a strange miniature world of marvel.

And gone in the flicker of a lash!

In a breath the city blurred—faded—and was gone. The huge gem clouded again with swirling mists of jade shot through with dazzling coils of silver sparkles. The boy frowned in bafflement and stepped away from the squat cube of black stone and the glittering globe of mystery it bore.

Had it been a dream—a vision—an enchantment?

Whatever it was, it was gone.

5. Dreams in Jade and Silver

The boy growled a wordless oath and fingered a small idol of white stone that hung about his throat suspended on a leathern thong. His tribal fetish, a crude thing, like a bearded face crowned with a circle of stars.

His scalp prickled with superstitious awe. Wild young Barbarian that he was, a scorner of cities, a battler from birth, reared in a harsh land of ignorant savages where every phenomenon of nature is an inexplicable wonder, he instinctively hated and feared magic and dark wizardry.

And that weird gem, that glyph-inscribed circle of ominous dark stones—*stank* of wizardry!

He stood warily, like a young animal at bay, before the twinkling stone. Its inner fires were quiescent now, calm, dully glittering. And yet he feared it and the unknown forces that had fashioned it, and which perhaps lurked within it.

Should he quit this strange place that even the dragons feared? Should he dare the grim dangers of the night beyond, the prowling predators, great black shapes that crept through the broken waste of stone, hunting hot flesh?

Sunset had died to faintly glowing coals by now; the plateau was deep in darkness; the sky a mass of turgid vapors, hiding the few faint stars that had dared to emerge at the sun's death. To venture forth from this curiously protected place into the unknown dangers of the plateau might be foolhardy.

Soon the great golden moon of old Lemuria would rise over the edges of the world to flood all the land in light; then he could traverse the rocky tableland in relative safety. He would still be prey to all the roaming monsters of the dark, but at least he could see them and protect himself against their attack with the great sword that he still clasped in his hand.

Perhaps the wisest thing to do was to wait here behind this ring of standing stones which, for some reason, the beasts seemed to fear. Wait here for the moonrise, and then set forth upon his long journey to the Dakshina, to the lush and jungled Southlands, with their golden cities and mighty kings. There was his goal and his destiny.

He would wait for the moon.

But he was still bone-weary from being hunted down the mountain passes by the twin dragon-hunters. He would rest here, stretch out his aching limbs, ignore the thirst that raged within his throat like a flame, the hunger that growled in his empty belly. He lay down on the smooth rock, between the black cube of the altar and the soaring pylons.

And, of course, he slept. . . .

Strange dreams filled his brain with curious visions.

It seemed that as he lay there in the darkness a cold radiance bloomed within the enormous mass of crystal; a weird luminance of mingled jade and silver that pulsed like a living heart—a heart of throbbing light!

Waves of green and silvery glare swept over his sleeping body, and from somewhere within the huge pulsing core of light that the magic gem had become a far, faint voice called to him in a language he did not understand.

But the message of those words he understood all too well.

The voice lured, sang, beckoned. It was sirenic; it called to him irresistibly. It sang of marvels and wonders, of impossible beautiful things, of unguessable mysteries . . . and he yearned to obey that mystic summons.

Like chiming silver bells the voice spun a net of magic about his sleeping mind . . . and drew him . . . drew him, on and on . . .

And in that strange, haunted dream it seemed to the boy that he opened his eyes and rose lithely to his feet, for all that he still slept. Step by step, entranced, wide-eyed, but still deep in slumber, he approached the great jewel.

It was ablaze now, a throbbing sphere of radiance. An aura of crackling power stood out around it like a huge glittering gateway—and through that gateway the tiny elfin city could be seen clearly now, yet it was somehow no longer small, but large . . . large enough for him to enter and to walk those crooked winding streets, to stroll those cool enchanted gardens, to quaff chilled sparkling wine in those ivory palaces. . . .

Step by step he strode up to the burning gate—

—And came awake in a ringing silence!

6.   Through the Crystal

Shock sluiced over him like a cold, unexpected shower. In his sleep he had, in truth, risen and approached the great gem and now he stood frozen, his extended hands only inches from the glistening crystal, which was, even as in his dream, ablaze with whirling lights and a beating aura of throbbing force.

Rage flamed in the heart of the boy savage. This vile witchery aroused his wrath. His scowling brows contorted. His lips drew back in a challenging snarl, baring white wolf-like teeth. A deep menacing growl rumbled in his deep chest.

"Gorm!"

Growling aloud the name of his primal god, the youth reached forward deliberately and seized hold of the huge sparkling crystal, as if challenging it to work its secret wizardries!

An icy tingling ran through him as he touched the chill,

slick crystal. An electric shock that numbed him as it flickered along his nerves. Waves of cold dazzle buffetted his mind, dulled his sight. He staggered on numb limbs—he fell—

Into the crystal!

It was as if in the instant he fell forward the hard sparkling surface melted into a glittering mist that swirled about him in icy coils but offered no resistance to his warm flesh. He fell forward and down and through the crystal . . . and hurtled into the dark throat of a spinning vortex of swirling jade and silver motes of light.

The odd thing about it all was that he felt neither surprise nor fear. It was like some weird occurrence within a dream —too fantastic and improbable to be real, and hence nothing for him to fear, since it could not really be happening.

He fell through the whirling vortex of moted light and now, it seemed, he fell slower and slower, as if the whirling vaporous diamond spangles of jade and silver radiance beat up and somehow sustained his weight.

In the next instant he struck a sloping surface with stunning force and went rolling down an incline.

Crisp, dew-wet, emerald grass slid across his limbs and he came to rest in a mass of drowsy flowers under an amber sky of dim, luminous vapors.

Dazed and uncomprehending, he stared about him wide-eyed at clumps of strange feathery trees that loomed up against the topaz twilight . . . trees without leaves, whose slick black boughs bore fantastic peacock-plumes of metallic green and gold and lapis.

Beyond them, weird, impossibly slender animals of snowy white grazed the dewy sward. Earth, he knew, had never bred those strange yet lovely creatures with their silken hide and long thick gold manes. If not earth, then—where was he?

Then a vagrant glitter caught his gaze and drew it beyond the feathery trees and the grazing unicorns . . . to the exquisite soaring minarets and swelling domes of a faërie city that lifted in the haze of distance.

The city in the jewel!

This was no dream, but strange reality.

As real as the fantastically clothed, bird-headed warriors who stood ringed about him—dissolved from emptiness in a twinkling—as real as the spear-blades of cold blue steel leveled at his naked breast!

7.   *The Man with No Face*

They took from him the great broadsword and its scabbard and baldric, and they bound his wrists behind his back with tinkling brass chains, or chains of what looked like ruddy, glistening brass, and all the while he stared at them with wonder.

At first he thought they had in very truth the heads of birds; later he determined that they wore curious avian head-dresses or helmets. They were very lifelike: plumed at the crest, with sleek gleaming feathers down over the face, glittering soulless eyes, and cruel hooked beaks.

Birdlike, too, the fantastic costumes they wore: robes and cloaks of woven plumage; hooked gauntlets affixed to their hands like the claws of winged predators. Even their tunics were woven of the soft breast-feathers of hawks.

The bird-warriors moved like automatons, without a sound, stiffly. They spake utterly no word to him, not deigning to reply to his questions. Neither did they handle him with rough, uncaring manner . . . it was as if someone had commanded them to seize him, disarm him, and render him helpless, but taking all the while the greatest possible care to see that he was not harmed.

It was odd. It was very odd. Thongor filed it away for future thought: just another of many mysteries.

Then they led him through the glittering streets into the impossible city.

Dawn—pearly, nacreous, rosy-pale—lit the strange amber skies as he was led captive into the weirdly beautiful city. But like no dawn that ever Thongor had seen on earth, for there was no sun, no orb of fiery light, but merely a gradual brightening of the vaporous sky into sourceless dim radiance.

He had not yet in his young life ever seen a city of men, save for the crude villages of his native Northlands; but he somehow knew no terrene metropolis was like to this.

He became aware, just then, of yet another strangeness.

The air was cool and clear and scented faintly of blooming flowers. But the honey-hearted warmth of verdant summer lay beneath the dewy coolness of dawn. And that was—*madness.*

For when he had come pelting down the great Jomsgard Pass that cleft in twain the Mountains of Mommur, it had been Phuol, the third month of winter. Yet no snow locked this land in its icy grip, and from the scented air and dewy lawns and flowering trees he had already seen, it seemed more like late spring—the month of Garang, say—or the month of Thyron in early summer.

Which reminded him of another unanswerable mystery.

For it had been in the very hour of sunset he had lain down beside the weird jewel. But here it was—*dawn!*

Thongor shook his head with an angry growl, as if to clear his mind of these mysteries. But already he suspected the truth: he was no longer in the world he knew, the world wherein he had been born, but in—another. Or mayhap within the magic jewel the sequence of day and night were curiously reversed, and the seasons of the year as well. Mystery upon mystery!—but their answers were of no importance. Whether or not he had been reduced in stature by some weird enchantment and now dwelt within the jewel, or whether the jewel was itself but the magical gateway which led to this strange new world, these did not matter.

What mattered was that, wherever he was, he was prisoner of those that ruled this ensorceled world of timeless summer.

As he went on between his bird-masked captors, he stared about him with dawning wonder, forgetting his superstitious fears and the grim fact of his captivity. Everywhere he looked, vistas of radiant and enchanting loveliness opened before him: dim arcades of slender, twisting columns wherein small shops offered trays of fabulous gems, gorgeous broideries, flagons of precious vintages.

Beautiful beyond belief the city lay in the dim morning, and yet a shadow of unseen horror haunted it. For in the pale golden faces of the robed and bearded inhabitants he caught the look of—fear.

Fear, too, lurked in their low musical voices as they conversed, covertly eyeing the boy as his captors led him through the streets. Fear, and a glint of something else: perhaps—pity?

The boy stared about him, and he knew the city could not be real. Oh, it seemed solid enough, and doubtless was, but—unreal, for all its solidity.

He was led past a bell-shaped dome that glittered and flashed in morning radiance. All of rock crystal it was, and never yet has this earth produced a cliff of pure crystal so vast as that curving and unbroken dome.

And the tower, the white minaret, builded all of one shaft of solid ivory. The seas and forests of the earth gave birth to no lumbering behemoth so vast as the unthinkable beast whose *single horn* supplied the snowy ivory for that solid tower!

Into a great, turreted citadel of sparkling jade and marble the warriors led him, and thence to an immense domed hall where his shackles were affixed to a ring in the floor. Food in a shallow bowl of some dark crimson wood, and a crystal flagon of water, were set at his feet. Then the soldiers left him.

Being Thongor, the first thing he did was to eat and to drink as much as his belly could hold.

And, when at length his hunger and thirst were assuaged, he attempted to break either his shackles, his chains, or the ring in the floor.

Tough young thews swelled along his strong arms; bands of iron muscle writhed and stood out in sharp relief across his deep chest and broad shoulders; his scowling face blackened with effort; but the sparkling metal, which looked like brass, was of an unbreakable hardness.

So—being Thongor—he lay down, resigned his problems to the turn of future events—and slept.

A gentle hand on his shoulder brought him to full instant wakefulness like a startled jungle cat.

The man who bent over him was old and lean and robed in white silken stuff. The cowl or hood of his gown was drawn, covering his features.

"Are you awake, boy? Do not fear me, I am a captive—a slave, like yourself," the aged one said in a quiet, cultured voice.

Thongor relaxed. "Why do you ask? Do I look asleep?" he growled curtly. The old man shrugged, seating himself tailor-fashion on the floor.

"Alas, I cannot tell. I have no eyes with which to see whether you sleep or wake," he said. Thongor bit his lip, angry at his own rudeness.

"Your forgiveness, grandfather," he grunted. "I did not know you were blind."

"Not blind, my son—without eyes. There is, you will perceive, a difference."

Thongor shrugged. "I do not understand."

"I will show you, then, if you will promise not to be

afraid of me. For, however dreadful my appearance, it is not of my doing, and I am no enemy of yours, however horrible to your sight my visage may be," the old man said.

And lifting one slender, wasted hand he drew aside his cowl and laid bare to the horrified gaze of the boy a sight of unthinkable terror. For he had no face, no face at all, merely a blank and featureless oval of pale unwrinkled skin: no eyes or nose or mouth, or, if mouth there was, a veil of tight skin was stretched over the opening.

"*Gorm* . . ." Thongor said hoarsely; if it was a curse, it was also half a prayer.

"Our Lord Zazamanc is sometimes . . . capricious," the old man said gently.

8. *Ithomaar the Eternal*

"How did you come to be—like that?" Thongor asked in a low voice. The old man veiled his horrible, blank visage behind that merciful mask of white silk and began to speak in a low, quiet voice.

"Listen to me, my son, we have little time. I cannot answer your questions now, not all of them. In a very short while you will be taken from this place and brought before the Lord of this city, and it is my task to prepare you for that meeting. So do not interrupt, but let me speak swiftly of that which you must know in order to be spared such horror as I have endured.

"My name is Yllimdus, and I came to this place even as did you—through the crystal. My city is Kathool of the Purple Towers; in my youth I was a jewel merchant, and oft led caravans into the Mountains of Mommur, seeking for gem fields. On one such expedition, I achieved a rocky plateau and discovered, amidst the level tableland, a circle of standing stones and within that circle, a great gem: but I need not detail my discoveries and my experiences further, for you have known them, or you would not be here. Is it not so?"

"It is," said Thongor. Yllimdus nodded.

"Ages ago, when the world was young and the Seven Cities of the East flourished, there arose a powerful sorcerer, a strange man of deep wisdom and uncanny mastery of the occult sciences: Zazamanc the Veiled Enchanter.

"This strange being achieved heights of power unguessed

at by mortal men; his lifespan he extended far beyond the endurance of human flesh; his searching gaze probed the hidden crannies of the moon, the surface of distant worlds, the dark gulf between the stars. Yet for all his learning and magistry, he was a thing of flesh and blood, and death comes to all that liveth, be it ne'er so wise. Zazamanc brooded long over his impending mortality, and at length perceived a method whereby he might cheat Death itself and outlive the eons.

"With his magical arts he constructed a crystal of perdurable substance; within that crystal he built a private universe where Time could not come and Death was not nor could enter therein. A gorgeous city he constructed, raised by the hands of invisible and captive spirits, and therein a magic land was created, whereover Zazamanc shall rule forever, an undying king, immortal and omnipotent as a god.

"This city he named Ithomaar the Eternal, for that nothing within it can ever age or die. And the kingdom whereover Zazamanc rules is the dwellingplace of captive peoples such as you and I—unwary travelers, lured by the mystery of the crystal and its singing voice—who have entered into this magical land and cannot ever leave."

"These things are fantasies, grandfather!" Thongor growled.

"Alas, my son, they are utter truth," Yllimdus said gently. "Tell me: what year is it in the great world beyond, the world from which you came?"

"Why, let me see; it is winter in the six thousand nine hundred and ninety-ninth year of the Kingdoms of Man," Thongor said. There ensued a silence of some duration. Then—

"So long . . . so very long," whispered the old man with no face. "Ah, lad, it was spring in the Year of the Kingdoms of Man 4971 when I came hither on that venture . . . *for two thousand years have I dwelt here in this accursed paradise beyond the reach of Time!*"

"Gods! Can this thing be true?" Thongor muttered.

Yllimdus sighed: "All too true, lad; here we can never die. O, I have prayed for death in my centuries . . . but we are beyond Death's hand, here, aye . . . and beyond the power of the Nineteen Gods themselves!"

"This sorcerer, this Zazamanc," the boy asked. "What will he do with—me?"

A dim echo of horror entered the gentle tones of the ancient man.

"He will . . . play . . ."

9. *The Veiled Enchanter*

In this dim world where no sun shone to light the day nor moon to shed her pallid radiance by night, it was impossible to guess the passage of time. Thongor soon discovered this strange truth. Tall windows, narrowed, pointed, barred with thick grilles of that strange brasslike metal which Yllimdus had named *orichalc*, let in the dim opal light. Thongor thought to observe the movement of time by the shifting across the floor of the patch of strangely colored radiance cast through that pointed narrow window . . . but it did not move; neither did it wane.

At some unguessable time later, the warriors came to take him before the Enchanter for . . . judgment?

Yllimdus had warned that to the proud, cold immortal who ruled this minuscule world, lesser men were slaves, toys, naught but cattle. Here in this world his art had made he was a very god, and could play with his human toys as he wished. Men could not die in this dim eternal world, but they could —suffer. So, as the whim struck him, Zazamanc the Veiled Enchanter transformed them—mutilated them into weirdly horrible monsters. Some were quaint, droll hybrids: men with the heads of insects, women with flower petals instead of hair, dwarfed little beings, gaunt giants, men with neither arms nor legs who wriggled about like naked pallid fleshy serpents.

Yllimdus himself had been a courtier until his Lord wearied of his cautious advice and sage counsel. And thus, with a potent cantrip, the old man had been transformed into a faceless thing of horror. Thongor's eyes smouldered with rage and the nape-hair bristled on his neck like the hackles of some jungle beast. The wild boy was no stranger to cruelty. Nature herself is cruel, and men are her children and have inherited much of her ways. But the boy knew only the sudden, savage cruelty of swift death, or red roaring war, of man battling against man or against brute.

This sort of cruelty, casual, cold, cynical—this was new to him. And it chilled him with an unsettling mixture of horror and nausea and contempt. He wondered what sort of a man could so negligently and carelessly disfigure another man who had done him no greater ill than merely to bore him . . . if, indeed, Zazamanc was only a man.

For this was of the species of cruelty man usually suffers at the hands of playful and uncaring gods. Was, then, this Veiled Enchanter a god? True: he had created all of this miniature world within the jewel, and that was godlike.

And—a thrill of dread went through the boy at the thought —if he was a god, could gods be slain?

The warriors who escorted the savage boy through the magnificent palace of the Enchanter were curious beings themselves, and as he paced along in their midst, young Thongor stole many curious glances at them in a covert fashion.

They were not bird-warriors like those who had arrested him beyond the city.

These were cold-faced, pale, expressionless men. They were automatonlike, even as had been the warriors in the fantastical avian costumes. But most of all they were like dead men somehow embued in some grisly and necromantic fashion with the uncanny semblance of life, but devoid of life's animation.

Old Yllimdus had spoken of these, back in the prison hall. He had used a curious word to describe them—*avathquar* —"living dead." An odd, uneasy, disturbing word. Thongor's hide crawled at the touch of them, cold and flaccid, like the puffy flesh of corpses.

Yllimdus, who had been imprisoned for more than a year within the great hall, having incurred the dislike of his Lord, had warned him of these, and had said that not everyone came through the Jewel Amid the Seven Pillars—alive. Some were drawn through, and were dead when they materialized within the miniature world. Perchance it was these fresh cadavers, magically animated by some occult science, that became the *avathquar*. It was a peculiarly unsettling thought, and he eyed them with frank curiosity as they led him along.

They seemed completely drained and empty, and they had none of life's warmth and passion. He wondered if they truly lived, or if they were but automatons of dead flesh vitalized in some weird manner by the power of the Enchanter. They were splendid specimens of manhood, surely, tall and strongly built and handsome in a regular sort of way. But they strode along like puppets, looking neither to the right nor to the left, their pale stern faces hard and blank, their cold eyes empty of alertness.

Bemused by such thoughts as these, Thongor saw little of the superb corridors and halls and chambers through which they led him; ever after he retained but a blurred impression of blazing tapestries seething with color and motion, or glowing figurines and statuettes of unearthly grace and lifelike detail, or of carven marble walls and fretted screens of ivory and soaring columns and arched and vaulted ceilings painted with weird and mythological frescoes.

At length they led him into a colossal hall floored with black marble like a gigantic mirror.

Far above, lost in dim shadows, an enormous dome reared atop thick columns of a sea-green stone unfamiliar to him. About the walls more of the zombilike warriors stood, motionless as graven images, immaculate in dazzling sun-gold armor.

For these things he had no attention.

It was that which occupied the very center of the gloomy hall which seized and held his fascinated gaze.

A tall, tall chair of scarlet crystal, three times human height.

And in the chair . . . a man was seated.

10. *Burning Eyes*

Zazamanc bore the appearance of a slim, tall, youthful man with strong arms, long legs, and a coldly beautiful face which bore no slightest sign of age.

He was attired in complicated and fantastic garments of many colors: puce, canary, blood-scarlet, lavender, mauve, subtle gray, deep violet.

His raiment was unlike any costume that Thongor had ever seen or heard of. Tight hose clothed his long slender legs; a tunic or jerkin, gathered and tucked and folded according to the dictates of some alien fashion, adorned his torso; sleeves of various lengths protruded one from the other. Long gloves were drawn over his lean strong hands, and strange rings of metal and stone and crystal twinkled and flashed as he moved his fingers.

A cowl, trimmed with strange purple fur, was drawn about his head but did not cover his face.

His face held and fascinated the boy. It was of a supernal, an unhuman, beauty. A high, broad white brow, arched and silken-black eyebrows, long imperial nose, firm, delicately modeled chin, thin-lipped but exquisitely carved mouth—these were his features.

They were flawless; without blemish. No wrinkle marred the purity of that godlike brow. No slightest shade of emotion lent warmth to the cold perfection of that face. It was like an idealized sculpture: cold, beautiful, pure, but inhuman.

It was the eyes alone that held life and expression.

Strange eyes they were . . . black and cold as frozen ink . . . depthless as bottomless pits . . . cold and deep, but burning with a fierce, unholy flame of vitality.

Behind their enigmatic gaze the boy somehow sensed a vast, cool, limitless intellect as far removed from the ordinary mind of mankind as man is from, say, the groveling insects or the squirming serpents.

They brought him before the tall scarlet throne and he stood erect and unbowing as that black, burning gaze swept him slowly from head to foot. With careful, judicious deliberation the Veiled Enchanter scanned him slowly.

When he spoke, and then only, did Thongor understand his cognomen. For, from brow to chin, his coldly perfect visage was delicately veiled behind a transparent membrane of some slight fabric, thin almost to the point of invisibility. Why a man should wear a veil which veiled nothing, and through which the eye could clearly see, was but the least of the mysteries Thongor had yet encountered in this tiny world of magic and beauty and depraved horror.

"It is a savage boy; doubtless from the Northlands; I believe I recall a race of strong Barbarians who dwelt of old on the wintry tundras of that portion of Lemuria," the Enchanter said idly. His voice was like his face: cold, perfect, clear, but devoid of warmth or animation.

"I recall the race; but that was . . . long ago."

For an instant it seemed to Thongor that the black flame of those eyes bore within their fierce depths a measureless weariness, an age-old boredom. Perhaps even something of —futility?

"He is young and strong, bred of brave warriors, I doubt me not. It might be amusing to see that strength . . . take him hence to the Arena Master. We shall see this youthful prowess on the Day of the Opal Vapors. Take him away now. . . ."

The guards saluted with mechanical perfection, and led Thongor from the silent hall.

Behind, sitting tall and straight and regal in the scarlet chair, the Veiled Enchanter continued staring straight ahead, into nothingness, with no expression on his cold and beautiful face.

11.   In The Speculum

Zazamanc stood in his magical laboratorium. Corrosive vapors swirled about him, caught in twisted tubes of lucent glass. Fiery liquors seethed in crucibles of lead over weird fires of glowing minerals. Trapped forever between two panes of quartz, a mad phantasm screamed soundlessly, caught in a two-dimensional hell. Strange and terrible was this place of many magics: the air stank of dire wizardries; the brimstone odors of the Pit reeked therein.

The square stone chamber was oddly lit. Wandering, ghostly globes of insubstantial luminance drifted like bubbles of light, to and fro, ice-blue, scarlet, blinding white.

Their shifting radiance cast eerie black shadows crawling over the uneven walls, clustering like frightened bats in the darkest corners.

A vast globe of silvery metal bore a strange image: a huge insectoid thing, with a naked, exposed, and swollen brain, and black, glittering, compound eyes, squatting in green caverns of porous rock, where glassy stalactites and strange crystal outcroppings caught and flickered with vagrant wisps of light.

This was one of the Insect Philosophers who dwelt in the dead core of earth's moon, and with whom, by his art, Zazamanc sometimes conversed.

With a white crawling fungoid intelligence, on the twilight zone of the planet Mercury, he also communicated betimes; and with a crystalloid but sentient mineral being on one of the moons of Saturn.

The insectoid thing with the monstrous brain faded slowly from the surface of the silver sphere.

The image was replaced with a different scene. A sweltering area of burning sand whereon a half-naked boy struggled with a huge crimson beast. Zazamanc drew in his breath sharply, watching in suspense. The boy held, for weapon, a hooked sickle. His wild black mane streamed about his yell-ing, contorted face; his strange gold eyes glazed lionlike through the tangle of his locks.

The crimson thing roared and foamed, and batting wildly at the nimble, leaping figure with heavy paws bladed with black claws like scythed razors. At length the boy darted within the reach of those grasping arms.

Zazamanc sucked in his breath and held it.

The sickle flashed, catching the light, as it swung in a wicked arc. It slashed through the distended throat of the roaring crimson brute and in an instant it lay gasping out bubbling gore on the wet sands, while Thongor stood panting, sweaty, streaming with blood, but triumphant.

Zazamanc uttered a curse and permitted the image to lapse into its component atoms of light. The surface of the silver sphere went blank and dull.

Turning away from the speculum, the Veiled Enchanter crossed the cluttered, crowded chamber to a huge desk that was a cube of gray, cracked stone. Atop this a jumble of parchment scrolls lay sprawled in a litter of amulets, periapts, talismanic rings, and instruments peculiar to the magician's art.

Shoving aside two of these, an arthame and a bolline, the Enchanter uncovered a vast and ponderous book.

This tome was of peculiar and alien worksmanship: no terrene product of the bookwright's art, surely. The leaves were bound between two plates of perdurable metal, but a rare, unearthly metal, blue as sapphire stone, and filled with radiant flakes of gold light. The twin plates were deeply embossed with large glyphs of geometric complexity. And the leaves within were even more strange: of flexive lucent stuff were they, glassy and crystalline and yet supple.

The pentacles, wherewith these leaves were inscribed, were of red-orange, green-black, silver, violet, and a strange throbbing color that seemed somehow to belong between the hues of heliotrope and jasper, but which was a color not elsewise found on earth and belonging to no spectrum of normal light.

In some odd fashion, these magical diagrams had been inked *within* the very substance of the flexible crystal leaves.

Zazamanc opened the ponderous volume and began an intent perusal of the sorcerous lore.

The boy Thongor must die. And in a grim and bloody manner.

And—soon!

But *how?*

12. Jothar Jorn

The arena stood on the further edge of the city of Ithomaar, a vast, circular amphitheater like an enormous crater. This bowl-shaped depression had been scooped out of the ground by captive genii, its sloping sides terraced into tiers and fitted out with curved marble benches. The gladiators themselves, and the cages that held the beasts they were to fight against, dwelt in subterranean crypts below the arena floor. To these, the bird-masked and unspeaking warriors conducted the youthful Barbarian.

They brought him to a huge, fat, half-naked man who had been working out with the swordsmen. He was crimson from his exertions, his massive torso glittering with sweat, and as Thongor came up to him he was toweling himself dry and emptying an enormous drinking horn filled with dark ale. One of the bird-guards proffered a slim ivory tablet to him. It was inscribed with a brief directive, written in emerald inks, in queer, hooked characters such as the barbarian boy had never before seen. The man scrutinized them quickly, then raised thoughtful, curious eyes to Thongor.

"A Northlanderman, eh? Tall for your age, and built like a young lion. Well, cub, I doubt not those strong arms will provide merry entertainment for our Lord, come the Day of Opal Vapors!" His voice was hearty and genial, and his great, broken-nosed slab of a face, beefy-red, glistening with perspiration, was cheerful and honest. His little eyes were light blue and good-humored. Thongor rather liked the look of him, and slightly relaxed his stiff, guarded stance. The gamesmaster noted this, and chuckled.

"My name is Jothar Jorn, and I be gamesmaster to the pleasure of our Lord," he said. "You've naught to fear from me, lion cub, so long as you do as you be told, and quick about it, too."

"I am Thongor of Valkarth," the boy said. The gamesmaster nodded, looking him over with quick, keen eyes.

"Valkarth: I might have guessed, from the color of those eyes. Snow Bear tribe?"

Thongor bristled and a red glare came into his strange gold eyes. "My people were the Black Hawk clan, and the Snow Bear tribe were—are—their enemies," he said fiercely. The big man eyed him with frank, friendly curiosity.

"You be somewhat mixed on your tenses, lad. 'Were—are'
—which would you have?"

Thongor's head drooped slightly and his broad young
shoulders slumped. In a flat, listless voice he said: "My people
are dead, fallen in battle before the dogs of the Snow Bear;
my father, my brothers . . ."

A sympathy rare in this primitive age shone in the small
blue eyes of the big man. "*All* . . . of your people slain in war
by the other tribe?" he asked in low, subdued tones.

Thongor's head came up proudly and his shoulders went
back. "All are dead; I am the last Black Hawk," he said
bleakly.

"Well . . . well . . ." Jothar Jorn cleared his throat loudly,
and shook himself a little. In that case, you will be hungry,"
he said in his hearty way. "Hungry enough to—eat a Snow
Bear, shall we be saying?"

The boy grinned soberly, then laughed. And they went in to
dinner.

Jothar Jorn bade an underling lead the Barbarian to the
commonroom where the gladiators ate at long benches, and
set a repast before him such as the boy had not seen for
weeks. A succulent steak, rare and bloody, swimming in its
own steaming juices, tough black bread and ripe fruit and a
tankard full of heady ale. Thongor fell on this feast raven-
ously, reflecting that if *this* was captivity, then it might not be
so bad, after all.

13. The Pits of Ithomaar

Ten days passed, and busy days they were. As a newcomer
to the City in the Jewel, Thongor was curious about everything and kept his eyes and ears open. He soon learned that
Jothar Jorn had entered the magic crystal only twenty years
before: he had been gamesmaster of the arena of Tsargol, a
seacoast city far to the south, head of an expedition into the
mountain country of Mommur trapping beasts for use in the
games then to be held in celebration of the coronation of
Sanjar Thal, Sark of Tsargol. He, too, had glimpsed the jewel
from afar, having left his trappers behind, hot in pursuit of a
mountain dragon, and had been caught by the sirenic lure of
the crystal even as had the Valkarthan boy.

As for the gladiators he trained, they were all Ithomaar-
born and knew nothing of the outer world from which Thon-

gor and Jothar Jorn had come. The boy soon found his place
among them, but not without a few lumps and bruises. For
the most part, the gladiators of Ithomaar the Eternal were
full-grown men, and a mere stripling cast into their midst was
fair game for a bit of good-natured hazing. But the young
Barbarian did not take very well to the playful roughhouse in
the manner to which his fellow-gladiators were by now accustomed.

The first man who tried to shove the boy around was a big,
cold-eyed bully named Zed Zomis, the acknowledged leader
of the gladiators. He ended up flat in the corner with his jaw
broken in three places and a mouthful of shattered teeth—for
all that he was ten years older than the boy Thongor, a head
taller, and outweighed him by thirty pounds.

Three of Zed Zomis' comrades, who had gathered to watch
their leader have a little fun with the surly outlander youth,
promptly jumped on the wild boy from behind when they
saw him dispose of their friend. Within the first few seconds
of the tussle they discovered they had picked a fight with a
lion cub in very truth. The *vandar,* as the jet-black lion of the
Lemurian forest-country was called, is twelve feet of steely,
sinewy strength from fanged jaw to lashing tailtip, and a
juggernaut of fighting fury: and Jothar Jorn had nicknamed
the young Barbarian aptly.

To a boy from the savage Northlands, war is a way of life,
and, for all his young years, the Valkarthan lad was no
stranger to the red art, having been raised virtually from the
cradle with a weapon in his fist. Northlandermen of Thongor's people dwell in a bleak and hostile land of bitter wintry
snows, and life is one savage and unending struggle against
rapacious brutes, scarcely less rapacious human foes, and Nature herself, who is cruel and harsh toward weaklings north
of the Mountains of Mommur.

Thus, to Thongor, fighting was no game but deadly serious.
And no one attacks a warrior of his kind in play, only in
earnest. Thus, when Zed Zomis' bullyboys sprang upon him
from behind, it was no mere laughing tussle he gave them,
but a grim, vicious battle to the death, from which they
emerged with a number of broken bones; and one of them, at
least, would limp forever.

Thus he made for himself a place in the Pits of Ithomaar,
and it was a place of considerable respect. The gladiators
treated him with care thereafter, and not a few of them were

quick to hail him as a friend. As for Thongor, he bore no ill will to the four men he had beaten and was as ready to be friends with them as with any man who treated him with dignity.

The boy thrived on the hearty meals the gladiators were served. These consisted of immense steaks swimming in hot gravy, raw vegetables, sweet pastries and a variety of good, strong wines. Of this menu, the last two items were new to his experience, and after a prolonged bout with the winecups, from which he emerged a bit unsure of his footing and with a head, the next morning, that throbbed with queasy pain, he treated the fruit of the vine with much the same gingerly respect with which the older gladiators had learned to treat him.

From Jothar Jorn he learned something of the fighting skills as practiced by civilized men. The warriors of the Black Hawk clan had schooled him in the use of bow and arrow, spear and javelin, war-axe, and, of course, in the art of using the great two-handed broadsword. He missed that broadsword, taken from him by the bird-masked guardsmen when they captured him. The sword was old, ancient, really, and it had passed down his line from father to eldest son from time immemorial. Some said the great sword—its name was Sarkozan—had been wielded by none other than Valkh the Black Hawk himself, the famous hero who had been the founder of Thongor's nation—Valkh, Valkh of Nemedis, one of the immortal heroes who went up against the Dragon Kings at the close of The Thousand-Year War—Valkh, who was of the blood of Phondath the Firstborn, in the twentieth generation of the direct male line.

That sword had, ages agone, drunk of the blood of the Dragon Kings, reaping a red harvest there on the black beaches of Grimstrand Firth. Mayhap the Nineteen Gods themselves had blessed it, when the heroes went up from Nemedis in the Last Battle, for it is written in *The Lemurian Chronicles* how of old They went among the men of the First Kingdoms.

Jothar Jorn trained the savage boy in such "civilized" weapons as dirk and dag, rapier and hooksword, cutlass and scimitar. But the strong hands of the Valkarthan yearned for the loved, familiar heft of Sarkozan. And at last he revolted.

"But, cub! We don't fight with broadswords in Ithomaar—and, look, you can have your pick of weapons," the gamesmaster argued. Thongor set his jaw grimly.

"They have taken my sword from me. I want it back," he said stubbornly. Something in the set of that jaw and the stubborn glint in those blazing eyes told Jothar Jorn it did no good to argue, but argue he did, and plead, and even threaten. But to all his bellowings and coaxings, Thongor made but one reply:

"They have taken my sword from me. I want it back."

At length, Jothar Jorn talked himself hoarse and gave up. Who could say? Maybe a Barbarian brandishing a broadsword would be a sensation in the Games. At least it would be—different.

"Get him his sword," he said, and shrugged, and left.

14. The Secret Gate

Now that Sarkozan was in his possession once again, Thongor began to plan his escape. He had no idea how he had come here, but he intended to return to the world he knew, one way or another. He was willing to die trying. For besides his appetite for red meat, his berserker courage, and his fighting ferocity, he shared another trait with the great cats of the jungle: he would not be shut in a cage. And Ithomaar was a cage—a very beautiful one, but a cage nonetheless. He had taken the measure of the folk of this fabulous realm, and he did not like what he saw, neither the dainty, gilded fops of the court who came to watch the gladiators at sword practice because it titillated them to see real men work up a sweat in brutal combat, nor the commonfolk of the city's shops and ways, with their listless faces, dead eyes, and hearts empty of hope.

The Pits were not guarded because there was no need to guard them. They were underground, hewn by invisible hands from solid bedrock, and there was no escape. Most gladiators never thought of trying to escape, because the life they had here was better than the one they had escaped from, with excitement and pride in their prowess, good meat and drink, and even women, occasionally brought in to serve their needs. But even at seventeen, Thongor knew he would rather die than live in a cage.

It was not long before he discovered the door in the wall. It was a slab of brassy orichalc and it bore, embossed upon its center panel, a hieroglyph whose meaning he did not know. What interested him was that the door was unlocked—had, in fact, no lock. In a roundabout way he questioned the other gladiators about it, eliciting little information. It was on the lowest level of the Pits and it was behind the beast-cages. Finally, drinking wine with Jothar Jorn, who had taken a liking to him, he mentioned the door. The brawny gamesmaster stiffened, his good-humored slab of a face paling.

"You do not be wantin' to find out what's behind that door, cub. Never go near it!" he grunted, eyes sober and almost fearful.

"I do not understand why it has no lock," Thongor said. "Where does it lead?"

"To the Tower of Skulls," said Jothar Jorn. And that was all he would say. His warning meant nothing to Thongor; the young Barbarian knew only that it must lead down into the city itself, for there was no tower near the arena. Once in the city, he knew it should not be difficult for him to escape to the woodlands beyond, for Ithomaar the Eternal had no walls, which meant no gates, which meant no guards.

So that very night he made the attempt. He had eaten a good dinner at the long tables of scarlet *lotifer* wood with his comrades, but some of the meat and bread and fruit he had not eaten, but had hidden away in a sack he had fashioned from a scrap of cloth and kept hidden behind his cloak. As his comrades strolled into the commonroom, where lute players and dancing girls waited to entertain them at their wine, he sought out the jakes and, once alone in the winding corridors of stone, turned aside to the level of the beast-cages and the secret door of orichalc that went unguarded and unlocked.

He thrust the door open, finding a long narrow corridor of damp stone. He went in, the door closing softly behind him.

He went forward, the great Valkarthan broadsword naked in his hand.

15. The Thing in the Smoke

In a vast chamber beneath the Tower of Skulls, Zazamanc the Veiled Enchanter sat enthroned in Power.

This throne stood on a dais composed of nine tiers of black marble, and it was carven from the ivory of mastodons. Set within the broad arms of this throne were the sigils whereby the Veiled Enchanter summoned the demons and genii and elementals that served his wishes in all things. At this hour he wore the Green Robe of Conjuration, and his left hand was set upon Ouphonx, the ninth sigil of the planet Saturn, which the Lemurians of this age knew by another name. Under his right hand lay Zoär, the third sigil of the Moon. Before him, on a tabouret of jet, lay the Crossed Swords and the wand called Imgoth.

Amulets were clasped about his wrists and throat. Pendent upon his brow hung the talisman the grimoires name Arazamyon, and upon it a certain Name was writ in runes fashioned of small black pearls.

The face of Zazamanc went masked this day behind a single tissue of pale-green gauze; through it the cold pallor of his handsome visage gleamed like an ivory mask, and his eyes glittered with frozen malice.

Sprawled upon the lower tiers of the dais lay the naked body of a sixteen-year-old slave girl, and beneath it a wet scarlet pool spread slowly. Beside the corpse lay a razory dirk that had, only a few moments before, cut her heart from her naked breast. As for the heart itself, it had been hurled—a gory, dripping thing, still warm and throbbing with unquenched vitality—into an immense bowl of bronze, curiously engraved, wherein red flames slithered slowly.

Seated rigidly in his ivory throne, the Veiled Enchanter now called upon the Name Alzarpha. As the echoes of that name died shuddering in the rafters of the high-roofed chamber, he began to enunciate in solemn, portentous tones the frightful names of the genii that ruled the Twenty-eight Mansions of the Moon. Strange and uncouth were these names; many were never meant to be spoken aloud by the lips of men, and these were difficult to pronounce. However, as the green-robed figure spake them one by one, the red flames that crawled and rustled within the brazen bowl turned first a sickly yellow and then a virulent green, the color of pus and corruption and decay.

From the ensorceled flames there began to issue forth a thick, oily smoke. It coiled through the darkness of the mighty chamber, heavy and sooty, and within it was the stench of hell.

" . . . Zargiel! . . . Maldruim! . . . Phonthon! . . . Ziminar!" Name after name came rolling from the Enchanter's lips in slow thunder. As they rang through the somber silence of the subterranean vault, the nauseous vapor grew dense, coalesced, and began to assume shape and substance. Gradually there took form a weird, towering figure that loomed up against the gloomy rafters far above.

Thrice the height of mortal man it was, and manlike in form, but only in that it stood erect upon two limbs and had a single head. For it was gaunt as a dead thing, covered with gray, greasy hide, wrinkled and bewarted like that of a toad.

This demon was known to the grimoires as Xarxus of the Crawling Eye, and the Veiled Enchanter had long since bound it to his service by a terrible and unbreakable vow. Its long, lean arms ended in grisly pincers, like a gigantic crab, and its head was unspeakably hideous. But one eye it had, and that was a hollow, fleshy pit from whose center slim tendrils sprouted: these flexed and slithered in a loathsome manner, and from this repellent and unnatural organ the demon's name was derived.

"I have the boy," Zazamanc said, when the demon had taken form. "But I cannot comprehend your warnings concerning him: he knows naught of me and is but a rough, untutored savage. I want you to read the future again, to discern if by his capture I have altered or averted the doom whereof you have foretold."

The demon stared down at him, tendrils crawling in the hideous, empty socket that was its only eye. When the tall thing spoke it was in a voice deeper than ever came from human throat, but curiously flat and unresonant. It spoke even though it had nothing remotely resembling a mouth, but this did not disturb Zazamanc, who knew that such as Xarxus did not require organs of speech but could resonate the very molecules of the air itself, or cause their thoughts to sound within the minds of those with whom they had uncanny converse.

I have warned you against having aught to do with this one, the demon said. *I have foretold that there approacheth down the paths of future time one who is destined to be your bane and the cause of your death. You would be wise to send him hence from this universe you rule.*

Brooding upon his ivory throne, Zazamanc seemed not to have heard the words of the demon.

"You can see further into future events than can I," he mused. "In my Speculum I have foreseen what will eventuate if he fights in the arena against my monstrous hybrids: his fighting prowess is such that he will escape victorious from every combat, if permitted an even chance and a good weapon. But it would be so easy to slay him . . ."

The demon shook its awful head, a familiar human gesture suddenly made horrible by his lack of human features. *There is little of the future that I may foretell with any degree of certitude, but this much I can say: the life of that one is linked with your own, and if you slay him, or order him slain, or set him in such danger that his death ensues, your own death will follow swiftly.*

Naked fear glittered in the cold, inscrutable eyes of the Veiled Enchanter. His death was the one thing in all the many worlds and universes that he feared, for he knew all too well that which would befall him thereafter, and his soul shrank shuddering from the knowledge. His gloved hands crawled uneasily on the arms of his throne.

"Why do you refuse to read my future in any detail?" he queried in a thin, petulant voice. "You are bound to serve my will by the nature of the vow between us . . ."

It is not that I refuse, but that I am unable to comply, the demon said. *You are naught but a human, for all your magistry, and the true nature of time remains hidden from your knowledge, a secret shared only between the Lords of Light and . . . mine own kind. Know, then, that time is like unto a maze of many thousand intersecting paths: at each single step you face a choice of paths to follow. Which path you may select in any given instance may be calculated, but to project the pattern of your choices further into the maze involves a geometric progression of possible choices, until the further ahead one seeks to predict, one is baffled before an infinite multiplicity of possible paths.*

"Read, then, what you can of my future," Zazamanc commanded.

Xarxus complied. *Every mortal hath seven assassins, appointed by inscrutable Fate to be his doom. One or another or a third he may elude. Few men elude all seven. The youth you have so unwisely drawn into your realm beyond space will be the doom of Zazamanc.*

"Then I will slay him first! And thus avert the destiny you foretell for me . . ."

The crawling eye of the demon stared at him sightlessly, tendrils writhing obscenely in the naked socket.

Death has never entered this universe of yours, Xarxus said
tonelessly. *Gladiators mangled in the arena regain their
strength, their torn flesh knits: even this girl-child whose
heart you fed into the flames will rise again. To strike down
the savage boy with a bolt of force would be to let Death in
. . . and once Death has entered here, he will not willingly
leave. Beware, O Zazamanc, and guard thy portals well: for
too long have you evaded the hand of the Destroyer of All,
and he shall seek you out if once you let him in. . . .*

With those words, the demon began to crumble and disperse, his pseudobody dissolving into the primal elements
from which he had been formed. Zazamanc sat stiff and
straight, his face an expressionless mask. But his eyes were
shadowed with a terrible fear. He knew that a magician may
defend his mortality with a thousand spells, but that the
Powers that rule Creation have foreseen a loophole through
even the most cunning defense. He knew, as well, that it is
forbidden to flesh and blood to assume the prerogatives of
divinity, the first of which is life eternal. And however a wizard prolongs his life through arcane science, he never loses
the dread of death; quite the contrary—the longer he lives,
the more he savors life.

Zazamanc was afraid—for the first time in uncountable
ages.

16. *The Edge of the World*

The secret passage was interminable. As Thongor prowled
its length, Sarkozan naked in his hand, he expected to be attacked at any moment, but no such attack came. Doubtless
the Veiled Enchanter used this tunnel to communicate with
beast-cages, wherein many of his most extraordinary hybrid
monsters awaited their turn on the sands of the arena. It was
unlocked and unguarded for the simple reason that no one
would dare disturb the privacy of Zazamanc and rouse his
enmity by using it. But Thongor dared!

At last he came to its end, and found a sliding panel that
opened into an immense hall—the same hall in which he had
first been imprisoned. This vast, shadowy place must, then, be
within the Tower of Skulls.

The boy stood, glaring about him into shadows, the great
sword naked in his fist. If he could find his way out of here, he

thought it likely he could escape from the city unseen and un-detected, for Ithomaar had no gates or walls to detain him, and every boulevard led to the green fields and feathery forests beyond, and thence to the world's edge itself—the nar-row, circular horizon of lambent vapor that marked the term-inus of this microcosmos.

And were he to reach the world's edge uncaptured—what then? How to find his way back through the enchanted crys-tal to the land of Lemuria? The boy shook his shoulders, growling deep in his chest: it was not the way of the Black Hawk warriors to gnaw at more than one problem at a time. He would find or fight his way to the limits of this artificial world, and then worry about a way beyond it.

Suddenly he was not alone.

He knew it by the prickling of his nape-hairs, the way a jungle beast senses the presence of danger. The boy whirled in a fighting crouch, the broadsword flashing in his hand—to stare into the cold, inhumanly perfect visage of the Veiled Enchanter.

Zazamanc had melted from invisible air soundlessly, but the keen senses of the savage had detected his presence. In his right hand the magician bore an ominous baton of black wood, carven with twisting runes and capped at both ends with ferrous metal. Thongor would not have known it for a weapon, but such it was. It was the wand called Bazli-moth, the Blasting Rod. Within it, lightnings slumbered.

"You are strayed from the Pits, child," said the Enchanter in a cold, remote voice. Thongor made no reply, but his strange gold eyes blazed lionlike through tangled locks and his weight was on the balls of his feet, ready for action.

The Enchanter slowly extended the black wand until its tip pointed at Thongor's breast. The cunning brain of the En-chanter seethed in a turmoil of unanswered queries—*had* the demon lied to him? How could the destruction of the wild boy bring about his own doom? True, Death had never en-tered here, but what of that? He could shrivel the boy to ash in an instant—and how could the act endanger him? Upon his cold lips a Word formed unspoken; suddenly the wand was vibrant with force. It throbbed in his hand like a live thing, eager to kill.

And in that instant a hand fell upon his arm and Zazamanc shrank with amazement and fury to find the faceless horror of old Yllimdus by his side. In his frenzy to blast down the Barbarian, he had forgotten that his former councilor was imprisoned in this hall by his order. He shrugged off the hand of Yllimdus, his perfect visage a mask of fury. The old man fell back so that he stood between the rage of Zazamanc and the Valkarthan youth.

"Your end is near, Zazamanc," the old man said. "Your reign is over. Slay not this child, but permit him to return to the outer world from which you drew him: do this, and you may yet live."

"You dare lay hands upon your master?" Zazamanc cried, trembilng with wrath. "Stand aside, fool, or die with him you would shield in your folly!"

"I do not fear death, for it is but an end to an existence of weary torment," the old man said quietly. "It is *you* who fear, for all too well do you know what will follow in the instant of your demise."

Zazamanc flinched at these words, for he had never dreamt his councilors knew the nature of the vow between himself and Xarxus; for the demon was sworn to serve his will during his life, but upon the moment of his death, his spirit would enter the service of Xarxus . . . and Zazamanc knew all too well the horrors that awaited him beyond the grave. He shuddered, his face livid and suddenly lined and weary with age, as if his supernaturally prolonged youthfulness was fading already.

"Die, then, worm!" he snarled, lifting the rod and loosing its dormant fires.

17. Letting Death In

The shadow-thronged hall lit suddenly with a flash of supernal brilliance that seared the eye. A thunderclap shook the domed roof and echoes bounced from wall to wall. Caught full in the fury of the bolt, the faceless man crumpled and fell, robe blackening, breast burnt away, a hideous charred pit.

Old Yllimdus spoke no further word, his head falling to one side as life left his shattered body. Nape-hairs rising with primal awe, Thongor blinked away the afterimages of the flash and saw to his astonishment that in the moment of death the fleshmask crawled and shrunk and molded itself into the features of an old man. Noble of brow, weary and lined was that face, but, somehow, at peace.

Zazamanc shrank back at the sight. His enchantment was broken, but he understood it not, for it should have persisted beyond death. A cold hand closed upon his heart, for at last the grim premonition of doom he had for so long denied came home to him. He thrust his hands wide, face a writhing mask of naked fear.

"*No*—!" he shrieked, shrill and weak as a woman!"

And in that instant, Thongor struck.

He sprang over the charred corpse of Yllimdus, booming his savage war-cry. The great sword flashed as he swung it high above his head and brought it hissing down upon the shrinking, cringing form of the Enchanter.

Zazamanc staggered and fell to his knees, his face a crimson, torn thing. The black baton fell from nerveless fingers and rolled across the stony pave.

On his knees he swayed, staring blindly up into the grim face of the half-naked boy who loomed over him like a vengeful specter. With quivering fingers he dabbled at his wound, peering in horror at his own blood. His dazed brain could scarcely comprehend what had happened: a thousand spells rendered him immune to death, invulnerable to assault. The swordblade should have glanced aside from his magically protected flesh, leaving him unharmed.

Then it was that he saw the great glyphs acid-etched down the blade of the mighty sword, and knew their meaning— knew as well that no mortal hand had drawn those immortal and portentous sigils in the steel of Thongor's sword.

"*Aiii*," he moaned, rocking to and fro on his knees, while his life's blood leaked from him, drop by drop; "*Aaiii* . . . it is Sarkozan . . . Sarkozan . . . *Sarkozan, my Bane* . . ."

Again Thongor lifted the broadsword above his head and brought it whistling down. Bone crunched, snapped: gore splattered. The severed head of the Enchanter flew from his shoulders to plop like a grisly fruit against the pave. The headless cadaver fell sideways to sprawl in a spreading pool of scarlet.

Thongor's grim lips tightened. Beneath his bronze tan, his flesh whitened. His burning eyes widened in disbelief.

For even as he watched the bloody head . . . *shriveled.* The flesh tightened—dried—split, and peeled away from raw, naked bone that *browned* in moments. The fleshless skull grinned up at him from the gory pave. Before his unbelieving eyes, the gaunt bone grew pitted and sere; crumbled. The brainpan fell in; the jaw detached to clatter on the stone. In mere moments there was naught to be seen but a clutter of bony shards and dry dust . . . it was as if the centuries Zazamanc had denied had come rushing back upon him at the last.

It was even as the demon had warned. Zazamanc had let Death in and it had taken its toll, long overdue, at the end. . . .

And Ithomaar was free.

Thongor stood at the world's edge, where glittering mists roiled and crept endlessly, moving as with a life of their own.

"Will you not come back to the real world with me, Jothar Jorn?" he asked. At his side, the burly gamesmaster rubbed his beefy jaw reflectively.

"I don't know, lion cub," he grunted. "This world be a fair one, and snug enough, with *Him* gone from it. And belike all my old friends in Tsargol would be gone by now, or that changed with the years I'd not be more than a stranger to them. As for me, well, I'll stay here. Someone must take charge o' things, now; someone must keep order and rule here for those who will not go back to the world outside . . . it might as well be me, me and my stout lads."

"Will many stay, do you think?" the youth asked.

The big man shrugged, grinning. "Belike, some o' them. Many will leave, to find their places in the outer world; but many more will stay, for they were born here, and this be home to them, and a fair place it is, with an end to fear and evil magicking. But what of you, cub? Is't back to the frozen north?"

Thongor stared at the coiling mists, his grim bronze face unreadable.

"There is nothing for me there. Those I loved are dead, all, all of them. I will fare down the pass into the Southlands, to seek my fortune among the bright cities. Surely there will be a place for a man who can use a sword and can face Death unafraid . . ."

Jothar Jorn mused on the tall youth with thoughtful eyes.

"Go, then, lion—cub no more, but a lion now, in truth! And—may you find what you're looking for, in the end!"

Thongor clapped his shoulder and turned away, striding into the seething mists and through the magic crystal into the great world that lay beyond, bound for the jungle-clad Southlands and a host of new adventures.

Walter C. DeBill, Jr.

IN 'YGIROTH

*The author of this next story became a Lovecraft fa-
natic at thirteen. Now in his middle thirties, Walt De-
Bill is becoming one of the newer and more talented
writers to enter the Cthulhu Mythos after the death of
August Derleth. This is not a Mythos story, however, but a
poetic and thematically original addition to and comment
upon Lovecraft's early Dreamlands sequence. This is also,
by the way, the first story DeBill sold professionally: three
months before he died, Derleth accepted it for the short-
lived* Arkham Collector.

—L.C.

In 'Ygiroth, where once the vile
And hairy things that passed for men
In long forgotten elder times
Did strut in arrogance and bow
To nameless things from outer spheres,
Now only baneful shadows crawl
In 'Ygiroth.

High above him rose the city, deep in a shadowed cleft
where the gentle lower slopes of Lerion ended and the jagged, slender spire of her uttermost peak began its long thrust
into the hazy sky of Dreamland. Unpeopled and dreaming it
had lain through the slow centuries of solitude and decay,
and until now no man had come to seek out its dark secrets.
Only he, Nylron the Acolyte, had dared follow the sparkling

river Skai north to its headwaters in the high valley of Mynanthra between Lerion and craggy Dlareth and then travel the rock-strewn meadows on Lerion's northern shoulder around and upward to where brooding 'Ygiroth slumbered. He tilted the furred brim of his hat to shade his eyes from the setting sun and urged the wiry Bnazic pony on toward the low outer wall.

No one knew where the men of 'Ygiroth had come from or when they came, for the green shadows of Mynanthra had already flickered with their furtive stalking and echoed to their eerie hunting cries when Nylron's ancestors had come from the east forty centuries ago to settle the fertile valley of the Skai and build Ulthar and Nir and Hatheg. Those sturdy tribesmen had instinctively disliked the men of 'Ygiroth, finding them a little too short, a little too hairy, and a little too silent as they crept through the forests. Perhaps if their brow-ridges had not jutted so far forward, giving them an unpleasantly beady-eyed look, or if they had cooked the flesh of the buopoth before dining, the men of the Skai valley might have sought peaceful intercourse with them, but as it was, none but a few adventurers of dubious repute had ever bothered to learn their coarse whispering language. It was from these ill-regarded and invariably ill-fated individuals that such scraps of lore as were known to the men of the Skai had come.

Not clever were the men of the 'Ygiroth, and their stone spears and necklaces of wolves' teeth seemed ludicrously backward to the intelligent and inventive men of the Skai. Very arrogant they were about their skill in hunting the gentle buopoth, though most of their success came from the use of the half-tame kyresh as both hound and steed. This morbid relic of an older time, long extinct in other parts of Dreamland, had a basically equine body which could be ridden by the more intrepid chieftains, a long blood-hound muzzle which could scent prey at great distances, and enormous claws which, together with a mouth full of great irregular fangs, did much more damage in the hunt than the crude spearheads. It did not seem to bother the 'Ygirothians that the vicious and excitable brutes took as great a toll among the hunters as of the hunted—if the hunt succeeded it left fewer to divide the spoils, and if it failed, fallen comrades would not be wasted by the hungry survivors.

Even the domestication of this treacherous monstrosity had

been beyond the abilities of the 'Ygirothians themselves. They had been taught and aided by a more formidable and sinister being. Their notion of time was so vague that they could not say whether it was ten or ten thousand centuries since the Thing in the Yellow Mask had come to them and taught them to make spears and ride the kyresh and eat fresh-killed meat. And when asked what the Thing demanded in return, they smirked evilly and made crude evasions.

It was the Thing which had made them build 'Ygiroth to honor It and Its unseen brothers, eldritch abnormalities from outer spheres of time and space whose ineffable forms and non-forms could never have been made tolerable to men by any amount of yellow silk or hypnotic incense. It had taught them to place stone upon stone in a remote cleft on Lerion which had been a place of outer evil before men existed, and It had directed the labors of countless terrified generations until the inept beast-men had completed a citadel of horror unmatched in Dreamland (for grim Kadath is not truly contiguous with any space men know or dream of).

Only one man of the Skai had ever been within the walls of 'Ygiroth and returned, and Lothran the Necromancer had said little that could be understood. He had reached Ulthar at sunset, raving hysterically of formless horrors from which he fled, horrors which he refused to name. He had been quieted with a strong dose of poppy gum and left to rest in an upper room of the inn, but in the morning when the elders of Ulthar entered the room in hopes of a more coherent revelation, they found nothing but an open window and a stench of carrion, of lightning and of singed flesh. Nothing, that is, unless one credits the tale, whispered by foolish gossips, that old Atal found one of Lothran's boots behind the bed, and that the boot was not empty.

The men of Ulthar and Nir and Hatheg would have been content to leave such unpleasant neighbors alone in their high valley were it not for the disappearance of several of their young maidens each Walpurgis and Yule and of plump specimens of both sexes at odd times throughout the year. The people along the Skai were quick to connect the former with strange lights and drumming in the distant hills and the latter with the footprints in their gardens of short, broad-footed men. Thus from the earliest times small bands of brave men had set out to destroy 'Ygiroth and its inhabitants. Each time, as they approached the shadowy forests of Mynanthra, heavy clouds would gather and they would find themselves ringed with many-colored bolts of lightning. Most turned back at this point, but the survivors among those who did not told of discordant music heard beneath the howling and laughter of the unseen men of 'Ygiroth, of charnel vapors and a distant form draped in yellow silk. Few indeed lived to tell of the sentient whirlwinds that keened and rushed through the murky glades and set upon men like unseen hounds, rending and mangling body and soul.

It was in the reign of King Pnil of Ulthar that the warriors of the Skai had challenged 'Ygiroth for the last time. Every able-bodied man had marched, armed this time with charms and spells of the Elder Ones as well as tools of war. No resistance was met, although the vanguard heard padding feet retreating through Mynanthra and followed fresh claw-marks of the kyresh right up to the gates of the city. Arriving at sunset and not wanting to assault the unknown defenses in the dark, they camped before the walls.

No warrior of the Skai-lands slept during that long night of suspense and brooding menace, none could forget the night-long crescendo of asymmetric rhythms on drums of stretched hide and hollowed bone or the jeering and insinuating voices from the dark crowing of the incomprehensible horror to be unleashed at dawn. As the first saffron rays struck the spire of Lerion silence fell with the force of thunder. For an interminable moment no one breathed, no eye moved from the still shadowed walls of 'Ygiroth. Then began that hideous silent exodus which haunts the legends and fireside tales of Ulthar.

As the first of the men of 'Ygiroth came scrambling over the walls and the gates were flung wide to let out dozens, then hundreds and thousands, all running straight for the ranks of the Skai, it was taken to be a charge, an attempt to overwhelm the besieging forces. But men wondered why they ran in silence, and as the first of them drew near it was seen that they were unarmed. Then as they rushed heedless onto the waiting spears men at last saw their mad, mindless eyes and knew that a terror beyond knowledge or nightmare had come to 'Ygiroth, and that 'Ygiroth was doomed.

When the last beast-man lay crumpled on the gory meadow, the warriors of Ulthar departed in awe, not daring to enter the city and raze it. Since then no man had ventured there, and were it not for the whispers of Lothran the

Necromancer perhaps none ever would. But before he vanished Lothran had whispered certain things to the high priest Atal, and in his old age Atal had tried to banish these things from his dreams by writing them down on parchment. Too cleverly he had hidden that parchment, and the priests of Nodens had been unable to find and destroy it despite his incoherent deathbed pleas. And now Nylron the Acolyte had found it and had read things which should never be written down.

Among less mentionable things Nylron had read of the evil secrets taught by the Thing in the Yellow Mask to the priests of 'Ygiroth, secrets they had neither the wits nor the courage to exploit, secrets which could have made them masters of all Dreamland and perhaps even of the waking world. They had merely carved them on the walls of the labyrinth beneath their temple in the foul Aklo tongue taught them by the Thing. Unfortunately for Nylron, he was a true scholar of this primordial language, and not without ambition.

The journey had taken him four days; the first along the fertile banks of the Skai, whose shady fringe of willows bade him rest and delay; the second through gradually rising hills where spring wild flowers questioned the value of ambition; the third in dark and cool Mynanthra, where a silent buopoth warned that time may stand still; and the fourth up stony mountain paths where the sky grew inhospitable. As he entered the city black clouds were rolling in from the north and the sun lost sight of Lerion.

He found the city surprisingly well preserved. Few of the buildings had collapsed, the tread of time being shown more subtly by cracked stone, precariously leaning walls and an occasional fallen roof. Only twice were the narrow, tortuous streets blocked with rubble, forcing him to detour even narrower alleys. He thought of certain rumored corpses, in which decay is said to be unnaturally slow and circumspect.

The great beehive-shaped temple was on a high ledge at the rear of the city, and by the time he had threaded the convoluted streets up to the broad plaza in front of it the first heavy raindrops had splattered on the pavement. He paused only a moment to wonder how the vast dome had survived the centuries of mountain storms and led the pony up the gentle ramp through the only opening, a tall narrow trapezoid topped by a small capstone.

It was quite dark inside, but he kindled a resinous torch

and soon saw that the temple was one enormous chamber, cluttered with a gloomy forest of pentagonal columns. At first he saw in them no geometrical arrangement at all, but gradually he perceived an odd asymmetrical regularity which he found disturbing to contemplate. He could barely make out seven large statues of kyresh spaced along the circular wall, some blindfolded, others with staring eyes and open jaws. There was a peculiar sour smell in the air and each step echoed from the dome above. The only natural aisle among the columns led straight back to the rear of the temple and Nylron led the horse, skittish now from the approaching storm, as far as a small stone post of indeterminate purpose. Tethering the horse to the post and removing the heavy pack, he proceeded down the aisle to what appeared to be the main altar. It was a wide irregular heptagon surmounted by a statue of a robed and hooded figure holding a spear in one hand and a small figure of a buopoth in the other. Before the statue lay an oval opening and, climbing up on the altar stone, he found stone steps leading downward into the living rock of Lerion.

Downward he went in a huge spiral, circling until he had lost all sense of direction. At last the stairs ended and he found himself in an intricate labyrinth of narrow passageways whose moss-grown walls sloped inward at the top, occasionally opening into substantial low-ceilinged rooms partitioned with arcades of trapezoidal arches. To be certain of finding his way out again Nylron turned always to the right and found himself again spiralling, this time inward.

In the center of the labyrinth was a room almost as large as the temple above and arranged similarly with seven kyresh and a central altar. Before the statue on the altar was a large flat stone, suggesting a covered opening. But what arrested Nylron's attention was the circular wall of the room, for it was completely covered with an inscription in the Aklo tongue.

The uncouth characters of brutish scribes were not easy to read, but Nylron could follow most of them and knew that the rest would yield to patient scholarship in the archives of Ulthar. He read of the feeble gods of earth and how they can be manipulated. He read of the Other Gods who once ruled and shall rule again, of Azathoth, the centripetal impetus of all cosmic chaos, of Yog-Sothoth, the all-pervasive horror which lurks in the inner spheres of existence, of

Nyarlathotep, who sometimes shrouds his form in yellow silk and sometimes in mind-blurring illusion. He read of the rewards for their chosen instruments, and hints of what might befall those instruments which failed. And finally he read a terrible passage, carved in immaculate calligraphy on an iridescent plaque harder than Nylron's garnet ring, which told of the joke played by Nyarlathotep on his minions when they summoned him and he declined to come. For he had sent instead his half-brother and other face, a ravenous and by no means sane entity which could radiate intolerable horror like a poisonous vapor.

As he finished this vile postlogue his torch began to flicker wildly and he saw that it had nearly burned out. He thought of the difficult way back through the labyrinth and shuddered. His composure did not improve when, passing the altar, he saw the symbol carved on the flat covering stone and noted the recent disturbance of the moss around it.

The way back proved disconcertingly difficult. At times he almost believed that the arcades and passages had been shifted since his trip inward. Faster and faster he went, frantically exploring multiple branches and dead ends. The padding echoes of his soft-soled boots seemed to conceal more stealthy footsteps and a distant grating of stone on stone. Once he could have sworn he caught a glimpse of yellow silk disappearing into a trapezoidal archway. He found the entrance to the upward spiral just as the torch winked out.

He calmed down somewhat in the spiral shaft and made his way rapidly upward by feeling along the left-hand wall. Total lack of sight raised his other senses to an acute pitch and he could plainly hear the stamping of the horse after each burst of thunder. As he neared the top he could hear the rain itself and feel the dampness in the air. Emerging into the inky blackness of the temple he was unpleasantly aware that the moisture had brought out the odd sour smell much more strongly. He felt his way to the edge of the altar, climbed down, then moved out blindly toward the shuffling and stamping of the horse. He almost tripped over the pack and his reflexively outstretched hand touched the smooth hair of the pony's flank. He was patting and stroking it reassuringly when he heard the sound, so incongruous that he took a full second to identify it as the frantic whinny of his horse. What made it incongruous was the fact that it came from outside the temple. At that instant a lightning flash lit up the doorway, silhouetting the gaping jaws of the kyresh and the masked monster that held its reins. He felt its hot fetid breath just before the teeth closed on his head.

Outside in the rain and the dark the horse's hooves clattered madly away through the dead streets of 'Ygiroth.

Clark Ashton Smith

THE SCROLL OF MORLOC

Clark Ashton Smith has long been one of my favorite fantasy writers. I delight in his glittering, suave, lapidary prose, his luxuriant vocabulary, his ironic understatement, his mordant and mocking humor. Working from his unpublished notes, list of invented names and story titles, I have for three years now been writing what Derleth used to call "posthumous collaborations" in what I earnestly hope is a good pastiche of his unique style. Because I particularly enjoy the invented milieu of his Hyperborean cycle, I have made it the setting of the new series. It has also amused me to visualize each of these new stories as a chapter from the Book of Eibon, *Smith's response to Lovecraft's* Necronomicon. *This is the third story in the cycle, and is also the third chapter from that prediluvian tome of prehistoric lore.*

—L.C.

The shaman Yhemog, dejected by the obdurate refusal of his fellow Voormis to elect him their high priest, contemplated his imminent withdrawal from the tribal burrows of his furry, primitive kind to sulk in proud and lonely solitude among the icy crags of the north, whose bourns were unvisited by his timorous, earth-dwelling brethren.

Seven times had he offered himself in candidacy for the coveted headdress of black *ogga*-wood, crowned with fabulous *huusim*-plumes, and now for the seventh time had the elders unaccountably denied him what he considered his just

guerdon, earned thrice over by his pious and reverent auster-
ities. Seething with disappointment, the rejected shaman
swore they should have no eighth occasion whereon to by-
pass the name of Yhemog in bestowing the uncouth hierar-
chial miter upon another, and vowed they should ere long
have reason to regret the ineptitude of their selection of an
inferior devotee of the Voormish god over one of his unique
and excessive devoutness.

During this period many of the clans of the subhuman
Voormis had fled into warrens tunneled beneath the surface
of a jungle-girt and mountainous peninsula of early Hyperborea which had yet to be named Mhu Thulan. Their shaggy
and semi-bestial forebears had originally been raised in
thralldom to a race of sentient Serpent-people whose primordial continent had been reft asunder by volcanic convul-
sions and which had submerged beneath the oceans an eon
or two earlier. Fleeing from the slave pens of their erstwhile
masters, now happily believed almost extinct, the ancestors
of the present Voormis had wrested all of this territory from
certain degenerate, cannibalistic subhumans of repellent appearance and loathsome habits, whose few survivors had
been driven northward to dwell in furtive exile amid the
wastes of bleak and glacier-encumbered Polarion.

Of late, their numbers inexplicably in decline, their war-
like prowess unaccountably dwindling into timidity, and the
surly and vengeful descendants of their ancient foes growing
ever more ominously populous and restive in the north,
many of the Voormish tribes had sought refuge in these
underground dwellings for safety and protection. By now the
furry creatures were accustomed to the comforting gloomi-
ness and the familiar, pervasive stench of their warrens, and
seldom if ever did they venture into the upper world, which
had grown strange and frightening to them in its giddy and
disquieting spaciousness of sky, lit by the intolerable brilliance of zenithal and hostile suns.

In contemplating self-imposed exile from his kind, the dis-
gruntled shaman was not unaware of the dangers he must
surmount. This particular region of the peninsula would
someday be known as Phenquor, the northernmost province
of Mhu Thulan. During this period of the early Cenozoic
the first true humans were only just beginning to seep into
Hyperborea from southerly regions of tropical jungles whose
climate had grown too fervent for them to comfortably en-

dure, and all of Phenquor was a savage and primal wilderness, uninhabited save for the cavern-dwelling Voormis. Not without peril, therefore, would the shaman Yhemog traverse the prehistoric jungles and reeking fens of the young continent, for such were the haunts of the ravening catoblepas and the agate-breasted wyvern, to cite only the least formidable of the denizens of the prime.

But Yhemog had mastered the rudiments of the antehuman thaumaturgies and had gained some proficiency in the arts of shamanry and conjuration. By these means he thought himself quite likely to elude the more ferocious of the carnivora, thus achieving the relative safety of the Phenquorian mountains hopefully unscathed.

By dwelling subterraneously, it should perhaps be noted here, the Voormis were but imitating the grotesque divinity they worshipped with rites we might deem excessively sanguinary and revolting. As it was an article of the Voormish faith that this deity, whom they knew as Tsathoggua, made his abode in lightless caverns situated far beneath the earth, their adoption of a troglodytic mode of existence was to some extent primarily symbolic. The eponymous ancestor of their race, Voorm the arch-ancient, had quite early in their history promulgated a doctrine which asserted that their assumption of a wholly subterranean habitat would place them in a special relationship of mystical propinquity with their god, who himself preferred to wallow in the gulf of N'kai beneath a mountain to the south considered sacred by the Voormis. This dogma the venerable Voorm had pronounced shortly before himself retiring into chasms adjacent to the aforesaid N'kai in order to spend his declining eons in proximity to the object of his worship.

The tribal elders unanimously revered the opinions of this patriarch as infallible, especially in matters of a purely theological nature, for it was commonly believed that their supreme pontiff and common ancestor had been fathered by none other than Tsathoggua himself during a transient liaison with a minor feminine divinity who rejoiced in the name of Shathak. With this ultimate patriarchal teaching the tribal elders now, somewhat belatedly, concurred; to obey the last precept of their spiritual leader was, after all, a reasonable precaution when you considered the profound and disheartening desuetude into which the fortunes of the race had so recently, and so abruptly, declined.

In reaching his eventual decision to henceforward shun the dank and fetid burrows of his tribe in favor of a radical change of residence to the giddy and vertiginous peaks which arose along the northerly borders of Phenquor, over-looking the frigid wastes of drear Polarion, the shaman Yhemog discovered himself ineluctably sliding into dangerous heresy. Unable to reconcile his private inclinations with the several pontifical revelations handed down by the eponymous patriarch of his race, he was soon implicitly questioning the actual validity of the teachings, a tendency which resulted in his eventual denial of their infallibility. Now rejecting as essentially worthless the very patriarchal dogmas he had earlier revered as sacrosanct, he lapsed from the most odious condition of heresy into the lamentable and blasphemous nadir of atheism.

Thus disappointment soured into bitter resentment and resentment festered into vicious envy and envy itself, like a venomous canker, gnawed at the roots of his faith, until the last pitiful shreds of his former beliefs had utterly been eaten away. And naught now was left in the heart of Yhemog save for a hollow emptiness, which became filled only with the bile of self-devouring rancor and a fierce, derisive contempt for everything he had once held precious and holy. This contempt cried out for expression, for a savage gesture of ultimate affront calculated to plunge his elder brethren into horrified consternation and dismay. Yhemog hungered to brandish his new-found atheism like a stinking rag beneath the pious snouts of the tribal fathers.

At length he determined upon a course of action nicely suited to his ends. He schemed to steal into the deepest and holiest shrine of Tsathoggua and to purloin therefrom an antique scroll which contained certain rituals and liturgies held in the utmost degree of religious abhorrence by the members of his faith. The document was among the spoils of war carried off by his victorious forefathers from the abominable race which had formerly dominated these regions at the time of the advent of the Voormish savages into Mhu Thulan. The papyrus reputedly preserved the darkest secrets of the occult wisdom of the detested Gnophkehs, which name denoted the repulsively hirsute cannibals whom Yhemog's ancestors had driven into exile in the arctic barrens. This scroll contained, in fact, the most arcane and potent ceremonials whereby the Gnophkehs had worshipped their atrocious divinity, who was no less than an avatar of the cosmic obscenity Rhan-Tegoth, and was attributed to Morloc himself, the Grand Shaman.

Now the Voormis had, from their remotest origins, considered themselves the chosen minions of Tsathoggua, the sole deity whose worship they celebrated. And Tsathoggua was an earth elemental ranged in perpetual and unrelenting enmity against Rhan-Tegoth and all his kind, who were commonly accounted elementals of the air and were objects of contempt to those of the Old Ones, like Tsathoggua, who abominated the airy emptinesses above the world and by preference wallowed in darksome and subterranean lairs. A similar degree of mutual and irreconcible animosity existed between those races which were the servants of Tsathoggua, among whom the Voormis were prominent, and those who served the avatars of cosmical and uncleanly Rhan-Tegoth, such as those noxious protoanthropophagi, the Gnophkehs. The loss of the Scroll of Morloc would, therefore, hurl the Voormis into the very nadir of confusion, and contemplation of the horror wherewith they would view the loss caused Yhemog to tremble with vile and delicious anticipation.

The Scroll had for millennia reposed in a tabernacle of mammoth-ivory situated beneath the very feet of the idol of Tsathoggua in the holy-of-holies, its lowly position symbolic of the Voormis risen triumphant over their subjugated and thoroughly inferior enemies. In order for the Scroll of Morloc to be thieved away by Yhemog, ere he quit forever the noisome and squalid burrows wherein he had passed the tedious and unrewarding centuries of his youth, he must, of necessity, first enter the most sacred and solemn precincts of the innermost shrine itself.

For a shaman of his insignificance, but recently graduated from his novitiate a century or two before, to trespass upon the indescribable sanctity of the most forbidden and inviolable sanctuary was a transgression of the utmost severity. By his very presence he would profane and contaminate the sacerdotal chamber, and this horrendous act of desecration he must perforce do under the cold, unwavering scrutiny of dread, omnipotent Tsathoggua himself, for therein had stood enshrined for innumerable ages the most ancient and immemorial eidolon of the god, an object of devout and universal veneration.

The very thought of thus violating the sacred adyts of the shrine to perform a vile and despicable act of burglary in the awesome presence of the deity he had once worshipped with such excessive vigor was sobering, even disquieting. But fortunately for the inward serenity of Yhemog, the fervor with which he had embraced his newfound atheism enormously transcended the fervor of his former pious devotions. His iconoclasm had hardened his heart to such an adamantine rigor that he despised his own earlier temerities, and now disbelieved in all supermundane or ultranatural entities far more than he had ever believed in them before. The venerable eidolon was but a piece of worked stone and naught more, he thought contemptuously to himself, and the arch-rebel, Yhemog, fears no thing of stone!

Thus it befell that the traitorous and atheistical Yhemog slunk one night into the deeplier and nethermost of the shrines sacred to Tsathoggua, having prudently charmed into premature slumber the scimitar-wielding eunuchs posted to guard the inviolability of the sanctuary. By their obese, stertorously breathing forms, sprawled recumbent on the pave before the spangled curtain which concealed the innermost adytum from the chance profanation of impious eyes, he crept on furtive, three-toed, naked feet. Beyond the glittering tissue was discovered a chamber singularly bare of ornamentation, in dramatic contrast to the ostentation of the outer precincts. It contained naught but the idol itself, throned at the farther end, which presented the repellent likeness of an obscenely corpulent, toadlike entity. Familiar as he was with the crude images roughly hacked from porous lava by the clumsy paws of his people, the shaman was unprepared for the astonishing skill with which the nameless sculptor had wrought the edidolon from obdurate and frangible obsidian. He marveled at the consummate craft whereby the chisel of the forgotten artisan had clothed the bloated, squatting form of the god with a suggestion of sleek furriness and had blent together in its features the salient characteristics of toad, bat and sloth, in a dubious amalgam subtly disturbing and distinctly unpleasing. The ponderous divinity was depicted with half-closed, sleepy eyes which seemed almost to glitter with cold, lazy malice, and it had a grinning and lipless gash of mouth which Yhemog fancied was distended in a smile redolent of cruel and gloating mockery.

His new contempt for all such supernatural entities
dimmed, fading, somewhat, in its originally febrile intensity
before a rising trepidation. For a moment he hesitated, half-
fearing the hideous and yet exquisitely lifelike eidolon might
stir suddenly to dread wakefulness upon the next instant, and
reveal itself to be a living thing. But the moment passed
without any such an untoward vivification, and his derision
and denial of the transmundane rose within him, trebled
in its blind conviction. Now was the moment of ultimate
profanation upon him; now he would metaphorically re-
nounce his former devotions by abstracting from beneath
the very feet of the supernally sacred image its chiefest
treasure, the papyrus wherein were preserved the blackest of
the arcane secrets of the elder Gnophkehs. Summoning the
inner fortitude his atheistical doctrines afforded, thrusting
aside the last lingering remnants of the superstitious awe he
had once entertained toward the divinity the idol represented,
Yhemog knelt and hastily pried open the ivory casket and
drew therefrom the primordial scroll.

Whereafter there occurred absolutely nothing in the way
of preternatural phenomena or transmundane acts of vengeance. The black and glistening statue remained immobile;
it neither blinked nor stirred nor smote him with the leven-
bolt or the precipitous attack of leprosy he had almost
expected. The relief which upsurged within his furry breast
was intoxicating; almost he swooned in a delirium of exultant
joy. But in the next moment dire melancholy drowned his
heady mood; for he realized now for the first time the fullest
extent of the vicious hoax the preceptors of his cult had
perpetrated upon him. To so delude an innocent young
Voormis-cub, so that the noblest aspiration it might conceiv-
ably dream to attain was the *ogga*-wood miter of the
hierophant, was an action of such perverted and despicable
odium as to excite within him a lust to desecrate, with a
blasphemy transcending all his prior conceptions of blasphemy, this sacred place.

Ere spurning forever the moist and gloomy tunnels to seek
a new and solitary life amongst the steaming quagmires and
cycadic jungles of the upper earth he would commit a desecration so irremediable as to defile, pollute and befoul for all
eons to come this innermost citadel of a false and cruelly
perpetuated religion. And in his very clutches he held at that
moment the perfect instrument of triumphant and absolute

revenge. For how better to desanctify the temple of Tsathoggua than to recite before his most venerable eidolon, and
within his most sacred and forbidden shrine, the abominable
rituals formerly employed by the hated enemies of his minions in the celebration of their obscene and atrocious divinity,
his rival?

With paws that shook with the intensity of his loathing and
wrath, Yhemog unfolded the antique papyrus and, straining
his weak, small eyes, sought to peruse the writings it contained. The hieroglyphics were indited according to an antiquated system, but at length his scrutiny enabled him to
deduce their meaning. The dark lore of the Gnophkehs was
generally centered upon the placation and appeasement of
their grisly and repugnant divinity, but ere long the shaman
found a ritual of invocational worship which he judged would
be exceptionally insulting to the false Tsathoggua and his
self-deluding servants. It commenced with the uncouth and
discordant phrase *Wza-y'ei! Wza-y'ei! Y'kaa haa bho-ii,* and
terminated eventually in a series of mindless ululations for
the enunciation of which the vocal apparatus of the Voormis was inadequately designed. As he commenced reading
the liturgical formula aloud, however, he discovered that the
farther he progressed therein the more easily his pronunci-
ation became. He also was surprised to find, as he grew near
the terminus of the ritual, that the vocables he had earlier
considered jarring and awkward became curiously, even dis-
quietingly, musical and pleasant to his ears.

Those ears, he suddenly noticed, had unaccountably grown
larger and now were not unlike the huge, flapping organs of
the ill-formed and ridiculously misshapen Gnophkehs. His
eyes as well had undergone a singular transformation, and
now bulged protuberantly in a manner which resembled that
of the revolting inhabitants of the polar regions. Having
completed the final interminable ululation he let fall the
Scroll of Morloc and examined himself in growing consternation. Gone was his sleek and comely pelt, and in its place
he was now covered with a repulsive growth of coarse and
matted hairs. His snout, moreover, had in the most unseemly
and impertinent manner undertaken an extension of itself
beyond the limits considered handsome by Voormish stan-
dards, and was now a naked, proboscidian growth of distinctly and unmistakably Gnophkehian proportions. He cried
out, then, in an extremity of unbelieving horror, for he

realized with a cold and awful panic that *to worship as a Gnophkeh* must, under certain circumstances, be defined in terms absolutely literal. And when his hideous lamentations succeeded in rousing from their charmed drowsiness the gross and elephantine eunuchs beyond the sequined veil, and they came lumbering in haste to discover a detested and burglarious Gnophkeh squirming on its obscene and hairy belly, gobbling guttural and incomprehensible prayers before the smiling, the enigmatic, and the lazily malicious eyes of Tsathoggua, they dispatched the malodorous intruder with great thoroughness and righteous indignation, and in a certain manner most acceptable to the god, but one so lingering and anatomically ingenious that the more squeamish of my readers should be grateful that I restrain my pen from its description.

C. A. Cador

PAYMENT IN KIND

The power of "word of mouth" has long been recognized in advertising and show biz, where it is treated with gingerly, almost superstitious respect; now C. A. Cador ably demonstrates its potency in the Black Arts.

This deceptively brief story is an interesting and unusual debut by an author new to me. It appeared in an occult newspaper I have never seen or read, and it would have passed me by entirely had not Poul Anderson alerted me to it, seeing that I received a copy.

Thank you, Poul: I wouldn't have missed it for the world!

—L.C.

The cowled figure glided silently across the thronged Square of the King's Mercy, past the Platform of Execution at its center, and paused by the Temple of the Seven Vilni, which is called the House of Wrath, until his eyes rested upon the man he sought. Walking quickly past the great bronze doors of the Temple, cast in a thousand shapes of nightmare, he dropped a small black stone into the outstretched bowl of one of the beggars there, and moving quickly into the teeming crowds, was lost to sight before the beggar's bored "Blessings on thee, Lord" turned to a string of highly imaginative curses when he saw what the latest addition to his bowl was. He picked it up to throw it away, but stopped for a moment to examine it, for it was not merely black, but shining like a mirror, and jagged—no such stones were found near Khoros the City. A sudden noise attracted his attention, and he tossed the curious stone to the ground and went back to his business, nor did he think again of the Stone, or of the cowled man.

Shem the beggar was crossing a desolate valley. The sun beat upon his head, and the black stones of the valley floor held enough of its heat to cause discomfort even to his callused feet, which had here and there been slashed when he stepped on a particularly jagged stone. The fiery air was torture to his lungs. As far as he could see, there was no living thing save himself—not a flicker of motion that might indicate a lizard, not even the spiny desert plants grew there. Yet he felt himself the object of an unpleasant scrutiny, and had a sense of waiting, and gloating. The worst of it was that he had no desire to be there, was fighting desperately against the compulsion dragging him across that fearful valley—to what? He prayed fervently to all his gods he would never find out.

Shem the baggar awoke screaming, bolt upright upon his sweat-soaked pallet, and sat, shivering, in a heap upon the floor till morning.

Boaz was in the shop of Nissan the barber, being shaved. There were dark circles beneath his eyes, and a haggard look to his face that fitted ill with his image as a hired thug.

". . . And since Shem told me of that dream which came to him night after night, I have had the same dream, but by last night I had nearly crossed the valley, awakening near two great standing stones at its far end. Truly it is a terrible place. That misbegotten son of Erlik has put a curse on me!"

Nissan laughed, and said, "The mighty Boaz, frightened by a dream! Well," he added quickly, seeing the growing scowl on Boaz' face, "such a dream might frighten many. My advise is, go to Shaya's House of Pleasure and have your fill of wine and woman—you'll forget your ill dreams there soon enough, I'll wager."

Boaz smiled, and lifted one foot. "That may be as it may be, but look at this—" His feet were crisscrossed with slashes, some starting to heal, others fresh and raw.

A few days later, Nissan the barber was a badly frightened man. He hobbled to the square of the King's Mercy and found his way to the temple of Anahita, a river Goddess who was patroness of his tribe, and was soon closeted with a priest.

". . . And so I passed between the standing stones Boaz spoke of, and beyond them into a valley much like the first, save that it was rimmed with cliffs, and at its far end I could see a half ring of standing stones against the cliff face. Holy One, you must help me—to have your own body moving against your will . . . and every night it grows worse. Nor can I fight off sleep. I'm not a young man, my health is poor, and then this . . ." he said, lifting a foot which was cut and burned.

The priest recoiled in fear and said, "Surely this is no ordinary dream, but the work of a necromancer! Had this Boaz any grudge against you?"

"None, Holy One. He is one of Balthok's hirelings, who take a tithe of the earnings of beggars and pickpockets and temples . . ." He stopped in confusion, then began again. "He has come weekly to my shop to be shaved, for two years. In all that time, I have not so much as nicked him."

"Wait here," the priest commanded. He returned after a time with an amulet and a wand. First he used the latter to draw a circle around the barber, invoking the power of Anahita, then shook it thrice on him so that Nissan was sprinkled with water out of its tip, then placed a silver amulet about his neck, saying, "Take this, and wear it thus always; it is a holy charm, blessed by the High Priest himself, and graved with thrice holy symbols of protection. With it you are safe. The Goddess will accept an offering of twenty zard."

The barber pressed thirty on the priest, who was speechless at this indication of how truly frightened Nissan had been. He did not, however, neglect to pocket ten zard more than the five he had earned, before passing the remaining fifteen on to the temple treasurer.

Once out of the temple, Nissan heaved a deep sigh of relief. He felt so much restored that he stopped by the Platform of Execution to watch the King's Mercy.

When the dream did not return, Nissan was voluble in his praise of Anahita and her priests, filling his customers' ears with her praises for weeks, without even asking payment from the temple for his proselytizing.

Shamash the priest was not so jubilant. After the fourth night, he decided, in a sudden and unwonted fit of religiosity, that the Goddess had cursed him for pocketing the full ten zard, and decided to make a confession to Gudea, the chief priest.

He entered the sumptuous quarters of Gudea, who looked up from his desk, whose top was carven from a single slab of malachite, and said in a bored tone, "They say you wish to confess a fault. Have you sinned against the Goddess?"

"Yes."

"How?"

"I withheld ten zard from the treasury, because they were given me in excess of the customary fee. The Goddess has cursed me with . . ."

"Stop. The curse is between you and the Gods. Repay twenty zard to the Temple and seek peace with the Gods and the lifting of the curse from the priests of the House of Wrath.

"As you order, Holiest."

Shamash approached the Temple of the Seven Vilni, which is called the House of Wrath, with trepidation. He had always hated the place because of the swarms of beggars who hovered around it like flies, knowing that those who go to make their peace with the fearful wielders of divine wrath who dwell therein were more than commonly generous, as if they hoped their almsgiving would soften the anger of the Gods.

In consideration of his rank as a priest of Anahita, Shamash was not kept waiting, but was ushered into the main chapel to brood for a time upon the fearful visages of the Vilni whose huge statues reared above the altar in aweful splendor—they had each eight arms, holding whips and swords, flaying knives and the arrows of pestilence, severed heads and torturers' pincers. They had the wings of bats. One had the head of an eagle, another of a vulture, of a boar, a tiger, a dog, a kite, a dragon.

After a suitable time, he was ushered into a tiny cubicle where waited one of the seven priests of the temple.

"It is not often a priest must come here to lift the curse of the Vilni from his shoulders." He smiled grimly. "What God have you offended, and have you attempted to make any amends?"

Shamash explained his fault, and the restitution he had made.

"So. It is well. Now describe the curse."

"It is a dream . . ." Shamash began, describing it with great feeling, ". . . and the fear I felt within the ring of standing stones I cannot describe. I know that if I do not rid myself of this curse, I shall enter the cave in the cliff, and I shall never return from there. Holiest, I know not what dwells in that cave but it is a thing of evil, and terror."

"So. Perhaps in the future you will be more reluctant to rob the Gods. They care for their own. Go and bid the acolyte before the altar nick a vein in your arm and drain off a cupful of blood, and burn it mixed with incense before the Vilni, and make the temple an offering of twenty zard. The curse will be lifted as your blood is burned."

That night Shamash the priest slept well, and afterward was a most devout man—for the space of a month.

Zadok the Priest of the Children of Wrath was walking through a land of fire. His feet burned on the black stones, and their tender soles were so gashed he left a trail of bloody footprints behind him. His lungs shrieked agony with every breath, and the pounding of the sun upon his head was an unending torment. He had been walking forever.

With each step he struggled to stop, to turn around and go back and away from this fearful place, but his body followed another will than his own. He felt the presence of an unseen watcher, gloating, in an almost physical way, and something worse—he felt its hunger.

As he passed within the circle of standing stones, dragged inexorably towards the square opening in the cliff face, it was as if a veil had been lifted from his eyes. He saw that atop each of the stones was a nameless, blasphemous creature, nearly human in shape, but black and shining as a piece of obsidian, with curiously elongated ears and long, pointed teeth, hands that were like talons with vicious, tearing claws, on arms that reached down past their knees, and long tails, naked and hairless as the rest of their bodies. He heard their obscene titterings, and the music that some played on long flutes carven from human leg bones.

When he turned his eyes from this hideous spectacle, he saw before him, not a cliff, but a great palace of black stone, old . . . old . . . covered with carvings of myriad nameless beings of a thousand different forms moving in great processions, worshipping strange gods, dancing, and . . . feeding.

Another step . . . and another . . . and he was within the hideous gateway. He felt a thousand unseen eyes upon him, heard slitherings and rustlings and breathings, and once a hissing voice that made him dwell for a moment on the lizardlike nature of some of the beings carved on the palace facade.

Step by step he moved down that black corridor toward a great bronze door, behind which lay—what? He knew only that it was the master of this place, and that it would be more pleasant to serve the anthropophagous inclinations of the beings he had already seen than to pass through that door.

Zadok the priest awoke, and his terrible shrieks brought frightened acolytes running from all directions. As reason returned to him, he drank from the pitcher of wine by his bed and looked in disgust at the elaborate pentagrams drawn on the floor with silver and blood and flour ground from holy grain grown in the fields of the Corn Mother; at the candles, red and black and green; the censers belching forth clouds of incense smoke; at the Names and Signals; the seals of the Seven whose servant he was; and the four Great Seals of Protection; and cursed, long and elaborately.

For Zadok was more than a priest—he was a wizard versed in all manner of lore; yet every protection he had been able to devise, every attempt to break the curse, had failed. His power had served only to reveal to him that which had been hidden to others not so gifted. He knew, as he stared down at the useless paraphernalia of his craft, that there was but one way to save himself.

That day there came to Zadok the priest many people. To each he strove to tell his dream, that it and its doom might pass from him, but his tongue was locked in his head when he strove to speak of it. And that night was bad—very bad.

The next day there was but one man he was to see—Poros the merchant, one of the richest men in Khoros the City and a frequent visitor to the House of Wrath. He remarked on Zadok's condition, for the priest could hardly walk, and, incongruously for one who dwelt within the walls of a temple, his face and hands were burnt a brilliant red by the sun.

"What is it that you wish?" asked Zadok wearily, ignoring his questions. "Is it again the guilt for your wife whom you slew slowly, when you caught her with her lover?"

"No," said Poros. "That ghost is laid to rest and troubles me no more."

"Is it then he who as a young man you left to die in the desert, although he had saved you from thieves in Zalit?"

"Aye, priest, and more. I fear. My luck has been too good. A month gone I cast a great ruby into the desert, the finest gem I owned, to break the chain and restore balance; but it came back to me last night in the belly of a wild goat that was roasted for my supper."

"Truly the Gods are not mocked, neither are they deceived by such tricks." Zadok the Priest felt his tongue move of its own accord, and his voice was harsh. "What will be, will be," he said, and he poured forth his terrible dream to the merchant, who sat paralyzed, powerless to move, face gone white with terror, until the priest was finished. Then he fled without a word. And no more was the sleep of Zadok the Priest troubled by bad dreams.

But of the state of Poros the merchant, when a few days had passed, little need be said.

Now at heart Poros the merchant was not a bad man. True, he had drugged and robbed one who had saved him from thieves in the dives of Zalit, and left him bound in the desert to die of thirst, helped along by the efforts of the vultures, always eager to please, and none too inclined to wait until one is quite dead to begin their supper.

But he had robbed him of the precious gems he carried because to win the hand of Bharyeela the Beautiful he must needs be a wealthy man, a very wealthy man indeed; so her father had decreed. And, he reasoned to himself, he was in love, and are not all things forgiven in the name of love? Besides, who but the most beautiful woman in Khoros the City, and hence the world, was worthy to be his bride?

True, he had slain Bharyeela the Beautiful, slowly and with many torments, so that she had pleaded for death long before it was granted, but then was not the death he gave her at the end a most magnanimous act of mercy? After all, she had betrayed him. Worse, she had shown herself to be less than perfect, and none of his possessions might be less than perfect. So she had died, painfully, for the pain she had caused him, painfully for deceiving him, painfully for being thus imperfect, who had been the fairest gem of all. It was, Poros felt, only just.

Poros knew that he was loved by his slaves—they were never beaten, for to thus mar a slave was to render it unworthy of his ownership. And there was the care he took that each had his own perfection, unmarred—for example the boy Nat, who sang to him at supper—he had been gelded, that he might never lose the perfection of his voice, so sweet and high. True, such slaves as fell short of his expectations by fault of error, or accident, or a stubborn blindness to his benevolence, were sold—frequently to those who bought slaves for the mines. Poros treated all his property well, so long as it did not displease him.

Poros found one peculiar thing; try as he might, he could describe his dreams to none, try he ever so hard, beyond saying that they were frightening.

In desperation, he sent a servant to a certain house in a less than reputable zone of Khoros the City, and had brought to him the shabby figure of Nasirkhand the Magician. In a terrified torrent of words he poured out to the magician his tale of woe and fear, stopping short, time and again, when he strove to speak of the dream.

"It is apparent to me what has happened, Poros. This is no chance occurrence; this is *your* dream, sent to you by some enemy who is a sorcerer of great power. It will be your death, and, I think, something more than merely your death, and soon as well, if its power is not broken."

Poros shivered. "I know that well enough. Can it be done?"

"Perhaps. First I must trace it to its source. But the cost will be great—as great as the danger you are in. For I am no starveling hedge-wizard to use my talent for a few coppers, as well you know. Nor is this a matter without danger to me. Remember, if it pleases me to walk with pimps rather than with princes, and wear rags rather than velvet, it is the concern of none but myself."

"I will pay. Tell my steward to give you anything you want. Here—" said Poros, drawing the seal ring off his finger, "give him this. But tell me how I may be saved."

"I must trace the dream to its source, as I said, and send it back along the path it has traveled until it returns to him who sent it, and then, if I am able to do so much, he will suffer the doom he meant for you. I begin with Zadok the priest in the temple of the Seven Vilni."

In reality, though, Nasirkhand began by extracting a truly princely sum in gold and jewels from the steward of Poros the Rich.

It was the work of all that day and night to trace the dream from Zadok to Shamash, and find Shamash in the brothels and trace it from him to Nissan, and from Nissan to Boaz, and from Boaz to Shem. Many hours were spent finding Shem, who had been absent from his place outside the Temple of the Seven Vilni, which is called the House of Wrath, since he had had an unpublicized encounter with Boaz, and with his knife.

On being told that if he wished to seek Shem, it would not be in the house of Yeza, his former landlady, but in the House of Irkalla, which is the House of Death, Nasirkhand returned to his lair and worked the true necromancy, which is the raising of the spirits of the dead, and was presently rewarded with the thin, reedlike voice of that which had been Shem the beggar.

Long was the struggle, but at last he compelled that which once had been Shem the beggar to pass into a tiny bottle, and placed a seal upon it which the dead cannot break, for it is the seal of Life, and made his way with the bottle to the house of Poros, to transfer the dream to that which was in the bottle, and thence to him who had placed the curse on the beggar.

When he came to the house of Poros the Rich, he saw that the door stood open, unguarded; and when he passed within, he saw that the floors were strewn with precious things, and surmised that the slaves had departed suddenly, without more than perfunctorily looting the wealth of the house.

He came finally to the room of Poros, fearing what he would find within. And it was as he had feared, for there, sprawled on the bed, was the torn, headless body which had been Poros the merchant, whose very bones had been cracked for their marrow.

He shook his head sadly, released that which was in the bottle, and made his way home, pausing as he went out to select a few choice items of value from the disordered shambles which had been the house of Poros the Rich.

In a quiet corner of a tavern in Zalit, a cowled figure laughed.

Avram Davidson

MILORD SIR SMIHT, THE ENGLISH WIZARD

In my notes to the Clark Ashton Smith story I was speaking of one of the more interesting technical areas involved in fantasy writing, that of invented milieux. It's axiomatic that fantasies are set in surroundings—historical, cultural, geographical—made up by their authors. And it's traditional that most of these settings are prehistoric or legendary. The only major exception to this that springs to mind is Fletcher's Pratt's The Blue Star, laid in something resembling the eighteen-century Austrian Empire.

Or, sprung. Because now the mercilessly brilliant, clever, witty and inventive Avram Davidson has created a fantasy kingdom of his own, in the Balkans, in a time period resembling the late Victorian era, which completely one-ups Pratt.

So . . . welcome to Scythia-Pannonia-Transbalkania! . . . and right on, Avram!

—L.C.

The establishment of Brothers Swartbloi stands, or squats, as it has done for over a century and a half, in the Court of the Golden Hart. The inn, once famous, which gave its name to the court, has long since passed off the scene, but parts of it survive, here a wall, there an arch, and, by sole way of access, a flight of steps (so old had been the inn,

161

that Bella, Imperial Capital of the Triune Monarchy, had slowly lifted the level of its streets around about it). The shops in the Court of the Golden Hart are an odd mixture. First, to the right of the worn three steps, is Florian, who purveys horse-crowns, though the sign does not say so. (All, in fact, that it says is *Florian*.) There is nothing on display in the window, the window being composed of small pieces of bull's-eye glass set in lead, a very old window, with the very old-fashioned idea that the sole duty of a window is to let light in through a wall. What are horse-crowns? Has the reader never seen a funeral? Has he not noticed the crowns of ostrich plumes—black, for an ordinary adult, white for a child or maiden-woman, violet for a nobleman or prelate of the rank of monsignor or above—bobbing sedately on the horses' heads? Those are horse-crowns, and nobody makes them like Florian's.

To the left of the steps is Weitmondl, who makes and sells mother-of-pearl buttons in all sizes. However great must be the natural disappointment of the fisher in the far-off Gulfs of Persia when he opens his oyster and finds no pearl within, he can still take comfort in the thought that the shells, with their nacreous and opalescent interiors, must find their way to the great city of Bella, where Weitmondl will turn them into buttons: all the way from the great buttons which adorn the shirts of coachmen down to the tiny buttons which fasten children's gloves.

Facing the steps in the Court of the Golden Hart is the shop of Brothers Swartbloi, who are purveyors of snuff-tobacco.

There are other shops, to be sure, in the Golden Hart, but they are of a transitory nature, some of them lasting a mere decade. Florian, Weitmondl, and Brothers Swartbloi are the patriarchs of the place; and of them all Brothers Swartbloi is the oldest.

The shop contains one chair, in which scarcely anyone dares to sit, a wooden counter, and, behind the counter, a wooden shelf. On the shelf are five stout jars, each the size of a small child. One is labeled *Rappee*, one is labeled *Minorka*, one is labeled *Imperial*, one is labeled *Habana*, and one is labeled *Turkey*.

Should anyone desire a snuff of a different sort, some upstart sort of snuff, a johnny-come-lately in the field of snuff—say, for example, *Peppermint! Wintergreen!* or *Co-*

coa-Dutch!—ah, woe upon him, he had better never have
been born. Words cannot describe the glacial degree of cold
with which he will be informed, "The sweet-shop is across
the Court. *Here we sell only snuff-tobacco.*"

One day comes Doctor Eszterhazy to the shop in the
Court of the Golden Hart. He is not walking very fast, in
fact, as he has been following someone, and as that someone
was taking his own good time, it may be said that Engelbert
Eszterhazy, Doctor of Medicine, Doctor of Jurisprudence,
Doctor of Science, Doctor of Literature, etc., etc., was walking decidedly slowly. The man he was following was tall
and heavy and stooped and wore a long black cloak lined
with a dull brown silk. Now, long black cloaks were not
then the fashion, and Lord knows when they had been. It
would be supposed that anyone who wore one did so in order
to create a certain impression, to draw upon himself a certain amount of attention. In all of Bella, so far as Eszterhazy knew, there were only two other men who went about
in long black cloaks. One was Spectorini, the Director of the
Grand Imperial Opera. The other was Von Von Greit-
schmansthal, the Court Painter. And both had their long
black cloaks lined with red.

To wear a long black cloak and then to line it with brown
. . . with *brown* . . . this indicated an individualism of the
very highest order. And, as he could scarcely in good manners stop this strange man on the street and confront him
with his curiosity, therefore he followed him. Down the
Street of the Apple-pressers (no apples had been pressed
there in decades), left into the Street of the Beautiful Vista
(the only vista there nowadays was that of a series of dress-
makers' shops), down the Place Maurits Louis (containing
six greengrocers, two florists, a French laundry, a café, and a
really awful statue of that depressed and, indeed, rather
depressing monarch), and thence into the Court of the Gold-
en Hart.

And thence into the establishment of the *Brothers Swartbloi,* SNUFF-TOBACCO.

One of the brothers was behind the counter. He looked
at the first newcomer, from as far down as the counter permitted him to observe, all the way up to the curious hat (it
was made of black velvet and bore a silver medallion of
some sort; and, while it did not exactly appear to be a cap of
maintenance, it looked far more like a cap of maintenance

than it did like anything else). And he—the Brother Swart-bloi—permitted himself a bow. The first newcomer drew from his pocket an enormous snuffbox, set it down, and uttered one word.

"Rappee."

The brother took up a brass scoop, reached it into the appropriate jar, removed it, set it on the scales, removed it, and emptied it into the snuffbox.

The quantity was just enough. One hundred years and more in the business of estimating the capacities of snuffboxes gives one a certain degree of skill in the matter.

The tall man placed on the counter a coin of five *copper-kas* (the snuff of the Brothers Swartbloi does not come cheap) and a card, allowed himself a nod of thanks, and turned and left.

His face was craggy and smooth-shaven and indicative of many things.

When the door had closed behind him the Brother again bowed—this time more warmly. "And in what way may I help the August Sir Doctor?" asked he.

"By supplying him with four ounces of Imperial."

Small purchases at Swartbloi's are wrapped in newspaper, when not decanted into snuffboxes. Larger purchases are wrapped in special pleated-paper parcels, each supplied with a colored label. The label shows a gentleman, in the costume of the reign of Ignats Ferdinando, applying two fingers to his nose; his expression is one of extreme satisfaction. These lables are colored by hand by old Frow Imglotch, whose eyesight is not what it was, and the results are more than merely curious: they are proof of the authenticity of the label and of the product.

"I had the honor of seeing the August Sir Doctor some months since," said the Brother, "when I was at Hieronymos's"—he named Eszterhazy's tobacconist, the source of the famous segars—"obtaining of our usual supply of Habana clippings for our famous Habana snuff-tobacco. I am wondering if the August Sir Doctor is giving up segars in favor of snuff . . . ?"

He was a dry, thin sort of man, with a few dark curls scattered across a bony skull. Automatically, Eszterhazy took a sight reading of the skull, but it did not seem very interesting. "Ah, no," he said. "It is for one of my servants—a saint's-day present. However, were I to take to taking snuff, be assured that it would be the I-have-no-doubt-justly-famous snuff of the Brothers Swartbloi. Who was that gentleman who was just in here?"

The brother, with a bow at the compliment, passed the card over.

MILORD SIR SMIHT
Wizard anglais
Specializing in late hours & By appointment

In a very elegant copperplate hand had been added: *Hotel Grand Dominik.*

"One does hear," the brother said, "that the British nobility are of a high and eccentric nature."

"So one does. Often," Eszterhazy agreed. It might not have been high, but it would certainly have been eccentric for a member of the British aristocracy to put up at the Hotel Grand Dominik. He reflected, not for the first time, he knew, and not for the last, he expected, on the persistence of the Continental usage of *milord*, a rank not known either to Burke or Debrett. As for the name Smith, no one to the south or east of the English Channel has ever been able to spell it right, nor ever will.

He put down his money and prepared to depart; now that he knew where the stranger was to be found, it was no longer necessary to dog him about the streets.

He looked up to find a familiar, if not a welcome, expression on the face of the brother, who proceeded as expected: Might he take the very great liberty of asking the August Sir Doctor a question? He might. Ah, the August Sir Doctor was very kind. But still the question was not forthcoming. Eszterhazy decided to help him along; most such silences, following such questions, followed a certain pattern.

"If the question involves past indiscretions," he said, gently, "I should represent that Doctor LeDuc, who has a daily advertisement in the popular newspapers— It is not that? Well. If the question involves a failure of regularity, I should recommend syrup of figs. What? Not that, either? Then you must come right out with it."

But the man did not come right out with it. Instead, he began a sort of history of his firm and family. The first Brothers Swartbloi were Kummelman and Hugo. They were succeeded by Augsto and Frans. And Frans begat Kummelman II and Ignats.

"I am the present Kummelman Swartbloi," he said, with an air of dignity at which it was impossible to laugh. "My brother Ignats—he is at present in the mill, salting the Turkey—has never married, and it does not seem that he ever will. My wife and I—she is the daughter and only child of my late Uncle Augsto—we have been wed for fifteen years now. But there have been no children. After all, no one lives forever. And how would it be possible, Sir Doctor, for there to be no Brothers Swartbloi in Bella? How could we leave the business over to strangers? And . . . and . . . there are so many medicines . . . One hardly knows where to begin. Could the August Sir Doctor recommend a particular medicine, known to be both safe and effective?"

The August Sir Doctor said very, very gently, "I should instead recommend my colleague, Professor Doctor Plotz, of the Faculty of Medicine. You may mention my name."

The Hotel Grand Dominik has come down in the world since the days when it formed a stop on the Grand Tour. Long after having ceased to be fashionable among the gentry, it retained an affection on the part of the more prosperous of the commercial travelers. But it was at that time near the East Railroad Terminal. It is still, in fact, near the East Railroad Terminal, but since the completion of the Great Central Terminal, the shabby old East only serves suburban and industrial rail lines. Consequently, the commercial travelers who stop at the Grand Dominik either are very uninnovative or very old and in any event very unprosperous, or else they are merely unprosperous by reason of such factors as not selling anything worth buying. In fact, for some several years the Grand Dominik has stayed open solely because its famous half-ducat dinner, served between eleven and three, is deservedly popular among the junior partners and upper clerks of the many timber firms who still hold out in the adjacent neighborhood. The rooms are thus ancillary to the hotel's main business. So the rooms are, in a word, cheap.

They are also—no management having been vigorous enough to undertake architectural changes—rather large. Milord Sir Smiht sat in a chair and at a table in the middle of his room, lit by the late afternoon sun. The rear of the room was dim. One caught glimpses of an enormous bed, hugely canopied and reached by a small stepladder, of an antique clothes press, a washbasin of marble and mahogany, a sofa whose worn upholstery still breathed out a very faint air of bygone fashion—and a very strong odor of present-day Rappee snuff—although it was actually rather unlikely that this last came from the sofa, and vastly likely that it came from the *wizard anglais* himself.

Who said, "I've seen you before."

Eszterhazy said, "You left a card in the Court of the Golden Hart, and so—"

"—and so that was why you followed me halfway across Bella, because you knew I was going to leave my card in a snuff shop. Eh?"

The conversation was in French.

Eszterhazy smiled. "The *milord* is observant. Well. It is certainly true. My interest was aroused by the distinctive, I may say, distinguished appearance—"

The *milord* grunted, took out an enormous watch, glanced at it, shoved it across to where his visitor could see it. "My terms," he said, "are two ducats for a half-hour. It has just now begun. You may ask as many questions as you please. You may do card tricks. You may spend the entire time looking at me. However, if you wish the employment of the odyllic force, then we should commence at once. Unless, of course, you are willing to pay another two ducats for any fraction of one-half-hour after the first."

Eszterhazy wondered, of course, that anyone so seemingly businesslike should find himself a wanderer in a country so distant from his own—let alone a lodger at the Hotel Grand Dominik. He had learned, however, that the role which people see themselves as playing is not always the same role in which the world at large perceives them.

"To begin with," he said, taking one of his own specially printed forms from his pocket, "I will ask Sir Smiht to be kind enough to remove his hat for the length of time which it will take me to complete my examination—"

The Englishman gazed at the forms with the greatest astonishment. "Good God!" he exclaimed. "I did once, long ago, at Brighton, to be sure, pay a phrenologist to fumble and peer about my pate—but I never thought that a phrenologist would pay *me* for the privilege!"

"Ah, Brighton," Eszterhazy said. "The Royal Pavilions

—what an excursion into the *phantastique!* Do you suppose that the First Gentleman of Europe might have been the first gentleman in Europe to have smoked hasheesh?"

Smiht snorted. Then his face, as he began to take his hat off, underwent a certain change. He completed the gesture, and then he said, "Brighton, eh. I suppose you must speak English, although I don't suppose you *are* English?"

"As a boy I often spent my holidays with the family of my aunt, who lived in England."

"Then let us cease to speak in French. Much better for you to struggle than for me. *Furthermore*—if you have been in England you ought to know damned well that the title Sir never precedes the family name without the interposition of the Christian name, although in such instances as that of Sir Moses Montefiore one would employ another terminology —a point which I can*not* get across to the Continental mind, confound it! I consent to *milord*, because it is, I suppose, traditional, as one might say; and I submit to S-M-I-H-T because I realize how difficult the T-H is to speakers of any other language except Greek and I suppose Icelandic . . . speakers? spellers . . . ?"

Here he paused to draw breath and consider his next phrase, and Eszterhazy took the opportunity to approach him from behind and gently place his fingers on the man's head. He was slightly surprised when the other went on to say, "Anyway, the baronetcy absolutely baffles the Continent of Europe—small wonder, I suppose, when every son of a baron here is also a baron and every son of a prince here is also a prince. No wonder the Continent is simply *crawling* with princes and barons and counts and grafs—no primogeniture, *ah* well . . . Now suppose you just call 'em out to me and I'll write 'em down, can't read this Gothic or whatever it is, so you needn't fear I'll get me back up if you decide I'm deficient in honesty, or whatever. Just say, oh, second down, third over—eh?"

"First down, first over," said Eszterhazy.

Without moving his head, the Englishman reached out his long arm and made a mark in the first column of the first row. "I was christened George William Marmaduke Pemberton," he said. "Called me *George*, was what me people called me. Marmaduke Pemberton was a great-uncle by marriage, long since predeceased by the great-aunt of the blood. Made *dog*-biscuit, or some such thing, grew *rich* at it, or perhaps they were digestive biscuits, doesn't matter. As he'd never gotten any children on Aunt Maude and never remarried after *she* died, couldn't get it *up,* I suppose, rest of me people they thought, well, let's name this 'un after him and he'll leave him all his *pelf,* you see, under the condition of his assuming the name of Smith-*Pem*berton. Baronetcy was to go to me oldest brother. *Well,* old Marmaduke left me *beans,* is what he left me, rest of it went to some fund to restore *churches,* sniveling *par*sons had been at him, don't you see.

"Second down, fourth over, *very* well. Tenny rate, say what you will, always tipped me a guinea on me birthday, so out of gratitude and because I couldn't *stand* the name George, have always used the style Pemberton Smith. Can I get *any* Continental printer to spell Pemberton correctly? Ha! Gave up trying. *Now,* as to the odyllic force or forces, in a way it began with Bulwer-Lytton as he called himself before he got *his* title—ever read any of his stuff? *A*wful stuff, don't know how they can read it, but he had more than a mere inkling of the odyllic, you know. What's that? Fourth down, first over, dot and carry one. And *in* a way, of course, one can say, 't all goes back to Mesmer. Well, tut-tut, hmm, of course, Mesmer *had* it. Although poor chap didn't know what he *had.* And then Oscar took a Maori bullet at a place called Pa Rewi Nang Nang, or *some* such thing, *damn*able is what I call it to die at a place called Pa Rewi Nang Nang, or some such thing—sixth down and four, no five over, *aiwah, tuan besar.* Next thing one knew, Reginald had dived into the Hooghli, *likely story,* that, and never came up —'spect a croc got him, poor chap, better mouthful than a hundred scrawny *Hin*doos, ah well."

George William Marmaduke Pemberton Smith fell silent a moment and helped himself to two nostrils of Rappee snuff.

"And what's the consequence? Here is my sole remaining brother, Augustus, heir to the baronetcy. And here's *me,* poor fellow, name splashed all over the penny press, because *why?* Because of a mere accident, a Thing of Nature, here am *I,* as I might be *here,* demonstrating the odyllic forces before a subcommittee of the Royal Society, one of whom, Pigafetti Jones, *awful* ass, having kindly volunteered to act as subject, dis-a-*pears!*—leaving nothing but his *clothes,* down to the last brace-button, belly-band, and ball-and-socket truss — Well! *After all. Is* this a scientific experiment or is this *not?* Are there such things as the hazards of the chase or are there *not* such things as the hazards of the chase? *First* off, laugh, then they say, very well, bring him *back*, then they dare to call me a *char*-la-tan: ME! And then—"

Dimly, very dimly, Eszterhazy remembered having read, long ago (and it had not been fresh news, even then), of the singular disappearance of Mr. Pigafetti Jones, Astronomer-Royal for Wales. But what he was hearing now provided more details than he had ever even guessed at. It also provided, if not a complete explanation for, at least an assumption as to why "Milord Sir Smiht" was and had long been wandering the continent of Europe (and perhaps farther) a remittance man, as the British called it. That is, in return for his keeping far away and thus bringing at least no fresh local scandals to his family's embarrassment, the family would continue to remit him a certain sum of money at fixed intervals.

It was still not clear, though, if he were already a baronet or was merely assumed to be because his father was one. Or had been.

And as for the odyllic force . . .

"Forces," said the tall old Englishman, calmly. "I am quite confident that there is more than one."

And for the moment he said no more. Had he read Eszterhazy's mind, then? Or was it merely a fortuitous comment of his own, in his own disjointed manner?

"Or, for that matter," the latter went on, in a generous tone of voice, "take Zosimus the Alchemist, if you like. *Come in!"* The hall-porter came in, bowed with ancient respectfulness (the hall-porter was rather ancient, himself), laid down a salver with a card on it, and withdrew. "Ah-hah. Business is picking up. Fifteen down, three over . . ."

Eszterhazy had not stayed beyond the half-hour, but made a semi-appointment for a later date. The card of the further business awaiting Milord Sir Smiht was facing directly toward both of them, and he could hardly have avoided reading it.

And it read: *Brothers Swartbloi, Number 3, Court of the Golden Hart. Snuff-Tobacco.*

Third Assitant Supervisory Officer Lupescus, of the Aliens Office, was feeling rather mixed, emotionally. On the one hand, he still had the happiness of having (recently) reached the level of a third assistant supervisory official; it was not every day, or even every year that a member of the Romanou-speaking minority attained such high rank in the Imperial Capital. On the other hand, a certain amount of field work was now required of him, and he had never done field work before. This present task, for instance, this call upon the Second Councilor at the British Legation, was merely routine. "Merely routine, my dear Lupescus," his superior in the office, Second ASO on Glouki had said. Easily enough *said,* but, routine or not routine, one had to have something to *show* for this visit. And it did not look as though one were going to get it.

"Smith, Smith," the Second Councilor was saying, testily. "I tell you that I must have more information. *What* Smith?"

All that Lupescus could do was to repeat, "Milord Sir Smiht."

" 'Milord, Milord,' there *is* no such rank or title. Sir, why, that is merely as one would say *Herra,* or *Monsieur.* And as for Smith—by the way, you've got it spelled wrongly there, you know, it is S-M-I-T-H—well, you can't expect me to know anything about anyone just named *Smith,* why, that's like asking me about someone named Jones, in Cardiff, or Macdonald, in Glasgow . . . Mmm, no, you wouldn't know about those . . . Ah, well, it's, oh, it's like asking me about someone named Novotny in Prague! D'you see?"

Lupescus brightened just a trifle. This was something. Very dutifully and carefully, he wrote in his notebook, *Subject Milord Smiht said to be associated with Novotny in Prague . . .*

With his best official bow, he withdrew. Withdrawn, he allowed himself a sigh. Now he would have to go and check out Novotny with the people at the Austro-Hungarian Legation. He hoped that this would be more productive than this other enquiry had been. One would have thought that people named Smiht grew on trees in England.

Eszterhazy's growing association with the white-haired Englishman took, if not a leap, then a sort of lurch, forward one evening about a month after his first visit. He had sent up his card with the hall-porter, who had returned with word that he was to go up directly. He found Smith with a woman in black, a nondescript woman of the type who hold up churches all around the world.

"Ah, come in, my dear sir. Look here. This good woman doesn't speak either French or German, and my command of Gothic is not . . . well, ask her what she wants, do, please."

Frow Widow Apterhots wished to be placed in communication with her late husband. "That is to say," she said, anxious that there be no confusion nor mistake, "that is to say, he is dead, you know. His name is Emyil."

Smiht shook his head tolerantly at this. "Death does not exist," he said, "nor does life exist, save as states of flux to one side or other of the sidereal line, or astral plane, as some call it. From this point of view it may seem that anyone who is not alive must be dead, but that is not so. The absent one, the one absent from here, may now be fluctuating in the area called 'death,' or he or she may be proceeding in a calm vibration along the level of the sidereal line or so-called astral plane. We mourn because the 'dead' are not 'alive.' But in the world which we call 'death' the so-called 'dead' may be mourning a departure into what we call 'life.' "

From Widow Apterhots sighed. "Emyil was always so healthy, so *strong*," she said. "I still can't understand it. He always did say that there wasn't no Hell, just Heaven and Purgatory, and I used to say, 'Oh, Emyil, people will think that you're a Freemason or something.' Well, our priest, Father Ugerow, he just won't listen when I talk like this, he says, 'If you won't say your prayers, at least perform some work of corporal mercy, and take your mind off such things.' But what I say—" She leaned forward, her simple sallow face very serious and confiding, "I say that all I want to know is: Is he happy there? That's all."

Pemberton Smith said that he could guarantee nothing, but in any event he would have to have at least one object permeated with the odyllic force of the so-called deceased. The Frow Widow nodded and delved into her reticule. "That's what I was told, so I come prepared. I always made him wear this, let them say what they like, he always did. But I wouldn't let them bury him with it because I wanted it for a keepsake. Here you are, Professor." She held out a small silver crucifix.

Smith took the article with the utmost calm and walked over and set it down upon a heavy piece of furniture in the dimness of the back of the room. There were quite a number of things already on the table. Smith beckoned, and the others came toward him, Frow Widow Apterhots because she was sure that she was meant to, and Eszterhazy because he was sure he wanted to. "These," said Smith, "are the equipment for the odyllic forces. Pray take a seat, my good woman." He struck a match and lit a small gas jet; it was not provided with a mantle, and it either lacked a regulatory tap or something was wrong with the one it did have—or perhaps Smith merely liked to see the gas flame shooting up to its fullest extent; at least two feet long the flame was, wavering wildly and a reddish gold in color.

Certainly, he was not trying to conceal anything.

But *these* were interesting, certainly whatever else they were, and Eszterhazy took advantage of the English wizard's at the moment administering to himself two strong doses of Rappee—one in each nostril—to scrutinize the equipment for the odyllic forces. What he saw was a series of bell jars . . . that is, at least some of them were bell jars . . . some of the others resembled, rather, Leyden jars . . . and what *was* all that, under the bell jars? In one there seemed to be a vast quantity of metal filings; in another, quicksilver; in the most of them, organic matter, vegetive in origin. Every jar, bell or Leyden, appeared to be connected to every other jar by a system of glass tubing: and all the tubes seemed fitted up to a sort of master-tube, which coiled around and down and finally upward, culminating in what appeared to be an enormous gramophone horn.

"Pray, touch *nothing*," warned Milord Sir Smiht. "The equipment is *exceedingly* fragile." He took up a small, light table, the surface of which consisted of some open lattice-work material—Eszterhazy was not sure what—and, moving it easily, set it up over the horn. On it he placed the crucifix. "Now, my dear sir, if you will be kind enough to ask this good lady, first, to take these in her hands . . . ? And, to concentrate, if she will, entirely upon the memory of her husband, now on another plane of existence." The Widow Apterhots, sitting down, took hold of the *these*—in this case, a pair of metal grips of the sort which are connected, often, to magnetic batteries, but in this case were not—they seemed connected in some intricate way with the glass tubings. She closed her eyes. "*And*," the wizard continued, "please to cooperate in sending on my request. Which, after all, is *her* request, translated into my own methodology."

He began an intricate series of turnings of taps, of twist-ings of connections at joints and at junctions, of connect-ings; at length he was finished. "Emyil Apterhots. Emyil Apterhots. Emyil Apterhots. If you are happy, wherever you are, kindly signify by moving the crucifix which you wore when on this plane of existence. *Now!*"

The entire massive piece of furniture upon which the equipment for the odyllic force (or forces) was placed be-gan to move forward.

"No, *no,* you Gothic oaf!" shouted the *milord,* his face crimson with fury and concern. *"Not* the sideboard! *The crucifix!* Just the *cru-ci-fix*—" He set himself against the sideboard and pressed it back. In vain. In vain. In vain. In a moment, Eszterhazy, concerned lest the glass tubings should snap, reached forward to adjust them, so that the intricate workings should not be shattered and sundered—the wizard, panting and straining against the laboratory furniture as the heavy mass continued to slide forward . . . forward . . . for-ward . . .

—and suddenly slid rapidly backward, Milord Sir Smiht stumbling and clutching at empty air, Eszterhazy darting forward, and the two of them executing a sort of slow, in-sane *schottische,* arm in arm, before coming to a slow halt—

And then, oh so grumpy, wiping his brow with a red bandana handkerchief, of the sort in which navvies wrap their pork pies, hear Milord Sir Smiht say, "I must regard this session as questionable in its results. And I *must* say that I am not *used* to such contumacy from the habitants of the sidereal line!"

Frow Widow Apterhots, however, clearly did not regard the results as in any way questionable. Her sallow, silly face now quite blissful, she stepped forward and retrieved the crucifix. "Emyil," she said, "was always so *strong . . . !*"

And on that note she departed.

Herr Manfred Mauswarmer at the Austro-Hungarian Le-gation was quite interested. " 'Novotny in Prague,' eh? Hmmm, *that* seems to ring a bell." Third ASO Lupescus sat up straighter. A faint tingle of excitement went through his scalp. "Yes, yes," said Herr Mauswarmer, "we have of a certainty heard the name. One of those Czech names," he said, almost indulgently. "One never knows what *they* may be up to." Very carefully he made a neat little note and looked up brightly. "We shall of course first have to communicate with Vienna—"

"Oh, of course!"

"And they will, of course, communicate with Prague."

Herr Manfred Mauswarmer's large, pale, bloodshot blue eyes blinked once or twice. "A Czech name," he noted. "An English name. Uses the code cypher *Wizard*. Communicates *in French*." He briefly applied one thick forefinger to the side of his nose. He winked. Lupescus winked back. They understood each other. The hare had had a headstart. But the hounds had caught the scent.

One of the bell jars was empty—had, in fact, always been empty, although Eszterhazy had merely noted this without considering as to why it might be so. He did not ask about it as he listened, now, to the Englishman's talk. Milord Sir Smiht, his cap on his head, his cloak sometimes giving a dramatic *flap* as he turned in his pacings of the large old room, said, "The contents of the vessels in large part represent the vegetable and mineral kingdoms—I don't know if you have noticed that."

"I have."

"The *an*imal kingdom, now . . . well, each man and woman is a microcosm, representing the macrocosm, the *uni*verse, in miniature. That is to say, we contain in our own bodies enough of the animal and mineral to emanate at all times, though we are not aware of it, a certain amount of odyllic force—"

"Or forces."

"Or forces. Point well *made*. However. Now, although the average human body does include, usually, some amounts of the vegetable kingdom—so much potato, cabbage, sprouts, let us say—undergoing the process of digestive action," *flap* went his cloak, "as *well* as the ever-present bacteria, also vegetative, *still*. The chemical constituencies in our body, now, I forget just what they amount to. Four-and-six, more or less, in real money. Or is it *two*-and-six? One forgets. *Still*. Primarily, the human organism is an *an*imal organism." *Flap*.

Eszterhazy, nodding, made a steeple of his hands. "And therefore (Pemberton Smith will correct me if I am wrong), when the human subject takes hold of that pair of metallic grips, the three kingdoms, animal, vegetable, and mineral, come together in a sort of unity—"

"A sort of Triune Monarchy *in parvo,* as it were, yes, co-*rect!* I see that I was not wrong in assuming that yours was a mind capable of grasping these matters," *flap,* "and then it is all a matter of adjustment: One turns *up* the vegetative emanations, one turns *in* the mineral emanations . . . and then, then, my dear sir, one hopes for the best. For one has not as yet been able to adjust the individual human beings. They are what they are. One can turn a *tap,* one can open a valve or lose a valve, plug in a connecting tube or *un*plug a connecting tube. But one has to take a human body *just as one finds it* . . . Pity, in a way . . . Hollo, hollo!"

Something was happening in the empty bell jar: mists and fumes, pale blue lights, red sparks and white sparks.

Milord Sir Smiht, dashing hither and thither and regulating his devices, stopped, suddenly, looked imploringly at Eszterhazy, gestured, and said, *"Would* you, my dear fellow? *Awf'*ly grateful—"

Eszterhazy sat in the chair, took the metal grips in his hands, and tried to emulate those curious animals, the mules, which, for all that they are void of hope of posterity, can still manage to look in two directions at once.

Direction Number One: Pemberton Smith, as he coupled and uncoupled, attached and disattached, turned, tightened, loosened, adjusting the ebb and flow of the odyllic forces. Animal, vegetable, *and* mineral.

Direction Number Two: The once-empty bell jar, wherein now swarmed . . . wherein now swarmed *what?* A hive of microscopic bees, perhaps.

A faint tingle passed through the palms of Eszterhazy's hands and up his hands and arms. The tingle grew stronger. It was not really at all like feeling an electrical current, though. A perspiration broke forth upon his forehead. He felt very slightly giddy, and the *wizard anglais* almost at once perceived this. "Too strong for you, is it? *Sorry* about *that!*" He made adjustments. The giddiness was at once reduced, almost at once passed away.

And the something in the bell jar slowly took form and shape.

It was a simulacrum, perhaps. Or perhaps the word was homunculus. The bell jar was the size of a child. And the man within it was the size of a rather small child. Otherwise it was entirely mature. And "it" was really not the correct pronoun, for the homunculus (or whatever it was) was certainly a man, however small: a man wearing a frock coat and everything which went with frock coats, and a full beard. He even had an order of some sort, a ribbon which crossed his bosom, and a medal or medallion. Eszterhazy *thought*, but could not be sure, that it rather resembled the silver medallion which Milord Sir Smiht wore in his hat.

"Pemberton Smith, who *is* that?"

"Who, that? Or. Oh, that's *Gomes*—" He pronounced it to rhyme with *roams*. "He's the Wizard of Brazil. You've heard of *Gomes*, to be sure." And he then proceeded to move his arms, hands, and fingers with extreme rapidity, pausing only to say, "We communicate through the international sign language, you see. He has no English and I have no Portagee. Poor old Gomes, things have been ever so slack for him since poor old Dom Peedro got the sack. Ah well. Inevitable, I suppose. Emperors and the Americas just don't seem to go together. Purely an Old World phenomena, don't you know." And once again his fingers and hands and arms began their curious, rapid, and impressive movement. "Yes, yes," he muttered to himself. "I see, I see. No. Really. You don't say. Ah, too bad, too bad!"

He turned to Eszterhazy. Within the jar, the tiny digits and limbs of the Wizard of Brazil had fallen, as it were, silent. The homunculus shrugged, sadly. "What do you make of all *that?*" asked the Wizard of England (across the waters).

"What? Is it not clear? The ants are eating his coffee trees, and he wishes you to send him some paris green, as the local supply has been exhausted."

"My dear chap, *I* can't send him any paris green!"

"Assure him that I shall take care of it myself. Tomorrow."

"I say, that *is* ever so good of you! Yes, yes, ah, pray excuse me now whilst I relay the good news."

In far-off Petropolis, the summer capital of Brazil, the wizard of that mighty nation, much reduced in size (wizard, not nation) by transatlantic transmission, crossed his arms upon his bosom and bowed his gratitude in the general direction of the distant though friendly nation of Scythia-Pannonia-Transbalkania. All men of science, after all, constitute one great international confraternity.

The saint's-day gift of snuff was so well received by Frow Widow Orgats, Eszterhazy's cook (who had taken his advice to stock up on coffee), that he thought he would lay in a further supply as a sweetener against the possibility of one of those occasions—infrequent, but none the less to be feared —when the Frow Cook suffered severe attacks of the vapors and either burned the soup or declared (with shrieks and shouts audible on the second floor) her intense inability to face anything in the shape of a stove at all. So, on the next convenient occasion, he once more made his way to the Court of the Golden Hart.

"Four ounces of the Imperial."

He peered at the Swartbloi brother, who was peering at the scales. "You are not Kummelman," he said. Almost. But not.

"No sir, I am Ignats," said the brother. "Kummelman is at the moment—"

"In the mill, salting the Turkey. I know."

Ignats Swartbloi looked at him with some surprise and some reproof. "Oh, no, sir. Kummelman always grinds the Rappee, and I always salt the Turkey. On the other tasks we either work together or take turns. But *never* in regard to the grinding of the Rappee or the salting of the Turkey. I had been about to say, sir, that Kummelman is at his home, by reason of his wife's indisposition, she being presently in a very delicate condition."

And he handed over the neatly wrapped packet of pleated paper bearing the well-known illustrated label—this one, old Frow Imglotch had tinted so as to give the snuff-taker a gray nose and a green periwig, neither of which in any way diminished the man's joy at having his left nostril packed solid with Brothers Swartbloi Snuff-Tobacco (though whether Rappee, Imperial, Minorka, Habana, or Turkey, has never been made plain, and perhaps never will be).

"Indeed, indeed. Pray accept my heartiest felicitations."

The brother gazed at him and gave a slight, polite bow, no more. "That is very kind of you, sir. Felicitations are perhaps premature. Suppose the child will be a girl?"

"Hm," said Eszterhazy. "Hm, hm. Well, there is that possibility, isn't there? Thank you, and good afternoon."

He could not but suppose that this same possibility must have also occurred to Brother Kummelman. And, in that case, he wondered, would a second visit have been paid to the large, antiquated room in the Grand Dominik where the *Milord anglais* still prolonged his stay?

Herr von Paarfus pursed his lips. He shook his head. Gave a very faint sigh. Then he got up and went into the office of his superior, the Graf zu Kluk. "Yes, what?" said the Graf zu Kluk, whose delightful manners always made it such a pleasure to work with him. More than once had Herr von Paarfus thought of throwing it all up and migrating to America, where his cousin owned a shoe store in Omaha. None of this, of course, passed his lips. He handed the paper to his superior.

"From Mauswarmer, in Bella, Excellency," he said.

The Graf fitted his monocle more closely into his eye and grunted. "Mauswarmer, in Bella," he said, looking up, "has uncovered an Anglo-Franco-Czech conspiracy, aimed against the integrity of the Austro-Hungarian Empire."

"Indeed, Your Excellency!" said von Paarfus, trying to sound shocked.

"Oh yes! There is no doubt of it," declared Graf zu Kluk, tapping the report with a highly polished fingernail. "The liaison agent—of course, in Prague, where else?—is a man named Novotny. The password is 'wizard.' What do you think of *that?*"

"I think, Your Excellency, that Novotny is a very common name in Prague."

Graf zu Kluk gave no evidence of having heard. "I shall take this up with His Highness, at once," he said. Even Graf zu Kluk had a superior officer. But then, long years of training in the Civil Service of Austria-Hungary cautioned him. "That is," he said, "as soon as we have had word on this from our people in London, Paris, and Prague. Until then, mind, not a word to anyone!"

"Your Excellency is of course correct."

"Of *course*. Of *course*. See to this. *At once!*"

Von Paarfus went out, thinking of Omaha. Not until the door had closed behind him did he sigh once again.

Oberzeeleutnant-commander Adler had had a long and distinguished career in the naval service of a neighboring power. "But then," he said, stiffly, "I—how do you put it, in English? Than I copied my blotting-book? I of course do not desire to go into details. At any rate, I thought to myself, even if I shall not be actually at sea, at any rate, at least I shall be able to put my finishing touches on the revision of my monograph on the deep-sea fishes. But the High Command was even more loath with me than I had thought; ah, how they did punished me, did I deserved such punishments? Aund so, here I am, Naval Attaché in Bella! In *Bella!* A river port! Capital of a nation, exceedingly honorable, to be sure." He bobbed a hasty bow to Eszterhazy, who languidly returned it. "But one which has no deep-sea coast at all! Woe!" For a moment he said nothing, only breathed deeply. Then, "What interest could anyone possibly find in a freshwater fish, I do enquire you?" he entreated. But no one had an answer.

"Mmm," said Milord Sir Smiht. "Yes. Yes. Know what it is to be an exile, myself. Still. I stay strictly away from politics, you know. Not my pidjin. Whigs, Tories, nothing to me. Plague on both their houses. Sea-fish, rich in phosphorous. Brain food."

But the commander had not made himself clear. What he would wish to propose of the Milord Sir Smiht was not political. It was scientific. Could not Sir Smiht, by means of the idyllic—what? ah!—thousand pardons—the odyllic force, of which one had heard much—could not Sir Smiht produce an ensampling of, say, the waters of the Mindanao Trench, or of some other deep-sea area—here—here in Bella—so that the commander might continue his studies?

The *milord* threw up his hands. "Impossible!" he cried. "Im-*pos*-sib-le! Think of the pressures! One would need a vessel of immensely strong steel. With windows of immensely thick glass. *Just to begin with!* Cost: much. Possibilities of success: jubious."

But the Naval Attaché begged that these trifles might not stand in the way. The cost, the cost was to be regarded as merely a first step, and one already taken; he hinted at private means.

"As for the rest." Eszterhazy stepped forward, a degree of interest showing in his large eyes. "At least, as for the steel, there are the plates for the *Ignats Louis . . .*"

The *Ignats Louis!* With what enthusiasm the nation (particularly the patriotic press) had encouraged plans for the construction of the Triune Monarchy's very first dreadnought, a vessel which (it was implied) would strike justly deserved terror into the hearts of the enemies—actual or potential—of Scythia-Pannonia-Transbalkania! A New Day, it was declared, was about to dawn for the Royal and Imperial Navy of the fourth-largest empire in Europe; a Navy which had until then consisted of three revenue cutters, two gunboats, one lighthouse tender, and the monitor *Furioso* (formerly the *Monadnock*, purchased very cheaply from the United States after the conclusion of the American Civil War). Particular attention had been drawn to the exquisitely forged and incredibly strong steel plate, made in Sweden at great expense.

Alas, the day of the Triune Monarchy as one of the naval powers of the world had been exceedingly short-lived and more or less terminated upon the discovery that the *Ignats Louis* would draw four feet more than the deepest reaches of the River Ister at high water in the floods. The cheers of the patriotic press were overnight reduced to silence, subsidies for the dreadnought vanished from the next budget, the skeleton of the vessel slowly rusted on the ways, the exquisitely forged and incredibly strong steel plating remained in the storage sheds of the contractor; and the two gunboats and the monitor alone remained to strike terror into the hearts of, if not Russia and Austria-Hungary, then at any rate Graustark and Ruritania.

The downcast face of the foreign naval commander slowly began to brighten. The countenance of the English wizard likewise relaxed. And, as though by one common if semi-silent consent, they drew up to the table and began to make their plans.

"*Qu'est-ce qu'il y a, cette affaire d'une vizard anglais aux Scythie-Pannonie-Transbalkanie?*" they asked, in Paris.

"*C'est, naturellement, une espèce de blague,*" they answered, in Paris.

"*Envoyez-le à Londres,*" they concluded, in Paris.

"What can the chaps *mean?*" they asked each other, in London. " '*English vizar Milor Sri Smhti*'? Makes no sense, you know."

"Mmm, well, *does,* in a way, y'know," they said in London. "Of course, that should be *vizier.* And *sri,* of course, is an Injian religious title. Dunno what to make of Smhti, though. Hindi? Gujerathi? Look here. Sir Augustus is our Injian expert. Send it up to him," they said, in London.

"Very well, then . . . but, look here. What can this be

about *Tcheque novothni?* They simply can't *spell* in Paris, you know. Check up on the Novothni, what are the Novothni?"

"Blessed if I know. Some hill tribe or other. Not our pidjin. Best send it all up to Sir Augustus," they said, in London.

But in Prague they sat down to their files, which, commencing with *Novotny, Abelard,* ran for pages and pages and pages down to *Novotny, Zygmund.* They had lots and lots of time in Prague, and, anyway, it was soothing work, and much more to their tastes than the absolutely baffling case of a young student who thought that he had turned into a giant cockroach.

They had directed the old hall-porter at the Grand Dominik to inform all would-be visitors that Milord Sir Smiht was not receiving people at present. But Frow Puprikosch was not one to be deterred by hall-porters; indeed, it is doubtful if she understood what he was saying, and, before he had finished saying it, she had swept on . . . and on, and into the large old-fashioned chamber where the three were at work.

"Not now," said Smiht, scarcely looking up from his adjustments of the tubing system to the steel-plated diving bell. "I can't see you now."

"But you must see me now," declared Frow Puprikosch, in a rich contralto voice. "My case admits of no delays, for how can one live without love?" Frow Puprikosch was a large, black-haired woman in whom the bloom of youth had mellowed. "That was the tragedy of my life, that my marriage to Puprikosch lacked love—but what did I know then? —mere child that I was." She pressed one hand to her bosom, as to push back the tremendous sigh which arose therefrom, and with the other she employed—as an aid to emphasis and gesticulation—an umbrella of more use to the ancient lace industry of the Triune Monarchy than of any possible guard against rain.

"And what would Herra Puprikosch say, if he knew what you were up to, eh? Much better go home, my dear lady," she was advised.

"He is dead, I have divorced him, the marriage was annulled, he is much better off in Argentina," she declared, looking all around with great interest.

"Argentina?"

"*Some*where in Africa!" she said, and, with a wave of her umbrella, or perhaps it was really a parasol, disposed of such pedantries. "What I wish of you, dear wizard," she said, addressing Eszterhazy, "is only this: to make known to me my true love. Of course you can do it. Where shall I sit down here? I shall sit here."

He assured her that he was not the wizard, but she merely smiled an arch and anxious smile, and began to peel off her gloves. As these were very long and old-fashioned with very many buttons (of the best-quality mother-of-pearl, and probably from the establishment of Weitmondl in the Court of the Golden Hart), the act took her no little time. And it was during this time that it was agreed by the men present, between them, with shrugs and sighs and nods, that they had beter accomplish at least the attempt to do what the lady desired, if they expected to be able to get on with their work at all that day.

"If the dear lady will be kind enough to grasp these grips," said Sir Smiht, in a resigned manner, "and concentrate upon the matter which is engaging her mind, ah, yes, that's a very good grasp." He began to make the necessary adjustments.

"Love, love, my true love, my true affinity, where is he?" demanded Frow Puprikosch of the Universal Aether. "Yoi!" she exclaimed, a moment later, in her native Avar, her eyebrows going up until they met the fringe, so pleasantly arranged, of glossy black hair. "Already I feel it begins. *Yoi!*"

" 'Yoiks' would be more like it," Smiht muttered. He glanced at a dial to the end of the sideboard. "Good heavens!" he exclaimed. "What an extraordinary amount of the odyllic forces that woman conjugates! Never *seen* anything like it!"

"Love," declared Frow Puprikosch, "love is all that matters; money is of no matter, I have money; position is of no matter, I expectorate upon the false sham of position. I am a woman of such a nature as to crave, demand, and require only *love!* And I know, I know, I *know,* that *some*where is the true true affinity of my soul—where *are* you?" she caroled, casting her large and lovely eyes all around. "*Oo-hoo?*"

The hand of the dial, which had been performing truly amazing swings and movements, now leaped all the way full circle, and, with a most melodious twang, fell off the face of the dial and onto the ancient rug.

At that moment sounds, much less melodious, but far more emphatic, began to emanate from the interior of the diving bell. And before Eszterhazy, who had started to stoop toward the fallen dial hand, could reach the hatch-cover, the hatch-cover sprang open and out flew—there is really not a better verb—out flew the figure of a man of vigorous early middle age and without a stitch or thread to serve, as the French so delicately put it, *pour cacher sa nudité . . .*

"*Yoiii!!!*" shrieked Frow Puprikosch, releasing her grip upon the metal holders and covering her face with her bumbershoot.

"Good heavens, a woman!" exclaimed the gentleman who had just emerged from the diving bell. "Here, dash it, Pemberton Smith, *give* me that!" So saying, he whipped off the cloak which formed the habitual outer garment of the *wizard anglais,* and wrapped it around himself, somewhat in the manner of a Roman senator who has just risen to denounce a conspiracy. The proprieties thus taken care of, the new-comer, in some perplexity, it would seem, next asked, "Where on earth have you gotten us to, Pemberton Smith? —and why on earth are you rigged up like such a guy? Hair whitened, and I don't know what else. Eh?"

Pemberton Smith, somewhat annoyed, said, "I have un-dergone no process of rigging, it is merely the natural attri-tion of the passage of thirty years, and tell me, then, how did you pass your time on the sidereal level—or, if you pre-fer, astral plane?"

"But I don't prefer," the man said, briskly. "I know noth-ing about it. I'd come up from the Observatory—*damned* silly notion putting an observatory in Wales, skies obscured three hundred nights a year with soppy Celtic mists, all the pubs closed on Sundays—and, happening to drop in on the Royal Society, I allowed myself to act as subject for your experiment. One moment I was *there,* the next moment I was *there—*" He gestured toward the diving bell. Then something evidently struck his mind. " 'Thirty years,' you say? Good heavens!" An expression of the utmost glee came across his face. "Then Flora must be dead by now, skinny old bitch, and, if she isn't, so much the worse for her, who is this lovely lady *here?*"

The lady herself, displacing her parasol and coming toward him in full-blown majesty, said, in heavily accented but still melodious English, "Is here the Madame Puprikosch, but you may to calling me Yózhinka. My affinity! My own true love! Produced for me by the genius of the *wizard anglais! Yoi!*" And she embraced him with both arms, a process which seemed by no means distasteful to the gentleman himself.

"If you don't mind, Pigafetti Jones," the wizard said, somewhat stiffly, "I will thank you for the return of my cloak. We will next discuss the utmost inconveniency which your disappearance from the chambers of the Royal Society has caused me throughout three decades."

"All in good time, Pemberton Smith," said the former Astronomer-Royal of Wales, running his hands up and down the ample back of Frow Puprikosch—or, as she preferred to be called by him, Yózhinka. "All in good time . . . I say, Yózhinka, don't you find that corset *most* constrictive? *I* should. In fact, I *do*. Do let us go somewhere where we can take it off, and afterward I shall explain to you the supernal glories of the evening skies—beginning, of course, with Venus."

To which the lady, as they made their way toward the door together, replied merely (but expressively), *"Yoi . . . !"*

Standing in the doorway was a very tall, very thin, very, very dignified elderly gentleman in cutaway, striped trousers, silk hat—a silk hat which he raised, although somewhat stiffly, as the semi-former Frow Puprikosch went past him. He then turned, and regarding the *wizard anglais* with a marked measure of reproof, said, *"Well,* George."

"Good Heavens. *Augustus*. Is it really you?"

"It is really me, George. *Well,* George. I suppose that you have received my letter."

"I have received no letter."

"I sent it you, care of Cook's, Poona."

"Haven't been in Poona for years. Good gad. That must be why my damned remittances kept arriving so late. I must have forgotten to give them a change of address."

Sir Augustus Smith frowned slightly and regarded his brother with some perplexity. "You haven't been in Poona for years? Then what was all this nonsense of your calling yourself Vizier Sri Smith and trying to rouse the hill tribes with the rallying cry of 'No votny'? Votnies were abolished, along with the tax on grout, the year after the Mutiny, surely you must know that."

"I haven't been in Injia for eleven years, I tell you. Not since the Presidency cut up so sticky that time over the affair of the rope trick (all done by the odyllic forces, I tell you). As for all the rest of it, haven't the faintest idea. Call myself Vizier Sri Smith indeed, *what do you take me for?*"

Sir Augustus bowed his head and gently bit his lips. Then he looked up. "Well, well," he said, at last. "This is probably another hugger-mugger on the part of the Junior Clarks, not the first time, you know, won't be the last," he sighed. "I tell you what it is, you know, George. *They let* anyone *into Eton these days.*"

"Good heavens!"

"Fact. Well. Hm. Mph." He looked around the room with an abstracted air. "Ah, here it is, you see, now that I have seen with my own eyes that Pigafetti Jones is alive and playing all sorts of fun and games as I daresay he has *been* doing all these years, ahum, see no reason why you shouldn't come home, you know, if you like."

"Augustus! Do you mean it?"

"Certainly."

The younger Smith reached into the clothes press and removed therefrom a tightly packed traveling bag of ancient vintage. "I am quite ready, then, Augustus," he said.

There was a clatter of feet on the stairs in the corridors beyond, the feeble voice of the hall-porter raised in vain, and into the room there burst Kummelman Swartbloi, who proceeded first to fall at the younger Smith's feet and next to kiss them. "My wife!" he cried. "My wife has just had twin boys! Bella is guaranteed another generation of Brothers Swartbloi (Snuff-Tobacco)! Thank you, thank you, thank you!" And he turned and galloped away, murmuring that he would have stayed longer but that it was essential for him to be at the mill in a quarter of an hour in order to grind the Rappee.

"Do twins come up often in the chap's family?" asked Sir Augustus.

"I'm afraid that nothing much comes up often in his family at all, any more. I merely advised him to change his butcher and I may have happened to suggest the well-known firm of Schlockhocker, in the Ox Market. Old Schlockhocker has six sons, all twins, of whom the youngest, Pishto and

Knishto, act as delivery boys on alternate days. Wonderful thing, change of diet . . . that, and, of course, the odyllic forces."

Sir Augustus paused in the act of raising his hat to his head. "I should hope, George," he said, "that you may not have been the means of introducing any spurious offspring into this other tradesman's family."

His brother said that he didn't know about that. Fellow and his wife were first cousins, after all. Sir Augustus nodded, again lifted his hat, and this time gestured to the multitudinous items upon the heavy old sideboard. "Do you not desire to remove your philosophical equipment?" he asked.

Smith the younger considered. He looked at his own hat, the velvet cap of curious cut with the curious silvern medallion on it. He took it in both hands and approached Doctor Eszterhazy. Doctor Eszterhazy bowed. George William Marmaduke Pemberton Smith placed the cap upon the head of Engelbert Eszterhazy (Doctor of Medicine, Doctor of Jurisprudence, Doctor of Science, Doctor of Literature, etc., etc.). "You are now and henceforth," the Englishman said, "the Wizard of the Triune Monarchy, and may regard yourself as seized of the entire equipage of the odyllic force, or, rather, forces. Sorry I can't stay, but there you are."

The brothers left the room arm in arm, Sir Augustus inquiring, "Who was that odd-looking chap, George?" and his junior replying, "Phrenologist fellow. Can't recollect his name. Does one still get good mutton at Simpson's?"

"One gets *very* good mutton, still, at Simpson's."

"Haven't had good mutton since . . ." Voices and footsteps alike died away.

Doctor Eszterhazy looked at the equipage of the odyllic forces, and he slowly rubbed his hands together and smiled.

Appendix

THE YEAR'S BEST
FANTASY BOOKS

I. ORIGINAL FICTION

1. *Shardik,* by Richard Adams. Novel; 529 pp., endpaper maps by Rafael Palacios; Simon and Schuster. No rabbits this time, but straight heroic fantasy adventure on the epic scale. Superb entertainment.
2. *The Enchantress of World's End,* by Lin Carter. Novel; 192 pp., map by the author; $1.25, DAW Books. Humorous Sword & Sorcery, set on Earth seven hundred million years in the future. Second volume of the Gondwane Epic; when completed, the Epic will be over half a million words long.
3. *The Deep,* by John Crowley. Novel; 180 pp.; $5.95, Doubleday. Strong first book by a new writer with a style and viewpoint, plot and setting, cast and mood unique and very refreshing. Strongly recommended.
4. *The Enquiries of Doctor Eszterhazy,* by Avram Davidson. Collection; 206 pp., maps by John E. Westfall; $1.25, Warner. Eight curious stories set in an imaginary turn-of-the-century Balkan empire, ranging from occult and macabre, to quaint Victorian detection. Eszterhazy obviously shares the same world as Mr. S. Holmes, Esq., of Baker Street.
5. *Wandor's Journey,* by Roland Green. Novel; 188 pp.; 95¢, Avon Books. Straightforward heroic fantasy—with a bite to it. Sequel to *Wandor's Ride.*
6. *The Birthgrave,* by Tanith Lee. Novel; 408 pp.; $1.50, DAW Books. Absolutely magnificent fantasy epic by a new writer of amazing skill, subtlety and dramatic power. Not the least of her skill is in the handling of

human characters, with a rich range of mood and emotion. The best debut in years.

7. *The Forgotten Beasts of Eld*, by Patricia A. McKillip. Novel; 208 pp., $1.50, Avon. Originally (in hardcover) as "for older children," the paperback reprint makes no mention of this limiting factor. Hence I am able to recommend this magical, lean, very moving fantasy of a witchgirl forced to leave her enchanted garden of fabled beasts and cope with the outside world of men. Splendid book, winner of the Lovecraft Award for best original novel of the year, given at the First World Fantasy Convention.

8. *The House of the Worm*, by Gary Myers. Collection; ix + 77 pp.; illustrated by Allan Servoss; $5.50, Arkham House. First book collection of Myers' marvelously Dunsanian/Lovecraftian fantasies. Ten tales in all, and every one a miracle.

II. IMPORTANT REPRINTS

9. *Lost Continents: The Atlantis Theme*, by L. Sprague de Camp. Nonfiction; x + 374 pp., illustrated; $1.95, Ballantine. A long, clear-eyed, steady look at Atlantis, Lemuria, Mu—and other imaginary civilizations on fabulous continents—and what legend, occultism, history, archaeology and even fantastic fiction have to say about them. An absolutely indispensable reference work, a sheer delight to read, and possibly the finest single book de Camp has *ever* written.

10. *She and Allan*, by H. Rider Haggard. Novel; xii + 303 pp., illustrations by Maurice Greiffenhagen; $3.45, Newcastle Publishing Company, 1521 North Vine Street, Hollywood, Cal., 90028. Softcover reissue of a hard book to find which is a towering fantasy and also a rare tour de force, which teams the hero of *King Solomon's Mines* and the heroine of *She* together in one story. Bravo, Newcastle!

11. *Almuric*, by Robert E. Howard. Novel; 217 pp., illustrations by David Ireland; $7.00, Donald M. Grant, Publisher, West Kingston, R.I. First hardcover edition ever of Howard's posthumous novel, a game try at

a fantastic adventure story on another planet in the Burroughs/Kline tradition, which *Weird Tales* serialized after Howard's death.

III. FANTASY ART

12. *The Book of Virgil Finlay*. 128 pp., 127 illustrations; $15.00, Gerry de la Ree, Saddle River, N.J. Generous sampling of the Master's work in black-and-white from 1932 to 1968, splendidly reproduced on glossy paper in hardcover. Includes many rare or previously unpublished studies, woodcuts, etc., plus scores of professional works from his peak years, printed from the original drawings.

13. *The Fantastic Art of Frank Frazetta*. 96 pp., 44 illustrations; $5.95, Rufus Publications/Peacock Press/Bantam Books. A fabulous feast for Frazetta freaks! Includes thirty paintings used for paperback covers, including six from the Lancer Conan series—one of them the famous *Conan the Adventurer* cover painting, published here for the first time in its final, finished form. Exquisite color reproductions of some of the best work by the greatest fantasy artist alive.

14. *Fantasy: The Golden Age of Fantastic Illustration*, edited by Brigid Peppin. 192 pp., 214 illustrations; $25.00, Watson-Guptill. 150 black-and-whites and 64 color plates by magazine and children's book illustrators from the turn of the century into the teens, at least. Seldom-seen work by the likes of Kay Nielsen, Dulac, Rackham, etc. A sumptuous survey of superbly fantastic art, at a hefty price, but actually worth it. Highly recommended.

IV. NONFICTION AND RELATED

15. *The Letters of James Branch Cabell*, edited by Edward Wagenknecht. xvii + 277 pp., with photographs, and frontispiece portrait by Frank C. Papé; $15.00, University of Oklahoma Press, Norman. Intelligent, witty, informative letters to friends, editors and colleagues,

among them Sinclair Lewis, H. L. Mencken, F. Scott Fitzgerald, Arthur Machen, Philip Wylie, Nelson S. Bond. A wealth of autobiographical data, interesting sidelights on the writing of *Jurgen* and the other fantasies, and fascinating opinions on and reactions to Lovecraft, Dunsany, *The Worm Ouroboros*, Haggard, etc. A valuable associational item by the greatest fantasy writer America has yet produced.

16. *Lovecraft: A Biography*, by L. Sprague de Camp. xvi+510 pp.; illustrated with 15 photographs, two drawings, and a map of the Dreamlands by Jack Gaughan; $10.00, Doubleday. A formal, full-scale life of the late and great (also the first genuine biography of Lovecraft ever done, and likely to remain the "standard life" for many years). De Camp's fluent, entertaining style, and scrupulous scholarship and research, make this lengthy tome readable, interesting and invaluable. His original research has turned up many previously unknown items of information (such as a lost, and very important, Cthulhu Mythos story about Tsathoggua), controversial new opinions on Lovecraft's health, racial views, etc. One of the most important books of the year in our field, and a brilliant job of work.

17. *Sir Gawain and the Green Knight/Pearl/Sir Orfeo*, translated (with an introduction, glossary and appendix) by J. R. R. Tolkien. 149 pp.; $8.95, Houghton Mifflin. Verse translations of three famous medieval poems, discovered in manuscript after Professor Tolkien's death. The *Gawain* romance, at about two thousand lines, is a miniature Arthurian epic, lively, vivid and stirring.

These books seem to my taste the best published in the fantasy field during 1975. But this is only my personal opinion, and does not necessarily reflect the thinking of my publisher.

To make certain that *your* book, brochure or publication comes to my attention during the coming year, send a copy to me care of DAW Books.

And if, in the course of your own reading, you run across a new book that you consider worthy, by all means drop me a line and let me know about it. It is my ambition to make this annual honor roll as complete and authoritative as I possibly can.

Happy Magic for 1976!

LIN CARTER